The Shattered Door

Morrison Investigations, Case One

Lisa Bouchard

The Shattered Door

First Printing, September 2012

ISBN (Print Version): 978-0988382602

For Paul, my beloved.

Chapter 1

Seven o'clock and Kathleen Harrison was alone. She checked her hair in the mirror. It looked as good as it had ten minutes before. Sleet battered the roof. She shivered as the cold seeped through the window casing. *Get a grip on yourself, you look fine.* She pulled her cardigan closed, thankful she'd decided to dress casually for dinner tonight.

She flinched at the sudden ringing of the oven timer. Barefoot, she padded through the drab front entryway to the kitchen to check on dinner: roast pork with baby vegetables and potatoes. George often complained about never having a home-cooked meal; she was confident he would love the delicious simplicity of this one. She leaned against the counter and smiled, tingling with the audacity of having her lover spend the night while her husband was away. After tonight there would be no going back, no pretending her marriage could be salvaged. She and George would pack her belongings in the morning, and then she would call her attorney and have him begin the divorce proceedings, setting herself and Steve free to find the happiness they each deserved.

She walked through her home, seeing it as though for the first time. She didn't like what she saw. The house was dark, an ugly combination of cherry furniture and gray-brown carpeting. Steve had chosen the colors to camouflage the inevitable dirt children brought into a house, but they'd had no children. She never felt the urge so many of her friends shared to bring children into the world. The strong colors had suited her when she thought she'd be spending her life with Steve, reflecting the strength of their future together. But now, trapped in a loveless marriage, the dark colors mirrored her despair. When she thought of George and their life together, she imagined bright whites and open windows. She couldn't remember ever feeling that way with Steve.

The doorbell rang, and her heart skipped a beat. *An entire night with him!* She opened the door, and reality came crashing back down on her. *Not this man.* This one could ruin her whole night. "I thought we agreed to meet tomorrow."

His smile was calm and reassuring. "This couldn't wait. I'm sure we can work out our differences quickly."

"I'm not available now. I'll see you in the morning."

She tried to slam the door shut, but he blocked it with his foot. "It will just take a minute. Please. Let me in."

She sighed. Why did he have to choose *tonight* for their confrontation? Resigned, she grimaced. The sooner she let him in, the sooner he would leave and the sooner she and George could toast their new future. Looking at her watch, she said, "Five minutes."

He closed the door behind him, and the smile on his face vanished. His usually genial eyes now flashed with anger. "Nice place you got here." He knocked the crystal bowl that held her keys off the table and smiled as it shattered on the tile floor. "Your telepath's money buys a lot of nice things," he sneered. "I guess he'll have to buy you another bowl."

"What the hell do you think you're doing? Get out of here." She tried to push him back toward the door, but he grabbed her arm and held her in place. "Let go of me!" She pulled her arm out of his grip, painfully aware she was free only because he let her go.

She stepped back until her hip hit the handrail leading upstairs.

"I'm not going anywhere. You and I have a lot to talk about right now, Kathleen."

Doing her best to keep her voice level, she said, "You'll have to leave now. I'm expecting a guest. I'll see you tomorrow, in my office, where we can both be reasonable and act like professionals."

"You're expecting someone?" Realization crossed his face. "But not your husband. You're meeting him here, aren't you, in the house you share with your husband?"

She tried to keep the fear out of her voice. "I don't see that this is any of your business."

He stepped forward, his face uncomfortably close to hers. "You filthy slut. You dirty, disgusting whore! It's bad enough you accept a telepath as a client, but to invite him into your home ..."

"My husband will be home any minute, so you should leave. Now."

He laughed. "Not even a credible bluff. He's in Texas all week."

Color drained from her face. "How do you know that?"

"I've been keeping an eye on you. Rather, I've hired someone to keep an eye on you. Oh, yes, I get regular reports on all your activities, from the late-night home-shopping binges to the time you spend with your favorite client. And let me tell you, you look foolish, like his trained pet human, coming whenever he calls."

She balled her hands into fists, hoping he wouldn't notice them shaking. "Just tell me what you want and then get out of here."

He smiled at her, once again becoming the genial man who had rung her doorbell. "Your work with telepaths has to stop. The telepathic scourge needs to be eliminated, permanently, for the good of humanity. Some people are calling for camps, but I say extermination if we can get away with it. Either way, they must be removed from society."

"But they're people," she said, horrified by what she'd heard. "People with families, children, jobs, just like the rest of us."

"No. They're not Homo sapiens—*not* like us." His eyes flashed, and he grabbed her arm again before she had time to move away. "And people like you—collaborators, dirty, filthy telepath lovers. Your minds have already been tainted by theirs. You've probably been scanned so many times by now that your thoughts aren't your own any more. People like you are the first who need to go."

He twisted her arm back, and she realized that if she wouldn't agree with him, he would hurt her.

He stood between her and the alarm panel next to the front door. Her mind raced. *What should I do? Damn you, George, for being late.*

"You want to put us away in camps too?"

He smiled at her. "No. Anyone scanned by the telepaths will have to die. Once there's no one left to stand up for the mind-stealers, the untainted humans will start seeing things my way. Once I get enough humans on my side, then we can demand what our society needs—to stem the anarchy telepaths are causing. By eliminating them."

He stepped to the side and lowered himself to the bottom stair, pulling her down next to him. She flinched forward, away from him, but the stairs were too narrow for escape, and he pulled her back.

He's crazy! All I can do is keep him talking until George gets here.

"Society is falling apart. There's no trust. No one knows who is in their brain and what they'll do with the information they steal from us. We have no reliable means of detect a telepathic intrusion. The Telepathic Corps is laughable at best. They have a terrible recovery rate, probably because they're telepaths and therefore can't be trusted. With no reliable human way to test for telepaths, we're at their mercy."

"I … I think I see your point." She took a chance, hoping to bring him back to some degree of sanity. "And that's where I come in. I am working to build trust, and once we have trust, we can start to institute safeguards to keep us from their prying minds."

"You!" he laughed. "You're a collaborator. You want us all to live together in peace and harmony, oblivious to their master plan."

"I don't think they have a master plan. I think they just want to live like everyone else, with simple human dignity."

"And there's your problem." He leaned over and whispered in her ear. "They're not human." He straightened and continued. "Do you know, do you even care, what they are doing to us?"

"What do you mean?"

He stood up and began pacing the seven steps between the staircase and the front door. "They plan to drive this country to its knees! Now that the world knows telepaths aren't welcome in the United States, the United Nations is preparing sanctions. No one buys American products anymore, and foreign tourism has ground to a halt. We're pariahs now when we have always been leaders."

Hardly able to comprehend this rant, she frowned and blinked. "Tourism is down because of our human rights abuses of our own people. No one wants to come here and risk being labeled as a telepath. It's too dangerous. The global boycott of American products is because of people like you, not because of the telepaths. People like you who want to kill telepaths – you're ..." She jumped up to face him. "You're nothing but terrorists."

He punched her in the jaw. "Bitch! Terrorists rule through fear. That's not what I want at all. I'm trying to save humanity from these freaks of nature."

She crumpled and fell against the banister, covering her head with her arms and tasting the blood on her lip. *Not again.* She had sworn she would never accept another beating from any man. She turned to him, forcing her shaking arms down to her sides, and stared defiantly at him. "No. You want to kill humans who are different from you. You are nothing but another Nazi incarnation."

She shrank away from the rage erupting across his face. Her momentary strength crumbled in his harsh glare. Desperate, she began to plead. "Please don't hurt me. I'm sure we can work this out. Just tell me what you want me to do."

"I came here to talk you into seeing reason, but I can see you aren't going to be persuaded. They must have already reprogrammed your mind. I can't save a woman who would willingly choose one of these mind-stealers over her human husband. You've already betrayed your people." He shook his head. "I suppose there isn't anything else to be done." He drew a gun from the back of his waistband. "I wish it didn't have to be this way, but you've left me no other choice."

Adrenaline surged through her. She sprinted up the stairs, barely evading his grasp, and slammed the door to the master bedroom behind her. Her fingers fumbled with the lock, but she managed to turn it before he made it up the stairs. She had laughed when her husband insisted they have a separate upstairs alarm, but now she praised his paranoia. She slapped her hand against the numbers, knowing any wrong code would prompt a call and a visit when she didn't answer the phone.

She heard his feet pound up the stairs after her. His voice was muffled by the locked door between them. "Now why'd you have to go and do that? There's no escape."

She shrank back from the door, fear churning her stomach and doubt creeping into her mind. Then she scrambled into the master bathroom. Locking the door behind her, she climbed into the tub, hoping the old-fashioned claw-foot beauty would protect her for a few more moments, until someone came to rescue her. The bedroom door lock was a flimsy thing and she knew he only had to push against the door for it to release. She had moved a bedside table in front of the door, hoping to slow him down.

"You don't want to do that. Come on out here so I won't have to break down this door."

She heard him kick the door open and cringed. She heard the table crash to the floor. If she had never taken George as a client, none of this would be happening now. If she had listened to Steve, she could have been happy enough with him, made their marriage work.

She pushed that thought away. She could never be happy with Steve again, not after the night he hit her. She was right to choose George.

She looked at her watch. It was 7:05. *He should be here by now.* Would he walk in on this maniac and be killed, too?

She heard the phone in the bedroom ringing. *The security company is checking up on me.* It would take them a few minutes to call the police to investigate. She sobbed; she knew she didn't have even a couple of minutes left. So much time wasted with Steve, so many regrets.

He broke a hole through the cheap bathroom door and continued to batter it with the pistol, the sound of splintering wood sending new panic into her heart. When the hole was large enough, their eyes met. "There you are. Nice and neat, so your grieving husband won't have to clean up much. Very thoughtful of you."

Desperate, she climbed from the tub and looked for something she could use to defend herself. She grabbed a can of hairspray, held it to the hole in the door, and pressed the button. *If I still smoked, I'd take my lighter and turn this can into a flamethrower.*

He backed away from the door, sputtering. "Now why do you want to make me angry?" He choked once, caught his breath, and aimed the gun through the hole.

"Please, no …" she whispered. "I can drop him as a client. I'll never see him again."

As he reached through the hole and unlocked the door she backed up and fell into the tub, thumping her head against the side. She gasped. As she opened her eyes, she saw him sitting on the edge of the tub, penning her in. She sat up and tried to speak, but he cut her off as soon as she opened her mouth.

"I tried. I was reasonable with you. You're trying to lie to me again. You don't see the error of your ways, and so you need to be put down."

He stood, walked backward to the bathroom door, and shot her between the eyes.

Chapter 2

George Wynton was running late. He was perpetually late, but this was the most important night of his life and he didn't want to miss a moment of it. He waved a fifty at the cabbie. "An extra tip if you can get me there by seven."

"I'll do my best, sir, but it will be close."

He sat back in the cab, closed his eyes, and imagined how his night would go. Her husband was gone. Texas, she said, and they would have the entire night together. Until now she had only dared to give him an hour, two at most, before she had to be back in the office, afraid her jealous husband might suspect. That was no way to start the greatest relationship of their lives.

He had dreamed of the time they would finally be able to spend an entire night together, but the dream had taken on a nightmarish quality when she had insisted they stay at her house. He wanted nothing to do with the house she shared with her abusive husband. But she was moving out, starting a new life on her own, and she needed his moral support.

Even though they'd be in that house, he knew he could make tonight perfect. No rushing, no looking over their shoulders, no hiding in dark corners of restaurants. No reason to talk in code or not to kiss. No reason to pretend they were just working. Tonight would be about the two of them, alone and crazy in love like teenagers.

He smiled. *Crazy in love.* Even though neither of them had said it, they were in love. Maybe tonight would be the time to finally declare it. Tonight, or tomorrow morning. Yes, morning would be the time to convince her to start her new life with him. He had already found the perfect house for them. Once she woke up with him and felt what it was like to start the day with someone who treasured every moment he spent with her, she wouldn't be able to turn him down.

How would her family react when she eventually told them? Leaving your husband for another man was common enough, but to leave him for a telepath would be shocking. Most people, even people who considered themselves fair and open-minded, weren't ready for that sort of mixed marriage. She must have thought about it, though. She'd know how to deal with them. She was a PR genius. Once they saw how happy she was with him, he hoped her family would accept him, if begrudgingly.

"This your place?" the cabbie asked.

He looked up at the beige colonial. 254 Wilding Street. Hers was the only house with faded Christmas decorations still up, even though Valentine's Day was last week. "Yup, this is it." He looked at his watch. Seven ten. *Not too bad. Close enough.* "Have a great night." He handed the cabbie the fifty and bounded up the front stairs. He rang the bell, but there was no answer. He turned the knob. The door was unlocked.

"Kathleen?" The house was silent. He could smell the home-cooked meal she had promised him. The aroma made his stomach growl in anticipation.

Until he'd met Kathleen, his personal life had

been empty. He'd never lied about being a telepath, and his honesty put a quick end to almost every first date he'd ever been on, whether she was a telepath or not. It was strange, most telepaths were just as afraid to be scanned as non-telepaths. Friends were just as difficult to keep once they knew his secret. Now that everyone knew he was a telepath, most of his normal friends were suddenly too busy to take his calls and his telepath friends were too much in awe of him.

"I'm here!" he called. "Where are you?"

He looked right, toward the living room. He noticed the broken glass on the floor and her keys in the corner. "Kathleen? Are you all right?" He waited, but there was still no answer.

He walked toward the back of the house, creaking floorboards announcing his progress. He followed the scent of dinner, thinking she might have gone to the kitchen for a broom.

She wasn't in the kitchen, or the pantry either. "Darling, did you hear me?" The dining room was empty, the table set for dinner, a bottle of pinot noir waiting on the sideboard. He finished walking through the first floor without finding her. *She must be upstairs.*

He called for her again as he climbed the stairs to the second floor, but heard nothing. He rushed into the bedroom when he saw a bedside table was toppled over. "Kathleen?" Chills raced down his spine when he saw the hole in the bathroom door. He rushed forward, then stopped, his heart refusing to beat.

"No!" he whispered.

Her beautiful face was marred by a bullet hole. Her open eyes seemed to stare at him, blaming him for being late. Behind her, blood painted the wall and tub. As he crumpled to the floor, his vision narrowed until all he saw were her eyes. But he couldn't faint, not when she needed him. Avoiding the sight of her pale face, he scrambled to his feet.

Burning rage fueled his muscles as he tore the mattress off the bed and then ripped through the closets looking for the murderer. *Steve. It has to be him. There was no trip. The bastard set us up.*

"Steve!" he raged. "Get out here and face me!" There was no sound but his panting breath. Instinctively, he reached out with his mind, searching for the killer. There was no one in the house. The neighbors were wrapped up in their petty lives and had no idea about the horror that had just occurred in their neighborhood. Once he realized the shocking invasion he was perpetrating, he shut his powers down. Even in a crisis, he knew, reading other people's minds without permission was unacceptable.

Convinced he and Kathleen were alone, he went back to the bathroom and sat next to the tub. "Oh, Kath. I'm so sorry. I didn't know." He put his head in his hands. "How could I know?" he sobbed. "I was only ten minutes late. That's nothing for me. Ten minutes, and I could have protected you. Ten minutes, and we could still be together.

"I wanted tonight to be special, to be perfect for us. I had it all planned out. I wanted you to see how it could be, sharing a life with someone who actually loves you, someone who knows how amazing you are, someone who cherishes his time with you."

He took a quick glance at her, but the blame he imagined in her eyes drove him to look away.

"If I hadn't been late, if I could just have been on time for once in my life, I could have saved you."

A tear trickled down his cheek, followed by another. He wiped them away and continued. "I thought we could get married, have children. I even found the perfect house for us. I never thought that could be possible, not for a person like me. But then I met you, and against all reason, you fell in love with me. Completely, totally, head-over-heels in love. And I was just as powerless to resist loving you.

"We never said it, but I planned to tell you in the morning. I wanted the first words you heard to be, 'I love you, Kathleen,' because I do. I love you with my entire being. I will always love you."

He sat and talked to her until, startled, he heard another person enter the room.

"Sir?"

He looked up. Two officers were aiming their guns at him. "Sir, put your hands behind your head and stand up slowly."

George wondered how they knew to come. He heard the command to stand up repeated.

"She's dead," he said.

"Yes, sir. Come with us, and we'll take care of her."

He stood up and walked toward an officer. He peered at the man's name tag. "Detective Fraser, you've got to find who did this." Before he could comprehend what was happening, the cop shoved him against the wall and handcuffed and searched him. George stood there, his cheek against the cool tiles, held still by the two men.

"You can't think I did this. I love her ... loved her."

"No, sir. Of course not," the other cop said. "I have to read you your rights, anyway, just to make sure."

George looked away as Fraser read him his Miranda rights.

"You're that telepath, Wynton," said the other officer.

George nodded, wondering what that had to do with Kathleen's death.

Fraser pushed George out of the bathroom and down the stairs, leaving the other officer upstairs.

"Where are we going?"

"To the station. We need to ask you some questions."

"Can we do that tomorrow? We have to find her husband now. He's the one who did this."

"Leave that to us, sir. We're the professionals."

George climbed into the back of the unmarked cruiser Fraser led him to, sat back, and closed his eyes. *It has to be Steve.* Unbidden, tears flowed down his face. He had been planning their future together. He'd finally told her he loved her and revealed all his plans for their future. But she hadn't heard him. It was too late, and now there was nothing he could do. Police refused to work with telepaths in any capacity, even when the stakes were as high as they had been in the Sarin gas bombings in Los Angeles the year before.

He rested his head on the window, watching the police and EMTs go in and out of her house like so many ants on a hot summer day. His mind wandered, trying to avoid the image of her blank eyes staring at him, and the ugly bullet hole that marred her beauty. Then two men wheeled out a stretcher with a black body bag strapped to it.

"No!" he yelled. He sobbed and thumped his head against the cool glass, the feeling soothing him.

Fraser stood in front of his window. "Mr.

Wynton, stop that. You'll hurt yourself."

George looked up, confused.

"You'll hurt yourself if you keep slamming your head against the glass. It won't break, and you'll wind up with a concussion."

How could a concussion matter now? He would trade anything, a concussion, glass through the head, anything at all to know she had heard him tell her how much he loved her.

The officer looked concerned but said nothing else. He climbed into the cruiser and drove away.

Chapter 3

George rested his forehead on the cold cruiser window, watching people go about their normal evening activities, hurrying into their homes, uncomplicated by dead loved ones, blissfully ignorant that their lives could end at any second. Tears ran down his face and he didn't care who saw.

By the time they reached the Washington Street precinct he had stopped crying and collected his thoughts. As he exited the car cameras flashed in his face, blinding him with the glare.

Paparazzi shouted questions at him as they strained against the police cordon. "Why did you do it?"

"Is it true you can kill with your thoughts?"

"How many other women have you killed?"

He stumbled up the stairs, Fraser's firm grip on his arm the only thing keeping him from collapsing.

"Keep going. One foot in front of the other."

It was odd, George reflected, that Fraser's advice was so helpful. He had been walking for thirty-three years, but tonight his legs seemed to have forgotten how.

In a daze, he followed Fraser's lead through the booking process, and at some point he realized he had been officially arrested.

Fraser led him into the interrogation room. One long fluorescent light flickered over the gray table. George stared into the only thing that broke up the monotonous gray walls, the one-way mirror. He couldn't sense anyone behind the mirror, so he looked away.

Fraser removed the handcuffs and gave him a cup of coffee before leaving the room. As he took a sip his shaking hand spilled some on the table. The coffee tasted bitter, scorched from sitting on a hot burner all day. He stared at himself in the one-way mirror, trying not to think about the accusing look in her eyes. It was the last memory he'd have of her. The coffee was cold before anyone came back to question him.

A thin, scowling man with graying temples and a limp walked in to the interrogation room. "I'm Chief Taylor. You've been read your rights?"

George nodded.

"Good. I know who you are. Even though you found that missing girl last month, don't think your reputation will buy you much good will around here." Taylor put a notepad and pen on the table in front of George. "I want you to write out exactly what happened from the minute you got to the Harrison house this evening until Fraser brought you in. Include the location of your weapon and why you shot her."

Why didn't they understand he couldn't have done this? He could never kill anyone, not when he witnessed firsthand the good within each person. Decades ago, before he had developed a tight rein on his telepathic powers, he had looked into many minds. It was easy to see the ugly, hateful, petty nature in people. He had almost gone insane that summer, inundated with the ugliness of the world. If he hadn't met Chloe Nathan, allowed her to pull him back from the brink and teach him to look for the small pearl of beauty in each person, he might actually have become the killer the police now suspected he was.

He could find Kathleen's killer, ethics be damned. All he needed to do was scan that bastard of a husband, and he'd have all the proof anyone needed. He would be back on the ugly path to insanity, but it would be worth it. To catch her killer, he would sacrifice his soul.

"I don't own any weapons. I didn't shoot her." When Taylor looked skeptical, Wynton slammed his fist on the table. "Get a telepath in here to scan me. Once you see that I'm innocent, we can find the real killer. I am your best bet to find him and you're a damn fool not to use me."

"Settle down, or I'll have you restrained," threatened Taylor. He pointed at the paper. "Start writing. I'll send someone in with a sandwich in a little while."

George looked down at the blank paper. *Start with arriving at the house,* he thought. He picked up the pen and began to write.

Twenty minutes and six pages later the lock clicked, and an officer came in with food. George ignored the interruption and kept writing. Ten pages later, he looked up at the giant one-way mirror and said, "I'm done."

Chief Taylor came back in and took the notepad. "You writing a novel?"

Not likely, George thought. "I wanted to make it as detailed as I could for you. I thought everything I could remember would make it easier for you to find …" His breath caught. "To find who did this to her."

Taylor sat down. He pointed to the sandwich.

"You going to eat that?"

George looked at the sandwich and vaguely remembered someone bringing it in. "Yeah." He took a bite of the bologna and cheese and made a face. "Needs mustard."

Taylor ignored him. He flipped through Wynton's write-up. "Tell me about your relationship with Mrs. Harrison."

George smiled, remembering the day he met the love of his life. "At first, it was strictly professional. I was so sick of the bad publicity we telepaths were getting, the distrust—hell, the hatred and disgust—people have for us. I thought using a public relations firm could help. I thought she could help to paint us in a better light. You know, plant some news articles about telepaths doing good in the world, get us portrayed as fellow human beings. That couldn't happen without someone coming forward as the face of telepaths, and since it was my idea, it had to be me. I did good deeds. I helped people in strictly non-telepathic ways. I've done that all my life, but now I had her publicity team shouting it to the world."

Taylor nodded. "When did your relationship change from business to personal?"

"June fifth of last year. I had just received a request for an interview from the *Boston Globe*, and we were thrilled. This was the first major news outlet she was able to get an interview with that wouldn't treat me like a sideshow freak. The call came in around six, so I told her she'd earned a nice dinner out. She'd worked her ass off to get me that interview, so she agreed. We went to one of the small Indian restaurants in Central Square, hoping to just eat—you know, without being bothered. By then, you see, people were beginning to recognize me on the streets. Most people were horrified to be near me, but a few were kind enough to thank me for whatever I'd done recently."

He sat back, relaxing with the memory. "So— dinner. We decided we were sick of talking business, and we talked about our lives instead. She opened up to me. Her marriage was falling apart, and her husband was furious that she took me on as a client. I felt bad for her, having a jerk of a husband. I could make her career if it all went well, but her husband wanted her to keep working with the minor sports and music celebs on her client roster.

"After dinner, I put her in a cab for home. The next day, she came to work wearing dark glasses. Wouldn't take them off. They didn't hide all the bruising, but no one would say anything if she didn't bring it up." He clenched his fists, and his voice became a low growl. "That bastard of a husband had given her a black eye for having dinner with me."

"And what did you do?"

Wynton closed his eyes, reliving the desperation he'd felt that day. It was that day, he realized, that he failed her, and now she was dead. He put his head in his hands. "It's all my fault. She's dead because of me. I tried to make her go to the police, make her file a report and get a restraining order, but she wouldn't. She was afraid of him, afraid of what he'd do. What else could I do? I took a few pictures when she wasn't looking, in case he did it again."

Taylor's eyes narrowed. "It's your fault she's dead? You killed her?"

George pushed his chair back and started to pace. "If I hadn't been so weak, if I had forced her to get help, she'd be alive now. But she begged me not to. She said he would only get angrier."

Taylor leaned forward. "You still have those photos?"

"They're on my phone. Fraser took it earlier. Look at them, and then tell me he didn't kill her."

"I'll take a look. But how did you go from one dinner to today?"

Wynton sat back down, relieved Taylor would look at the evidence and not railroad him into a conviction. "It was slow, after that. She was afraid and wouldn't see me alone. But one week, her husband was away on business, and we had another dinner. She felt safe while he was gone. We wound up at my place. She didn't leave until three or four the next morning."

"And that was the turning point?"

"Yes. I fell in love with her that night."

"But she wouldn't leave her husband for you?"

"She thought he'd kill her. I think he did."

Taylor sighed. "There's no gunshot residue on your hands, but you could have been wearing gloves." He leaned forward and stared at Wynton intently. "Did you kill her?"

"Of course not. After all I just told you, how can you think—?"

"It's either the husband or the lover, seventy percent of the time. If his Texas alibi holds up, that leaves you. There's a small chance it was someone else. And if it wasn't you and it wasn't the husband, who could it be?"

"I don't know. She was spending a lot more time working with me, so she had to pass a few clients on to some junior associates. Maybe one of the clients took offense. But I still think it was her husband. If he really was in Texas, he could have hired someone to do it, and he'd have a rock-solid alibi."

"We're looking into that. We're going to have to keep you here, though."

"Why?"

"You're still the number one suspect. Whether you killed her or not, you know what the public will say, don't you? That if you didn't kill her, then you made someone else do it for you. That you're acting like you're in shock, but you're just manipulating us."

Wynton nodded. He'd heard it all before—fear manifested as hatred for anyone who was different.

"I can't force people to do what I want."

"Doesn't really matter, does it? People, normal people, are still afraid of your type. That automatically makes them think the worst."

George looked at Taylor. "Do you think I did it?"

"It doesn't matter what I think. But if you want my advice, get yourself a good lawyer, one you can't hope to afford, or else you'll rot in jail for the rest of your life, whether you killed her or not."

"Do I get a phone call?"

Taylor reached into his pocket and handed his cell phone over. "Be my guest."

George picked up the phone and dialed. "Hi, Joyce, it's me. I need the best lawyer you can get me. I'm at the Brighton police department. Murder."

George held the phone away from his ear as loud squawking filled the room.

"Joyce. Joyce! Listen to me. Kathleen's been killed. Of course I didn't do it. But they found me at the scene, and I need a lawyer. Call in whatever favors you can. Get me someone good."

He handed the phone back to Taylor. "My attorney should be here soon. I'd appreciate seeing him as soon as possible."

Taylor said nothing as he left the room.

#

Dan Stevens hesitated outside Interrogation Room Two. For the eighth time in the last two hours, he wondered what karmic misstep had led him to represent this man. *No, not a man — a telepath.* Gray and Shalek, the oldest law firm in Boston, had a strict human-only policy, and until now they'd no sooner represent a telepath than they would a farm animal. He was sure his boss, Stirling Philips, hated telepaths as much as he did. But with his widely recognized name, it seemed George Wynton could command the services of the most prominent firm in Boston.

The thing Dan most dreaded, the thing every human dreaded, was being read. Whenever he thought he was near a telepath, a humiliating, soul-stripping vulnerability would strike Dan. It was bad enough they were allowed to walk the streets, but at least in a crowd he could pretend he was among his own kind. In the interrogation room, with nothing but a few feet of table separating them, he could do nothing but hope his client would not scan him. The powerlessness, the absolute certainty that he was defenseless against this telepath and his ability to delve into Dan's deepest secrets if he wanted to, made Dan hesitate outside the door. He knew the contract he would have his client sign would not, for one moment, keep him safe. Dan shuddered. How could you trust someone you could not control?

He had already observed his client through the

one-way mirror, but the sleeping figure gave him no insights. He was left only with Wynton's PR image: an affable, quiet businessman with no visible vices and a penchant for helping other people. But PR, like all advertising, was nothing but a glossy coating over a much uglier truth.

"You going in?" asked Detective Fraser.

"Yeah." Dan turned to look at the officer approaching him. "Give me a minute. You the one who found him?"

Officer Fraser nodded. "Broadbent and I watched him for a minute before he noticed us. Creepiest thing I ever saw. He was just sitting there, next to the tub, talking to her like it was any regular day, making plans for their future."

"What do you mean?"

"He was talking about buying a house on the Cape for the two of them." He paused and looked sheepish. "You don't think he was really talking to her, you know, telepathically?"

"She was dead, right?"

"Had to be. Bullet right between the eyes. Maybe her spirit hadn't left the room yet?"

Dan frowned. *Spirit. Right.* "There's no such thing. It was just grief, or a good act."

"Didn't look like an act. It looked like he really expected her to answer him."

"That's crazy." He shook his head. But then again, sane men don't murder their girlfriends. "Okay," he said, "I'm ready to go in."

He steeled himself as Fraser opened the door and then cleared his throat in nervous anticipation of meeting his client. "Mr. Wynton?"

George lifted his head, his bleary eyes blinking away his exhaustion. "You're my lawyer?"

"I'm Dan Stevens, your attorney. I'm with Gray and Shalek." He handed George a business card. It was simple, displaying the company logo—an intertwined G and S—Dan's name, and a phone number.

George sat back, looking at Dan. It had to be three in the morning, but the attorney's suit was immaculate, and he was freshly shaven. Gray and Shalek, George knew, was the oldest law firm in the city; it thrived on the notoriety of its high-profile clients. It also fit Chief Taylor's criterion of a firm he could not hope to afford. "Joyce sent you?"

"I was assigned to your case and told to get down here ASAP. All the details have been worked out, because I was instructed not to bother talking to you about my fees. They're all taken care of. You must have some very powerful friends."

Dan sat down, opened his briefcase, and took out a pen and a piece of paper. "First, we have some preliminaries to go through." He handed George the sheet of paper. "This is our standard telepathic client agreement."

"Your standard agreement? How many telepaths have you represented?"

One side of Dan's mouth lifted in a wry smile. "You are actually the first. I suppose this will become standard if we ever take on another telepath. It states that you will not, under any circumstances, read my mind, or the minds of the police, or officers of the court, or employees of Gray and Shalek, or any other passersby." He pointed to the relevant lines as he said, "Please sign here and initial here and here."

Wynton scowled. He had done just that only hours ago, but he couldn't admit to his lapse in discipline. "Do you really think I'd do that? I don't scan minds without permission, and I'm a public-enough figure that you should know that. Does your firm always begin a business relationship by insulting its clients?"

"Of course not. But my company requires this agreement before I can begin representing you. Even though, realistically, we'd never know if you did scan someone or not, what are we if we cannot live by our word?"

"Fine," George said. He signed and initialed the paper, the pen taking the brunt of his fury as he smashed it down.

"Now that we've taken care of that, let me tell you that as your attorney, I'll do everything I can to prepare a strong defense for you. I'm on your side in this matter, and if we can just put this," he waved at the paper, "behind us and get to work, we'll see how we can get you out of here. Start by telling me what happened last night."

George ran through the entire night, from the moment he got out of the cab until Dan arrived in the interrogation room. Dan listened intently, taking a few notes, not speaking until George had finished.

"You're sure you didn't see anyone leaving the house?"

"No one, and I went through the whole house when I got there, looking for her. But I know someone else had been there because there was broken glass in the entryway when I walked in."

Dan smiled at his weary client. "We know someone else was there because she didn't shoot herself and then dispose of the weapon."

Anger replaced the grief and exhaustion he felt. "No, I suppose not. I just meant to say someone had come and gone before I got there."

"Of course," Dan said, trying to ease his client's tension. "I've got questions for you, and some of them will seem insulting. My questions are going to be nothing compared to what the prosecution will ask you, so be prepared."

George took a deep breath and nodded.

"Why did you kill her?"

George stared at him, a look of shock freezing on his face. "I just told you what happened. I did not kill her. What do you think I am? Some kind of monster?"

"Of course I don't. You'd be surprised at how many people lie to their lawyers. I have to ask. I gauge the truth from whatever response you give me. If you didn't kill her, who did?"

"Her husband. I don't know how he did it, but it had to be him. He came home early, flew into a rage because I was going to be there, and killed her."

"He was in Texas. He couldn't have."

"No one else could have been that angry with her. If he didn't do it, he hired someone. He beat her. Did you know that? I think it was only a matter of time before …"

Dan was quiet. Finally, he asked the ugliest question the prosecutor would ask. "What makes you think that an individual such as yourself has the right to date a human woman?"

Wynton's face flushed. Rage flashed in his eyes. He slammed his fist on the table and pushed his chair back. "You're fired. Get the hell out of here!"

"Calm down, Mr. Wynton. I told you there would be ugly questions. This question, more than any other, you'll have to answer over and over." He sat back and folded his hands. "Do you have a good answer?"

Wynton sat down and took a deep, calming breath. "No, I don't have a good answer. Your question is just as offensive as when a black man dared fall in love with a white woman a hundred and fifty years ago. The next thing you know, the public will be calling for a lynching."

"They may, if you can't answer the question."

Wynton put his head in his hands and closed his eyes. "I am human, just like you, just like Kathleen."

Dan judged that his client had clearly had enough for one night. "That's all I have for you now. It's too late to keep the media out of the story, but we'll do our best to get your side out. I'm not sure who will be listening, though. Your relationship frightens people, and frightened people are not known for rational thinking."

Wynton closed his eyes; his head slumped forward. When he didn't say anything, Dan snapped his briefcase shut. Wynton looked up, appearing startled.

"Is there anything else you should tell me?" asked Dan.

"I loved her," he whispered. "I wanted to take her away from that jerk, to make her happy. To make her smile every day, not just on the days her husband was away."

"I'll see about bail and getting you some food. You should sleep. Wherever they put you, try to get some rest."

"I can't rest now. Her killer is out there." He stood up and started pacing. "I've got to find him. Her husband needs to pay for doing this to her." He stopped and stared intently at Dan. "You've got to get me out of here."

"You've been up almost all night. You're exhausted and can barely keep your eyes open. You can't do anything from in here. You've been accused of a serious crime, and with your status as a telepath, I can't guarantee you'll be allowed out on bail. Regardless, no matter where you are, you'll need to be clear-headed to deal with the press, the police surveillance, and meetings with me." Dan put his hand on George's shoulder. "You need to sleep. And if I do get you out on bail, you will sit tight, stay out of the public eye, and wait for your trial date."

George nodded, too exhausted to argue.

"I'll be back later today. I'm sure I'll have more questions. If you're lucky enough to get bail, it will be high, so you need to think about how you can get the money together."

Dan shook George's hand and rapped on the door to be let out, leaving George to wonder if his lawyer would be able to prove his innocence.

Chapter 4

Although the meeting was scheduled for the ridiculously early hour of five in the morning, State Senator Aaron Hill arrived even earlier. Other than his contact, Smith, he had no idea who belonged to the Twenty, and he didn't want to walk into the meeting unprepared. Smith had insisted that secrecy was of the utmost importance throughout his initiation into the Twenty, and today was the first time Hill would meet the entire group. He loved the idea of a group of people dedicated to eradicating the telepathic menace, first in Boston, then the rest of the United States, and then the world. Exterminating the telepathic scourge was what he lived for, but he was a politician and tried to work in the system whenever he could.

He had reservations about joining the Twenty, and the initiation process had almost convinced him to back out. Clearing his schedule for forty-eight hours to remain awake and keeping his mind blank to protect himself against a telepathic attack had been almost impossible for him. He was just glad it was over.

From his car, he watched Francis Wallburton emerge from his black Escalade and stride to the front door of the Chestnut Hill Country Club. He knocked twice, and a uniformed doorman let him in. Hill sat back, astonished. Wallburton was Vice President of NationalGrid and controlled the power supply for all of Massachusetts. Rumors about the rolling blackouts instituted in 2015 not being fairly distributed were widespread, and Wallburton ultimately controlled who lost power and when in the state. Hill smiled. If he played his cards right, he would never lose power again.

A navy Lexus drove into the parking lot. Caroline Henning sprinted to the door, avoiding the sleet that had just begun.

Smith had told Hill he would make excellent contacts in the Twenty, which was what finally convinced him to join. He did not like secret societies; their secrets were rarely secret for long, and association with them generally went very badly once everything fell apart. But Henning's influence alone made the risk worth it. As news director for Fox News in Boston, she could ensure Hill received more favorable press. Where Fox News led, most of the other media in the Commonwealth followed.

Hill was so engrossed in planning his future with his new, powerful allies that he did not notice Smith pulling into the lot. Smith parked in the spot next to his and rolled down his window. "You ready?"

Hill nodded and collected his briefcase before getting out of his car.

"You won't need that. No notes, and no recordings of any meetings."

"How does that work?"

"Our secretary has an eidetic memory. He can recall anything we need to know from previous meetings so we have no need for written records. We've managed with him for years now."

Years? Hill had never heard of the Twenty until Smith had approached him last month. He relaxed a little, reassured that they closely guarded their identities and secrets. He set the briefcase back in the car and said, "All right, then. Lead the way."

Smith pulled out a golf umbrella, and the two men walked beneath it toward the building. "It's best if you keep quiet during your first meeting. Get a feel for how we do things. Answer questions people ask you, but don't volunteer anything unless I give you the nod."

"Right. Observe. Try to fit in. I can do that." *But not for long.* He needed an active position within the Twenty to start moving his agenda forward.

Smith smiled. "Good. I don't want to see you booted out. We've been short one member for too long."

A black limo pulled up to the front doors. The driver emerged and raised an umbrella. He opened the passenger door and an elegantly dressed man emerged. He was tall, Hill noticed, several inches over six feet, and slender in a way that Hill hadn't been since his high school track days.

"Sir."

"Smith." The man nodded. "Hill?"

Hill held his hand out. "Yes, I'm Senator—"

"Good. Glad to have you aboard." The man walked ahead of Smith and Hill and knocked on the door.

Hill dropped his hand, angered by the brush-off. When the man was out of earshot, Hill asked, "Who was that?"

"Our chairman, William Jacobs."

"I don't recognize him."

"You wouldn't. He stays out of the public eye. Very old money. People like us don't run in his circles."

Hill felt a wave of insecurity course through him. *What do they want with me?* These people held far more power than he did. As a state senator, he held some sway in Massachusetts, but he couldn't influence the country as a whole. Not before he won a national office.

Inside the private dining room, twenty of the most powerful people in Massachusetts sat around the long cherry dining table while the club's staff served coffee and pastry. Hill looked around the table, making a quick note of the people assembled. Steve Boyce, aide to Governor Larkin. *Does his presence mean the governor shares our position?* Emily Estershon, director of Boston's Federal Reserve; Willard Robinson, president of Boston College; and several other people he did not immediately recognize. He wondered if the Twenty had been in existence since the discovery of human telepathy.

Jacobs, dressed in an impeccably tailored navy suit, sat at the head of the table. Once the last server left and closed the door, he cleared his throat, and the room quieted down.

Jacobs opened the meeting. "We welcome a new provisional member today, Senator Aaron Hill. Senator Hill has worked tirelessly for the segregation of telepaths from human society. Now, with our resources behind him, we expect to see great progress within Massachusetts, and throughout the country."

Hill nodded gravely at the assembled men and women. *Throughout the country*, he thought. The assembled power and money in this room alone could catapult a national campaign. "Thank you, it—"

Smith kicked him under the table. "Listen, don't talk," he whispered.

Goddamn it. Would he ever get an entire

sentence out before he was interrupted? He was a politician; talking was his life.

"Today's business: Kathleen Harrison," Jacobs continued.

Wallburton shook his head. "Again? She's been a thorn in our side for months. What are we going to do about her now?"

Jacobs shook his head. "Nothing. She's dead. Last night she was shot in the head, in her home."

Hill said nothing, curious to see how the members would react to her death. Murmurs from all around the table continued until Jacobs cleared his throat again.

"In a great stroke of good fortune, George Wynton is in custody. Police found him sitting with the body. He says he's innocent." He paused to allow the group to chuckle at the thought of an innocent telepath. "We need to make sure no one else thinks so. This is our opportunity—we can capitalize on this and take Wynton off the playing field. Caroline, you will take the lead on this. I want nonstop coverage of Wynton until he is convicted."

Caroline Henning nodded. "We're already on it. I spent half the night on conference calls, setting up national coverage, making sure rallies are organized and our most outspoken allies are lined up for interviews this morning."

"Hill, you're in charge of the legal aspect. Find out what you can about his defense attorney, and derail him. Make sure we have the right prosecutor on our side. Use whatever means you think necessary to make sure Wynton is convicted."

Henning interrupted. "Are you sure? He's new here. What if he can't pull it off?"

Jacobs shot her a fierce glance. "Then we'll

know he doesn't belong, and he'll probably wind up going to jail himself for tampering with a murder investigation." Jacobs looked directly at Hill. "And jail can be fatal for a man like you. We would make sure of it."

Hill blanched. This was not what he had in mind when he had been approached to join the Twenty. He'd thought the Twenty would be like politics: lots of committees, lots of mission statements, but very little direct action and that's why he had agreed to join. He had certainly not expected threats to his life and freedom, but what could he do now? He was stuck here. Smith had already made it quite clear that there was only one way out, and if Wynton wasn't convicted Jacobs would see he took it whether he wanted to or not.

"What if he actually did it?"

Jacobs shook his head. "Justice is blind, and sometimes she makes mistakes. You need to make sure Wynton is convicted, no matter the truth."

As the meeting broke up, members of the Twenty approached Hill, shook his hand and introduced themselves. He smiled. He could accomplish anything with these people behind him. His dreams would see fruition. He would start pushing for more decisive action, more pressure on the telepaths, presuming the group let him speak at the next meeting.

He left the club and saw Smith waiting by his car. "A very good meeting," Hill said.

"Not bad. You did good keeping your head down. I'm sure we'll vote to keep you in the group after your probationary period."

"I thought I was already in. How long does it take to become a full member?"

"Relax. The last three candidates never made it this far," Smith replied.

Hill imagined the worst. "What do you mean?"

"We eased them out before they made it to the initiation. You don't need to worry. You're right on track, although some members came to me with concerns. You have a reputation as a hothead, hell-bent on getting rid of the scourge at any cost. We move cautiously here, to ensure we are not harmed. And we do not tolerate outside actions. Anything you do in relation to telepaths needs to be run through the Twenty first. We coordinate our actions, like a dance, to obtain the most favorable result with the least possible attention to ourselves."

"I understand. But, in the Senate, I'm not the only one who is concerned about telepaths. If a vote is called, or I'm asked to co-sign something, I can hardly stop and call the Twenty for permission first."

"Of course not. You are in a different position than the rest of us. You need to act as you always have. But if you personally want to introduce new legislation, it needs to be run through us first. Anything else should proceed as you think best. We've analyzed your beliefs, and we think your judgment is sound."

Hill nodded. "Good."

Smith got into his car and started it up. "Call me if you need any advice on how to embark upon your task," he said through the open window. "I'm an old pro at fixing juries."

Hill nodded and watched as the Supreme Court justice drove away.

Chapter 5

Darcy looked across Huntington Avenue toward her twin sister, Olivia. Olivia was being restrained by the man who claimed to love her, Dan Stevens. There was no traffic, no spectators, no noise at all. Darcy took one step into the street, toward Olivia.

"Please don't leave me. I can't live without you, Liv."

Olivia tried to take a step toward her, but Dan would not release her. "She's mine," he said.

Olivia reached her hand toward Darcy, "I'm sure he'll let me see you, if I'm a good enough wife." And then she vanished.

Darcy ran across the street; her Glock appeared in her hand. She raised the gun, aimed, and pulled the trigger. At that instant, Olivia reappeared with a bright red circle of blood on her shoulder. She crumpled to the ground and moaned.

"No!" Darcy yelled.

Dan looked toward Olivia but made no move to help her.

"She's better off with me. She'll die if she stays with you. You'll kill her," he said.

"Darcy! Wake up! You're having a nightmare."

Darcy opened her eyes. Olivia's panicked face was above her. Darcy was still groggy from the dream, and she instinctively reached for Olivia's shoulder. "I shot you. But you're not bleeding."

"I know. I saw everything."

"How ...? Oh, shit. I did it again." Darcy sat up and ran her hands through her short, black hair.

Olivia sat next to her on the bed and put her arm around Darcy's shoulders. "You promised me you wouldn't use your telepathy any more. If we get caught—"

"I hardly think the sniffers are out at this time of night, hunting telepaths. It's too late, and there's no way they could find us in this big building, anyway."

Olivia bit her lip. "You are so frustrating! The Telepathic Corps could be anywhere. They can pull us off the streets at any time. We might never see each other again, and Dan wanting to marry me will be the least of your troubles then."

Darcy just looked at Olivia, and shuddered at the rumors of what happened when the Telepathic Corps got hold of a telepath. Over the years, the rumors had grown from jail to torture and medical experimentation.

Olivia stood up and grabbed her bathrobe. "I'm going to shower. Trying to sleep tonight is useless."

"Liv, really, I promise it will be all right." *I'll make sure of it, no matter what it takes.*

"No, it won't. One of these days you're going to slip up, and then we'll both pay for it. We'll be taken away. We'll be tested, experimented on, and there won't be anything we can do about it. Every time you use your telepathy, we're in danger."

"But it was just a dream. I can hardly be blamed for reaching out for my sister when I'm scared."

"You know you will be blamed for anything you do that uses telepathy. You've got to start doing your exercises again."

"I hate those boring things," Darcy groaned. "My brain feels so numb and stupid when I'm done with them. I feel like I'll never think straight again."

"But they keep you out of trouble. They keep *us* out of trouble." Olivia sat back down next to Darcy. "Those exercises allow us to live a normal life, where we can do whatever we want." She took her sister's hand. "You really have to try."

Darcy looked into Olivia's teary eyes. "I promise I'll try. I'll do some of the exercises. I'll be extra careful, even when I'm asleep, to make sure I don't slip up." The dreams were far too frequent, and Olivia was right. Darcy knew it was dangerous to let their powers go unchecked.

"And I'll be careful, too. I'll try to wake up sooner when you're reaching out," Olivia promised.

The sisters hugged. "I'll make some coffee while you're in the shower," said Darcy. "I think we're going to have a long day."

In the kitchen, Darcy stared at the coffee pot and slammed her fist on the chipped counter. "Reckless," she sighed as she put coffee into the filter. If she could shake this feeling about Dan, she'd be able to release the nightmare, but the way he treated Liv … Darcy knew Dan didn't love her sister. Maybe it would have been easier for her to accept him if he had taken the trouble to show her the slightest respect as the sister of the woman he claimed to love. But early on, he made it clear his plans for Olivia did not include her.

She was staring at the cereal bowls in the cabinet when Olivia walked back into the kitchen, towel drying her long, blond hair. "Coffee's almost ready," Darcy said.

"Thanks." Olivia leaned against the kitchen counter, arms folded protectively across her chest. "Look, I know I'm hard on you, but I'm scared."

Darcy put her arm around her sister. "I know." She looked into Olivia's eyes. "Your eyes are puffy," Darcy said, a knot of guilt tightening in her stomach. Upsetting her sister wouldn't do either of them any good. They needed to stick together, now more than ever. "I've made you cry. I'm sorry. Look." She held up the tattered notebook containing the telepathic control exercises she'd used since she was a child. "I've got my book out, and I'll start working on the exercises tonight. I promise."

Olivia dropped her arms and nodded. She took two boxes of cereal from the cabinet and set them on the counter. "I'll do them with you. That way you won't be so bored."

Darcy released a relieved sigh. Every time she had the dream, she was afraid Olivia was going to leave her. Fighting with Liv made everything worse. "Thanks."

After they finished their cereal, Olivia said, "Since we're going to be up for the rest of the morning, we might as well get to work early."

"Ha! What work?" In Darcy's opinion, as long as Shaughnessey was in charge of finding cases for their fledgling P.I. firm, their workload was laughable at best.

The ceramic bowls clattered together as Olivia shoved them into the dishwasher. "I am sick of this! He's our biggest problem, but he's supposed to be our greatest help. I can't stand the thought of being stuck with him."

"Until we can find someone else, we've got no choice," said Darcy. After the brutal year it had taken to find someone to mentor them during their mandatory training period, she did not want to give up on Shaughnessey after only six months.

"Right. Like that'll ever happen," Olivia said. "We're going to have to finish with him to get our licenses. And we still need someone to teach us the finer points of the business. We can't keep making it up on our own. Some day we are going to get hurt." She fingered the diamond necklace Dan had given her. "Maybe I should ask Dan if he knows someone who needs us?"

"Dan is the least likely person to help us out," said Darcy. "You can ask him, but you need to figure out what to say before you go to him."

"He'll say the best way to protect me is for him to keep an eye on me." Olivia sighed. "Then he'll ask me to marry him, and I'll have to turn him down again, and it will be ugly for weeks."

"If he really wanted to help, he could throw some cases our way. We could use the money and the good reference. But he won't."

"I've asked, but he says they usually have internal people handle their investigations."

"I'm going to get dressed. Let's head in. Maybe we'll catch a good case today."

#

Olivia parked her six-year-old Audi in the spot labeled MORRISON INVESTIGATIONS. Of the eight tenants in the building, only Dr. Pak, the elderly dentist, was in. He specialized in early-morning and late-evening appointments, and his office never seemed to be empty during his unorthodox hours.

Louie sat near the corner of the building,

warming his hands over a tiny fire in a coffee can. He was a fixture in the neighborhood, preferring to spend his days and almost all of his nights outside. Nights when it was too cold, Olivia knew, Louie stayed with his sister over in Allston.

The sisters got out of the car. "Hey, Louie. What's the good word?" asked Olivia.

"Not much, Miss Liv. Been spending too many nights indoors, and I'm getting restless."

"Hang in there—spring's just around the corner."

Even though Shaughnessey never got into the office before noon, she asked, "Shaughnessey in yet?"

Louie scoffed. "Nah. It's not even seven. We won't be seeing him for a few hours yet."

She slipped him a five, which disappeared into the inside pocket of his duct-tape-patched down coat. "Too true."

"Have a nice day, Miss Liv."

"You too, Louie. I'll see you tomorrow."

They knew Louie got nervous when he was around too many people, so Darcy had been waiting at the door throughout the exchange. She smiled at Louie. "See you later," she called to him.

On the stairs to their office, Darcy said, "Every day, five dollars to Louie. For what?"

"He keeps an eye out for us, makes sure the building is left alone while it's empty. And he needs it more than we do."

"So he's a low-rent security guard?"

"I suppose so. But he's useful. Ask Dr. Pak. Last week he ran into a couple of kids trying to break into his office. Dr. Pak yelled, and Louie came running to save the day. Kids ran off, nothing was taken, and Dr. Pak wasn't hurt. That's got to be worth something. Since then, Dr. Pak has been squeezing Louie in to do some work on him when he's done with patients."

Morrison Investigations was located in a shabby third-floor walk-up in Brighton. When the sisters had originally rented the space six months before, they had been sure that by now they would have been able to afford better offices, maybe a secretary. Instead, Olivia's trust fund was paying their rent until the business started generating more clients.

Shaughnessey had promised them the stars when he agreed to be their mentor. It was his job, during the two-year training period, to teach them the business and make sure they could handle just about any case they came across. Instead, he took half the money they made, up front, and disappeared for days at a time, leaving them to work cases on their own.

Darcy breathed a sigh of relief when she opened the door to their office and saw that Shaughnessey really wasn't there. Olivia looked toward their mentor's desk as well.

"Probably sleeping it off somewhere," laughed Darcy.

"Coffee?" asked Olivia.

"Yeah. It's going to be a long day."

Olivia started the thrift-store Mr. Coffee and sat at the partner's desk the sisters shared.

Darcy threw the phone bill down on top of their latest case file. "Another overdue, stamped in red. We're not going to get much business without a phone," she said.

Olivia finished opening the envelope in her hand. "Or electricity," she said, tossing the overdue electric bill on top of the phone bill. "I can call them, maybe get us another extension."

Darcy sat back in her chair. "We have cases, we get the job done, but we still can't even pay our bills. Last week, five sick-day investigations, our best week yet, and we can only pay one of these bills."

"Our luck will turn around. We're paying our dues, getting our name out there. Someday soon a really great case will come through that door, and we'll be on the upswing. You'll see." *It's all about marketing and perseverance*, Olivia thought.

"Or someday we can get rid of that leech Shaughnessey, keep our money, and make this business at least pay our expenses, maybe even bring in enough to live on."

Olivia sighed. "I'd love that."

Darcy sat up, excitement in her eyes. "Maybe we can buy him out—just get him to sign forms for us but leave us alone. Maybe we could get a loan from Dad for that."

"I doubt even *I* could talk Dad into that. He doesn't want us to succeed here. He'd be too happy to see us come home and act like the proper daughters he thought he raised."

Before Darcy could reply, the phone rang. "Morrison Investigations, how may I help you?"

"Miss Morrison? This is Marcy Stone calling. I wanted to thank you for your work this week. I've fired my secretary and made sure she'll never work in this town again. I don't know what she was thinking, abusing her sick days like that. Anyway, good work. Your check is in the mail."

"Thank you, Ms. Stone," said Darcy. "Please keep us in mind for all your investigations. We are available for criminal and civil investigations, background checks, and a variety of personal investigations."

"I...I'll think about it," she stammered, "but I'm not comfortable using women for dangerous work. Good bye."

"Yes, but ..." When it was clear Stone had hung up on her, Darcy dropped the phone on her desk.

"What did she say?"

She grimaced. "She's not comfortable using women for dangerous work."

"Ridiculous!"

"It's bullshit. You'd think a woman would know better," Darcy agreed.

The door to the office opened, and the pot-bellied, unshaven man they knew as Miles Shaughnessey walked in, smiling. Darcy wasn't sure if that was good or bad, but when it came to his dealings with the two of them, it was usually bad.

"Good morning, girls," he said as he sat at his desk.

"What are you doing here so early?" asked Olivia.

He ignored her question. "Who was that on the phone?"

Darcy reeled as the smell of old beer and cigarettes wafted toward her. "Jesus, Shaughnessey! You didn't even bother to go home and shower the track off before you came in?"

"For you, darling, I saved my natural aromas. Knew they'd drive you wild." He laughed at the horrified looks on Darcy and Olivia's faces.

Olivia said, "It was Marcy Stone. She called to tell us what a great job we did and that the check is in the mail."

He smiled and said, "You made coffee. Good

girl."

Darcy stiffened. She hated his condescension, greed, and sloth. The only thing she liked about him was his absence. When he was gone, she could breathe easier, knowing he couldn't possibly ruin things for them from afar.

Shaughnessey dumped his three-day-old coffee into the ficus and poured himself a new cup. He looked in the tiny refrigerator, which was empty. "What, no cream? Now this is useless." He put the mug on the desk and took a bottle of beer out of the bag he had set on his desk. He cracked it open and said, "Nothing for me to do here. I'll just be taking my cut and heading out to the track."

"Check's not here yet," said Olivia, even though they'd been through this argument several times before.

"But it will be, and until it gets here, you'll front me the money. Your next progress report is due soon, and you don't want to get a bad score on it, do you? The licensing bureau can be very particular about these things." He swilled down a third of the bottle, belched, and leaned back, ready to argue with her.

Over Darcy's glaring face, Olivia said, "No, but if we don't pay the phone bill, we're not going to get any clients. They're threatening to shut the phone off in a week if we don't pay them."

"Then it sounds to me like you've got to find a new case or two before then, don't you?"

Olivia sighed and pulled out her checkbook. She wrote Shaughnessey a check for a hundred dollars and tossed it on his desk.

"There's a good girl." He finished his beer, stood, and took the check. "You know where I'll be if you need me." He laughed as he walked out of the office. "Like you'll find more cases," he snorted.

Darcy stood up, but Olivia grabbed her hand. "Let him go. We're better off without him anyway."

Darcy sat, concentrating on letting go of her aggravation. "What we need to do," she said as she closed the door to the office, "is work a few cases he doesn't know about. We could pay off these bills."

Olivia smiled. "I think we'll have to. I'm running out of money to keep this business going. And Shaughnessey deserves to be left high and dry. Maybe we should be making our own reports to the licensing bureau."

Darcy winced. "Tattling won't get us anywhere, and we'll just get a reputation for being hard to work with. No one will come near us." Her face lit up. "But maybe when we're done with him we can report all this, so he doesn't do this to some other unsuspecting fool."

"We can do that, but meanwhile ..." Olivia gestured to the unpaid bills, "what about these?"

"I don't know, Liv."

"Well, I have an idea. I've been thinking I could get a night job or a weekend job."

Darcy's face flamed. "No! You do enough as it is."

"But I could ..."

"If anyone should get a second job, it's me. You already put all your money into supporting us. Your trust fund shouldn't be used to keep me afloat."

"And you should never have been forced to use yours for college, just because Mom and Dad didn't approve of your choices," interrupted Olivia.

"I'll take a second job because you're a better face for the business. You're good with people; they like you and trust you. Me, they tend to avoid."

"But when do you have time?"

"Nights, weekends, days—it doesn't really matter. But you'll have to keep things running here while I'm away." She looked Olivia in the eye. "You'll have to deal with Shaughnessey on your own."

"I can handle that," she said with a shudder. "I think. Promise me it won't be for long. I might be good with people, but even I have limits with him."

"I know. I'll do everything I can. In the meanwhile, we should get back to stuffing envelopes."

Olivia picked up an envelope. "I don't know if this flyer is really doing any good. We haven't had a single call from any of them, and we're about out of stamps."

"Don't give up hope. Even if we have to send one to every lawyer in Massachusetts, sooner or later one of them is going to call us, and we'll get more work."

Chapter 6

Olivia smiled at Dan's ringtone, the opening lines from Cream's "Sunshine of Your Love" and then she picked the phone up from their desk. "Hi, sweetie."

"Good morning, beautiful. Is Shaughnessey with you?"

"No, he's gone to the track."

"You get paid for another job?"

"No, but a client called to say the check was in the mail. That's good enough for him."

"Liv, really—you should consider working for me. We make a great team."

"I know we do, but I'm sure that's not why you called this morning," she said. "How can we help you?"

"Put me on speaker. I've got a case for you."

Olivia smiled as she pushed the speaker button. "Really? Tell us about it."

"I can't tell you anything until you come down, sign some standard nondisclosure forms, and have lunch with me."

"Lunch?" asked Darcy.

"Oh ... uh, sure. You can tag along, too, Darcy."

"No, thanks. I've got plans." *Plans to avoid you at all costs.* "I'll come down and sign the forms, but then I've got to head out."

"All I can tell you right now is that my client is a telepath."

Damn, thought Darcy. She'd known this day would come. She was torn between wanting to help a fellow telepath and fear that their secret would be exposed. No one except their parents knew they were telepaths, and they agreed to keep it that way.

Dan took a deep breath. "If you're squeamish and don't want to work with that kind of person, I completely understand. I wouldn't have taken the case at all—no one in the firm would have—but Stirling assured me he's a high-profile client, the case is sure to set legal precedent, and we want in on the fame and glory."

What an ass, thought Darcy, unable to keep the thought from her face.

Olivia sent Darcy a distressed look. "We'll head to your office right away. I'm a little worried about working with telepaths, but I don't think it will be a problem. I mean, if you're brave enough to do it, I am too."

"Great. I knew I could count on you. I'll see you soon," said Dan.

When Olivia hung up the phone, Darcy said, "What do you think you're doing?"

"I'm taking a case that will pay us real money—money to keep the phones on, money for power, money to pay our rent on time. That's what you just said you wanted."

"But Liv, telepaths? How do we know we can trust them? What if …" Her voice trailed off.

"Let's just go talk to Dan, see what the case is. A telepath is in legal trouble, and we can help. How can we refuse?"

"It's too risky. We can't meet a telepath and hope to keep our secret safe."

Olivia dialed her phone. "Hi, Dan? Darcy and I

want to know if we will actually meet the telepath. The more I think about it, the more nervous I am about being scanned. What would a person like that do with the information in my brain?" She paused. "Oh, good. That's great to know. We'll be right down."

"Dan says he'd 'never subject the woman he loves to that kind of danger.' "

Darcy couldn't stand it. "I'm sure he wouldn't mind if *I* met the telepath. And besides that, how the hell will he be able to make sure we aren't scanned?"

Olivia shook her head. "He can't. I know that. He's just trying to look out for me."

"I don't know how you put up with him."

"Oh, Dar. He loves me. He thinks I'm special, a person to be cherished and protected. He's what I need. And he has a lot of really good qualities as well. He's loyal, smart, and dependable, and when it's just the two of us, he's a really great guy."

"But how can any of this matter when he doesn't know the real you?"

"He does know me. There's just one little secret he doesn't know."

"It's not a 'little secret'," said Darcy. "It's the core of your being. It's the one thing that makes you different—the one thing that would make you a completely different person if you took it away."

Olivia shook her head. "Let's just go. We aren't in any position to be picky."

They drove to the office of Gray and Shalek in silence, but Darcy's mind was reeling. *Dan has to have an angle. He's not the kind of man who offers to help out of the kindness of his heart. Everything he does is for his own personal gain. But how could he gain from having the two of us work on a case?*

Darcy broke the silence. "What do you think he wants?"

Olivia glared at her sister. "You can't let even a single opportunity to make a dig at Dan pass by. You never, ever give him the benefit of the doubt. He wants to hire us to work on a case for him, just like he said."

Darcy gripped the steering wheel tighter. "But what's his angle? He's told you that his firm has its own investigators and he doesn't need our services. Why the sudden change?"

Olivia turned toward Darcy. "We've been at this for six months. He's seen us struggle, and he's heard me talk about how tough it can be to make ends meet. Maybe he's just showing a little kindness."

"I doubt it." In the three years she had known him, Dan had never shown Darcy anything but contempt. He treated her like a problem to be ignored until it went away. There was no way he was being kind to her now.

Olivia shrugged. "Maybe their investigators are all busy."

"Or maybe they have the good sense to stay away from a telepath case."

#

Gray and Shalek's offices took up four floors of the Prudential Building. The receptionist on the fourteenth floor peered at Darcy's faded jeans and called Dan's office before she handed them visitor badges. "Mr. Stevens will be down to escort you. Please wait in the seating area."

Ignoring the delicate scent of the lemon topiary trees in the waiting area, Darcy chose a chair and started thumbing through the magazines provided. She didn't golf, she didn't own a yacht, and vacation home decor was not at all what she needed, so she threw the magazines back on the table. She spent the rest of the time Dan made them wait glowering at the trees, hating their pruned perfection.

A young woman approached them. "Miss Morrison and Miss Morrison?"

"Yes," said Olivia.

"If you would follow me to Mr. Stevens's office." She turned, not waiting for their reply, and escorted them to Dan's office, three floors up.

"I'm so glad you could make it," Dan said after they were all seated. "I think this case is a good opportunity for you and could really make your name in the business." He smiled at Olivia and took her hand.

It's as though I'm not even in the room, Darcy thought. How he could love one twin and completely dismiss the other was beyond her.

"I've got a new client. He's been accused of murder, and I'll be defending him. It's my first murder case, and I'm going to need every advantage—"

"So why are you hiring us?" Darcy broke in.

Dan looked at her, eyes blazing at being interrupted. He smiled the fake "I like you too" smile he always used to smooth over his true feelings for her. "As I was saying, I'll need the advantage of working with the most thorough and determined investigators I know." He looked back to Olivia. "If there's anything I've learned about you, it's how strong and persistent you are. I never thought you would make it this far in such a tough business, and I'm quite proud of you."

"Just to be clear," Darcy interrupted again, "you're proud of us for our miraculous feats in finding lost dogs? Or perhaps it was our sterling professionalism when we managed to cover ourselves with garbage, only to find out the husband really wasn't cheating?" She sat back and crossed her arms. *Let him talk his way out of that question.*

"Darcy, stop it!" said Olivia.

"As I said, you are strong and persistent."

Darcy looked at Olivia's smiling face. *Oh God,* thought Darcy. *She's eating this up. She thinks Dan actually respects her.*

"I am representing George Wynton. He's accused of murdering his girlfriend, and the police think it was a crime of passion."

"Isn't he the famous telepath? The one who's on the news?"

"Yes. The woman he allegedly killed was both his girlfriend and his PR agent."

"Why would he need a PR agent? He seems such a genuinely caring person," Olivia said.

Dan looked at her as if she were a small and stupid child. "First, I don't think we should get in the habit of calling telepaths people, Olivia. They're not like us, and unless it can be medically proven, I don't believe they're even human. Second, your opinion proves that his PR campaign was working."

Darcy felt enraged. It would be such a simple thing to walk across the room and punch that smug, disapproving face of his. She grabbed one hand with the other and attempted not to grimace. It didn't matter. Dan was ignoring her, as always.

"And he has no alibi?" asked Olivia.

"He was found at the scene of the crime, talking to the victim."

"What? She wasn't dead?"

"Oh, yes, she was dead. Shot in the tub. He was just sitting on the floor, talking to her about their plans for the future."

Olivia's face paled. "That's really strange. He had the gun?"

"The gun hasn't been found, but the ballistics report links the gun used to shoot her to three unsolved murders over the past twenty years."

"So you think he might have killed four people over twenty years?"

"I wouldn't put it past him. In fact, I have a theory. What if a telepath comes across a person he can't read, or a person he can't control? What can he do?"

"Oh, Dan, do you think that's possible? I didn't know telepaths could control people with their minds," said Olivia.

Darcy rolled her eyes. How Olivia could keep up this act was beyond her. Neither of them could control people with their minds, so it stood to reason that other telepaths couldn't.

"Not proven. But really, what makes you think they couldn't? So if a telepath ran across someone immune to them, they'd have to kill that person."

Darcy had heard enough. "That's a huge leap, Dan, to go from not being able to read someone to killing them. What possible reason could they have?"

He smiled at Darcy, no emotion showing in his eyes. "I have a theory."

Oh yes, Darcy thought. *Share with us, at boring length, yet again, your conspiracy theories about telepaths. Maybe I could just throw myself out the window instead.*

He began pacing his office. "Telepaths are in the minority, but that's not a threat to them, because they can control us. Right now, I think they're in the testing phase of control, but at some time, on some signal given by their leader—who may just turn out to be this Wynton—they're going to control us all, and we'll be nothing but slaves to their power." He paused and turned to Olivia, who wore a look equal parts fear of telepaths and awe of Dan. He took her look for encouragement and went on. "But the only flies in the ointment are those of us who are naturally immune to their powers. We can't be controlled, and, therefore, we're a threat."

Darcy was shocked at his arrogance. "You think you're immune?"

He smirked. "I'm certain I'm strong-willed enough to repel any mental attacks."

She couldn't resist. She knew it was wrong, but she had to look. In his mind, she read his absolute confidence that they would screw up the case and that Wynton would wind up behind bars for life, where Dan thought all telepaths belonged.

"So, can we get back to the case?" she asked.

"Of course. I have to provide Wynton with a vigorous defense, the best defense his anonymous benefactors can afford. To do that, we have to find other people who could also have had a motive to kill Mrs. Harrison and then pick apart their alibis until we have reasonable doubt as to Wynton's guilt. Can you do that for me?"

"I'm sure we can handle the case," said Olivia. "And when we find who did kill her, it will be a great day for us."

Dan smiled at her. "Olivia, you're making a rookie mistake. You can't believe your client when he says he's innocent. The first rule of the legal profession is that everyone lies, and absolutely everyone lies to their attorney, at least some of the time. The sad truth about our legal system is that it's not about who did what; it's about what can be proven."

Darcy interrupted. "I'd like to talk it over before we take the case. We'll call you this afternoon."

Dan turned to Darcy, anger flashing from his eyes. "You don't want the case? I think some gratitude is in order here. I had to go to my boss and talk the two of you up before he would allow me to hire you." He walked to Olivia and took her hand. "You want the case, don't you? I really need your help here, but I can't beg."

"I'm sure Darcy just wants to talk over some of the details. I'll call you in a few hours. Everything will be fine."

Dan looked at his watch. "Good. I was going to have to cancel our lunch anyway. I've got a meeting right now, so I've got to go." He buzzed for his secretary, but there was no response. "Where the hell did she get off to? Liv, remind me to fire her. She's missing, so now I have to take the time to walk you down to reception."

"I'm sure we can find our way back on our own," said Darcy.

"Not allowed. If you don't work here, you must always have an employee with you. Gray and Shalek take security very seriously. And with the billionaire clients we have, we can't be too careful."

Clients like John "The Fish" Pescado. Darcy remembered the case. Pescado had billions of dollars, some of which he used when Gray and Shalek helped him avoid prosecution for a toxic waste dump. Dan had made his name in the firm on that case. He had been the first associate to arrive and the last to leave each day, surviving only because Olivia took on the role of his unpaid and unappreciated assistant. Anything he needed, he called her, and she delivered — clean shirts, food, coffee — and not only for him. Anything the more experienced lawyers wanted, he made Olivia deliver at any time of the day or night. The stress and lack of sleep nearly killed her. In the end he merely took her out to dinner, and instead of showing his appreciation, he continued to take business calls all night.

He opened the door to his office and looked out; still no secretary. "Let's go. I can't be late to the meeting."

"There's no need to get angry. We're coming," said Darcy.

Dan glowered at Darcy in the elevator. "Look, either you want the job or not. Don't waste my time here. Are you going to take it, or should I find some real PIs who know a good opportunity?"

It won't kill him to wait. And do I really want to work for him? No way. Darcy looked over at Olivia and shook her head no, but it was too late.

Olivia gave Darcy's hand a squeeze and turned to glare at Dan. "So you don't want to hire us after all. All your talk of supporting my career, yet you're trying to bully us out of making a thoughtful decision. Getting cold feet, are you? Wishing you'd called someone else instead? Forget it. We're taking the case. I expect to be fully briefed when we meet tomorrow morning at eight."

"Good," said Dan. "I can't make eight. I'll have my new secretary call you tomorrow with a time. And if you are diligent enough to start today, he's being held at the Washington Street precinct. They've agreed to hold him there instead of bringing him to the Nashua Street jail. It'll be safer for him in a smaller lockup."

"There's no need to take that tone with us. Of course we'll start today," said Olivia.

Dan's expression softened. "I'm sorry, baby. You're right. I'll call you tonight."

The elevator doors opened. Olivia took a step toward him, but he put his hand up. "Not at work." He let the door close, leaving the women in the lobby.

"What the hell was that?" asked Darcy.

"He's just in one of his moods," said Olivia. "I'm sure by tomorrow he'll be all sunshine and happiness again."

Darcy rounded on her sister. "I meant *you*. I didn't want the job. I don't want to work for him, no matter how good it could be for us."

Olivia stopped walking. "Dar, this is a big step for him. You have to see beyond the surface. He's trying to help us. He wants to see us succeed. Finally, he's given in to the idea that I won't just be a trophy for him, that I am a serious woman with a serious job. In his way, he's showing his respect for me. For us."

"I don't see it. He's not a person who shows respect to anyone who can't give him what he wants. He's got none for me and none for his client. When you aren't doing what he wants, he doesn't treat you well, either. He's got an angle somewhere, I can feel it."

"You didn't—"

"I don't need telepathy to know he's a jerk," she said. "I don't need to read minds to know you can do a hell of a lot better. Nine out of any ten strangers on the street would tell you he's working some sort of angle. It's who he is." *And there's no way I'm going to tell you that I did look into his mind.* "I wanted nothing to do with this case, but now that you've committed us to it, I'll be damned if we're going to let him have the satisfaction of seeing us fail. Let's get back to the office and get to work. We can hunt down background on Wynton and Harrison so we'll be ready for whatever he throws at us tomorrow."

Olivia stopped walking. "Dar, I know you're going to hate this, but I think we need to see Wynton."

No chance in hell am I going near someone who might scan me. No chance will I allow our secret to escape. "No. Liv, he's accused of murder. A murderer isn't going to think twice about scanning someone. There's no way I'm placing myself in jeopardy like that."

"Then why do you go out? Why do you leave the apartment? You could be scanned at any time, by anyone. Every time you're in public, your secret is at risk, but you never talk about that."

"That's because I can at least pretend like no one is scanning me, and since nothing bad has ever happened, I think that on the street I'm safe — "

"That's exactly what Dan thinks. As long as he's anonymous and in a crowd, he thinks he's safe."

The idea that she and Dan thought the same way about anything clawed at Darcy's insides, but she continued. "As I was saying, in a one-on-one meeting with a telepath, what's to keep him from taking a peek?"

"What keeps you from taking a peek?"

Darcy turned away, hiding the guilty look she could not control from Olivia. "But we don't have to meet with him. All we have to do is provide reasonable doubt."

"No. I can't let it go at that. Without someone being convicted, too many people will still think he did it. Wynton has everything to lose. He's worked so hard to present an image of telepaths as being respectful of people's boundaries, of never reading anyone without permission first. He helps people. He's not that kind of man."

Darcy snorted. "If I trusted your ability to judge men ..."

"Just shut up, and let's go. I'll meet with him tomorrow, alone."

Chapter 7

Olivia woke the next morning to the sound of Dan's ringtone. Without opening her eyes, she grabbed her phone. "Goo—" She cleared her scratchy throat. "Good morning."

"Look, baby, I don't have time to meet on the Wynton case at all today. You'll have to come pick up my notes."

"Wait—what?" she said.

"Jesus, Olivia, it's six o'clock. You should be awake by now."

She cringed at the disdain in his voice. Sitting up, she opened her eyes. "So, we're not meeting this morning? And we need to go to your office to pick up your notes?"

"Right."

"Can't you send them by messenger?"

"No, I can't. And don't forget I need you to be ready by six tonight for dinner with Stirling and his wife."

Olivia rubbed the sleep from her eyes. She had forgotten about dinner with Dan's boss. *It's going to be a busy day.* "Six. I'll see you then."

"And wear the blue dress. It's more forgiving." He hung up before she could say anything else.

She looked over at Darcy, still sound asleep, and realized Dar hadn't had the nightmare last night. She smiled and decided to let her sister sleep in while she made breakfast.

Ten minutes later, when the coffee was brewing and the quiche was in the oven, Olivia began reflecting on Dan's call. He knew how busy they would be today. Refusing to use a messenger was his way of emphasizing his disappointment with her laziness. Anyone not up by five in the morning was lazy in his eyes. As for the blue dress being more forgiving — forgiving of what? Her figure? He was happy enough with her shape when they were alone. Was he really trying to tell her she was barely presentable?

She closed her eyes, took a deep breath, and slowly exhaled. She hated it when he got like this. The stress of his job forced him to say such cruel things. She knew he didn't believe them, not really.

The coffee maker beeped, and she opened her eyes. The sky outside her kitchen window began to lighten, promising another overcast day. She poured two cups of coffee and brought them into the bedroom.

"Wake up, sleepyhead," she said softly as she opened the curtains.

"Five more minutes," pleaded Darcy.

"In five minutes, I'll have drunk all your coffee."

Darcy groaned but pushed her blankets off and sat up. "Fine. I'm up." She smiled when she saw her cup of coffee on the bedside table. "Thanks, Liv." She took a big sip.

"No problem. Did you sleep well?"

Darcy nodded, her mouth full of coffee.

"You didn't have that dream again?"

"No … I don't remember having any dreams. I forgot that was one of the side effects of our exercises. I'd never appreciated it until now."

Olivia smiled and turned to make her bed. "Good. Breakfast will be ready in a bit. Oh, and Dan called earlier. He can't meet with us, so we need to pick up his notes before I interview Wynton."

Darcy rolled her eyes.

"Hey! I saw that. Cut him some slack. He's a busy guy. I'll do just fine working through his notes."

"It's not that. I'll go with you. It's not fair to let you assume all the risk. And if he scans you, he'll probably see we're both telepaths so what difference does it make if I don't go?"

#

Olivia sat on the couch, nervously clutching a pillow. When Darcy was out of the shower, she said, "Dar, we need to talk."

Darcy looked over at her from the hallway. "We do? What's up?"

Olivia turned to face her sister. "Can you come in here?"

Darcy nodded, walked over, and sat on the couch, looking very concerned. "Is there something wrong?"

"No, nothing's wrong, but I've made a decision." She took a steadying breath. "I don't want to hide any more. I want to be able to tell the truth about myself."

Darcy nodded. "I thought this might be it."

"First, there's a problem. I'd have to tell Dan." Her voice wavered. "The whole truth. And I'm afraid to. I'm afraid he will leave me because I represent all that he doesn't want in his life. He's afraid of telepaths, and if I don't approach him the right way, he'll never speak to me again.

Darcy reached out and took her sister's hand. "Oh, Liv. I don't know if that's such a good idea."

"My dream is to make telepaths more accepted, more trusted. I think that familiarity will finally bring telepaths and normals together. The way things are now, that will never happen. With George as the only spokesman, people can pretend he's the only telepath, or that he's the only good one,."

"And what do you want to do, exactly?" asked Darcy.

"I have to come out as a telepath. A female telepath out in public will help people see the softer side of us as well."

"Are you crazy? After all the work we've done to keep ourselves hidden, to blend in, you want to out yourself?"

Olivia nodded. "Yes, I think I do."

"You realize you'd be outing me as well?"

"That's why we're talking first. It doesn't necessarily mean people will think you're a telepath as well."

Darcy sighed. "We're identical twins. No one would believe you were a telepath and I wasn't, unless we were both tested. I am not subjecting myself to that kind of testing for your sense of community."

"But can't you see how important it is? How much good it will do for everyone?"

"I can't think of everyone else. We don't have that luxury. We have to consider what will happen to the two of us first." She stood up and began pacing. "I've spent my life protecting you. Remember when you read Tommy Freelander's mind to find out what he wanted for his birthday and he found out?

Olivia nodded. At the early age of six, she had

learned never to read someone's mind, not even with the best of intentions.

"And now it feels like you want to throw our safety away."

"Not true. I don't want to …" Olivia paused. Darcy was right. She would be throwing the carefully constructed lies her parents had built and lived with for more than two decades to the wind. Revealing her true nature would have implications for not just Darcy, but her parents, her extended family, for Dan. In her fervor, she hadn't fully considered that.

"You're right."

Darcy stopped pacing and sat back down. "We can't do this right now. If it really means so much to you, we'll have to find a way to do it without getting the rest of the family in trouble."

"You'd help me? You'd go public, too?"

"I'm not ready to go that far," Darcy said, "but I understand why you are. I'll do what I can for you. But no drastic actions until we figure this out, right?"

"Right. But I'm not willing to give up on this."

"That's fine. But be careful. We're not prominent enough to be safe from the sniffers. We could be snapped up at any minute."

"I know. But there haven't been any in Boston for at least a year," she said.

"Then we're about due for a visit, aren't we?" Olivia rolled her eyes. She'd been listening to tales of the Telepathic Corps since she was a small girl. She'd still never met one and had often wondered if they really existed.

#

Olivia studied the thin folders Dan's newest secretary

handed over. The woman was clearly pissed at having to come in early on her first day. *She's another secretary who won't last long,* Olivia thought.

The rush-hour drive from Dan's office to the Brighton police department frustrated Olivia. *Dan could have saved us this trip into the city if he'd just sprung for a messenger.*

The precinct was just winding down from the night's inevitable vice arrests — hookers, drunks, and a surprising variety of people strung out on anything to take their pain away. Olivia walked in and stopped. A wall of desperation flooded her mind. Somewhere near the precinct, a telepath was collecting and projecting all the panic and fear most people kept shut up inside. She held on to the door frame until the vertigo subsided.

"You all right?" asked Darcy.

"Yeah," she shook her head. "I'm okay. Can you feel that?"

Darcy nodded and took a deep breath. "Sniffers?"

Olivia bit her lip and nodded. "They must know Wynton is here."

A heavyset man with gray hair rose from his desk and called out to them. "Darcy, Olivia!" He waved them over.

They both smiled and hugged him.

"Uncle Joe! I didn't know you'd be here this morning," Darcy exclaimed.

"Hadn't planned on it. This is my vacation week. But when Fraser called to tell me you were interviewing Wynton, I canceled my plans. Someone has to watch over you two and make sure you don't get in over your heads."

Olivia faked a scowl at him. "Uncle Joe, do you

really think we'd do that?"

"Every day of the week," he laughed. "But listen, you two can't go around calling me Uncle Joe, not if you want to be taken for professionals."

"Uh, sure," said Darcy. "Joseph?"

He made a face. "Absolutely not. Only your grandmother called me that. Here I'm just Broadbent."

Olivia sat at his desk. "What can you tell us about the case ... Broadbent?"

"Absolutely nothing. You know the rules."

She smiled at him. "You can't blame a girl for trying."

Darcy walked into the interrogation room first. She extended her hand to the man sitting at the table. When he looked up at her, she was taken aback by the deep circles under his eyes. "Mr. Wynton? I'm Darcy Morrison, and this is my sister, Olivia. We work for your attorney and we have some questions for you."

He flicked his eyes toward Broadbent.

Broadbent nodded. "Just rap on the door when you're ready to leave."

Once he left, the sisters sat down. "I'd like to start with you telling us about your relationship to Mrs. Harrison," said Darcy.

Wynton sat back and sighed. "Kathleen and I were having an affair. It bothered me that we couldn't be out in public together. I was doing everything I could to convince her to leave that no-good bigot for me. She was happy with me, happier than she ever was with her husband."

"How long were you seeing her?"

"We'd been seeing each other for six months."

"Six months, and you thought she'd leave her husband of ..." she consulted her notes, "twelve years for you?"

"She said it was a relief to be with me. She didn't have to hide who she was with me."

Darcy looked at him, not understanding.

"I'm a telepath. She knew she couldn't lie to me. I'd be able to tell. The honesty, knowing I'd know everything about her ... she loved that."

Darcy couldn't keep the surprise out of her voice. "You read her mind?"

"She asked me to. She wanted me to. Whenever I felt like it, she wanted me to see what she was thinking."

"And did you?"

"Occasionally. When she seemed upset, I'd look to see what the problem was. I wanted to help."

"And what were her problems?"

"Her husband. Ugly, hateful little man. And bigoted. Hated telepaths, hated that she was working with us, hated that she loved her job. He hated it so much he began beating her."

"Did he kill her?"

"I think so. Get me into a room with him and I'll prove it."

She sat back, stunned. He had just offered to violate the first code of the civilized telepath: never, ever scan someone without permission. Sure, she'd done it occasionally, but Wynton? He had such a squeaky-clean reputation.

"A scan isn't admissible evidence."

"No, but if I knew, I could tell you where to find the evidence."

Olivia broke in. "That's disgusting. It's suborning the legal system."

"The legal system is broken. If you ask me, telepaths should be used. False imprisonment would plummet."

"And anyone with a strong enough mind could fake their way out of a legitimate prison sentence."

"It's never been proven that anyone can resist being scanned," he said.

"Can we get back to this case?" Darcy asked.

He leaned forward, looking intent. "It was her husband. He's the only one who could have done it. It was only a matter of time before he went off the deep end and killed her."

"Did she ever go to the police or hospital?"

He shook his head. "No, she never did. Like many abused women, she was too afraid."

"We'll look into that. Why did you go to her house that night? I presume it was off limits to you."

"Absolutely. But her husband said he would be in Houston, and she invited me over."

"Did anyone else know you'd be there?"

"Absolutely not."

"Did anyone see you go in?"

"Just the cabbie—but I don't remember what cab I took."

Darcy laughed. "You're the main suspect in a murder investigation. You're the only suspect right now, and you can't remember your only alibi witness?"

"Believe me," he sighed. "I spent all night trying. I gave the cabbie a fifty-dollar tip to get me there fast."

At least that's something, she thought. "Did anyone else see you?"

"No."

"All right, we'll start there," said Olivia.

"It might not matter anyway, Liv. He was

caught sitting with the body—she had just died. An alibi of a few minutes won't make a difference," said Darcy.

"Is there anything else you want to tell us?"

He shook his head.

"Are you aware of anyone else who would want to hurt her?"

"Her hus—"

"Besides her husband," Olivia interrupted. "You've had a lot of news coverage lately. She's really been pushing the telepath agenda. That may have made her some enemies."

"None that she told me about."

"But you looked into her mind."

"No one stood out." He sighed. "It takes a long time to fully read a mind. I wanted the surface thoughts—what she thought of me, how her day was, how I could make her happy. I didn't ..." He squeezed his eyes shut, too late to stop a tear from escaping. "I didn't take the time to look. It was all still so fresh and new. We were in love, and all I wanted was to make that feeling last for as long as I could."

Olivia reached over and put her hand on his. "You are not responsible for her death. You couldn't know someone was going to kill her."

He looked up, anger in his eyes. "Do you think that helps me sleep at night?"

"No," she soothed, "I'm sure it doesn't. But it may, in time. Is there anything we can get for you?"

"Just get me out of here. My secretary will bring me whatever I need."

Darcy stood up and knocked on the door. Fraser opened it and led Wynton out, back to his cell.

Broadbent came walking down the hall toward them. "You all set?"

"Yes, we've got enough to go on now," Darcy lied.

"Really? Did he tell you where he put the gun?"

"Broadbent, you know we aren't going to tell you anything. Our client is innocent, and once we prove it you can buy us dinner."

He smiled. "Sticking to the 'I'm innocent' story, is he?"

"He'd be a fool not to."

"You two need anything else here? Technically, it's my vacation, and I'd like to get some relaxation in."

"We're good. You going straight home, or can we buy you an early lunch?"

Broadbent laughed. "Bringing two beautiful women into the bar—I'd be the envy of every cop there."

Olivia laughed. "Yeah, until we call you Uncle Joe."

"No, you two go on ahead. I'm going to rearrange my vacation time."

Chapter 8

Senator Aaron Hill's office was small but well-appointed. A large office wouldn't suit his constituency, but he had to have nice things and a beautiful secretary to keep up appearances.

His chief of staff walked into his office. "Senator?"

Hill glanced up from the *Boston Globe*. He had been reading an article on the telepaths. "What is it, Jerry?"

"I got a call from my friend in the Brighton PD."

Hill looked at him, frustrated that he always had to pull information out of the man. "And?"

"Wynton has a lawyer."

"Of course he does. Everyone has a lawyer. Hell, my Chihuahua has a lawyer," he chuckled.

"Not just any lawyer. It's Dan Stevens."

"Who the hell is that?"

"He's a young up-and-comer with Gray and Shalek."

Hill sat up. "How the hell did Wynton get a real attorney?"

When it was clear his chief of staff had no answer, Hill continued. "Mind control, I tell you. He's making that lawyer take the case. Must be a weak-minded man. You get him on the phone for me. I'll check him out."

"Yes, sir."

"And get me a file on him!" Hill yelled as the chief was closing the door.

Hill jumped up and started pacing the room. *Wynton has a good lawyer. This can't be good. If I don't make sure he's convicted, I'll never be a full member of the Twenty. Jacobs will make good on his threat.* He took a deep breath and felt his pulse slow. *Now is not the time to panic. It's time to get back to work.* Back in his black leather office chair, he finished reading the article. It wasn't quite the angle he had suggested when he'd had the editor in last week, but it was close enough.

He called his secretary on the intercom. "Baby, send some flowers to that *Globe* editor we had in last week, and get her to come around again. I've got a new idea for an article."

"Yes, sir."

The next article had to explore telepaths' ability to control other people. Weak-minded people. Once the idea was out there, people would start to notice. Then the country would really see what they were dealing with.

His phone rang. "Sir, I've got Dan Stevens on the line."

Shit, he thought. He had no information about Stevens to work with. He hated dealing with people he had no leverage on. He picked up the phone and answered in his most congenial voice. "Mr. Stevens, how are you this morning?"

"Fine, Senator, just fine. What can I do for you?"

"I understand you've got a client, a telepath. Is this true?"

"Yes. I am representing Mr. Wynton. But of course I can't talk about the case."

"Of course. I don't want to talk about Wynton

but about telepaths in general. You understand what a threat these people are to our society?" Not pausing for an answer, he went on. "I understand there's going to be quite an investigation into how they control our minds."

"Really? You think they can do that?"

"Oh, you'd be surprised, Mr. Stevens. Look for it in the paper. But in the meantime, are you sure you're not being … manipulated to take this case?"

Dan laughed. "Not me. I just take the cases assigned to me. If he was manipulating anyone, he would have to be working much further up the food chain than me."

"How far up?" *How far does the infiltration go?*

"I'm not exactly sure. I know Stirling Phillips gets involved with some case assignments, but usually middle management hands out the cases."

"And why did they pick you?"

"Well, sir, I like to think they have confidence in my abilities."

"And have you ever tried a murder case before?"

"No. This will be my first."

"You ready for it?"

"Honestly, it's a little daunting, holding a man's life in your hands. But I've got the full backing of my firm, so we're forging ahead with his defense."

"And if you're successful, and he's acquitted?"

"Then I've done my job. Sir, what exactly are you driving at?"

"You know my position on these telepaths. You know what I think they can do. Is it really in the best interest of humanity to let these … things … roam free among us? If Wynton is convicted, if we take down the poster boy for the telepaths, won't we be sending a clear message to the rest of his kind to clear out and leave us alone?"

"Sir?"

Is this man stupid, or careful? I have to take a leap and lay it all out for him. "Mr. Stevens, you are in a unique position to save humanity from being controlled by telepaths. Taking out a local leader will shake them up, disorient them, and give us an opportunity to destroy their community. But if he's found not guilty and allowed back on the streets, telepaths will have won the battle—and maybe the war."

"I see."

"Mr. Stevens, do you have children?"

"No, sir."

"Well, let me tell you, I have two beautiful daughters, and I will do anything to keep them from being manipulated by these telepaths. They're young, they're innocent. The things an unscrupulous telepath could make them do … well," he chuckled, "it's enough to make a father buy a shotgun."

"Sir, I understand. Believe me, I do. But while I have this case, I need to put my personal feelings aside and provide Mr. Wynton with the best defense I can."

This call is not going well, thought Hill. "Professional ethics. I can see that you would hold to them. After all, what is a man if he can't hold to his own code? Perhaps we should meet in person? You'll have lunch with me today. I'll send a driver."

Dan said, "I'd be happy to, sir."

Hill hung up and sat back. This Stevens was obviously unhappy to be representing a telepath. It wouldn't take much to get him to see it would be best if Wynton was convicted.

#

Sitting in the car after interviewing Wynton, Olivia turned to Darcy. "That wasn't so bad, was it?"

Darcy screwed up her face. "No, I suppose not. I don't think he scanned us, but that could just be me hoping he didn't."

"So, where to first? Harrison's house?"

"We should go to her office. There's no way the police will let us into the house until they're completely done, and I'm sure the husband won't welcome us either. The only other lead we have is the cabbie, and we'll have better luck finding him if we wait for the night shift to start."

Darcy punched Harrison's office address into the GPS and headed east, into Boston.

Harrison's office was not at all what Darcy expected. Instead of a chrome industrial look that mirrored the building's exterior, the offices of Harrison Public Relations were warm and inviting.

They walked across the richly patterned Persian carpet to the receptionist's desk. Her nameplate read CAMILLE JOHNSON.

The receptionist dabbed her eyes as she spoke into her headphone. "Yes, Mr. Ryan. Of course, Mr. Ryan. We here at Harrison PR are committed to providing you with the same quality service during this," her breath caught, "difficult transitional period."

She hung up and did her best to smile at Olivia and Darcy. "May I help you?"

"Yes. Hello. I am Olivia Morrison, and this is my sister, Darcy. We're looking into Mrs. Harrison's tragic death and we'd like—" Olivia stopped speaking when the receptionist broke down in tears. She stepped to the other side of the desk and put her arm around Camille's shoulders. "There, there now. Take a deep breath." She waited until the woman complied. "We're so sorry. From everything we've heard, she was a wonderful woman."

The receptionist dried the tears from her face. "Thank you. Are you with the police?"

Darcy stepped forward. "No. We are working with an attorney. We're trying to find out who is responsible for her tragedy."

"You are? Do you have an ID or something?"

Olivia pulled Dan's letter out of her bag. "We're working with Mr. Wynton's attorney to determine who did this."

The receptionist took the letter and read it quickly. "Oh, good. I couldn't believe it when I heard on the news that Mr. Wynton had been arrested. It just didn't make sense that he would want to hurt her."

"You must see everything that goes on here. Is there anything you can tell us? Did she have any enemies?" asked Darcy.

"She's had threats, you know, since she took on the Wynton account. She said not to worry about them, that no one would really hurt her. But I still worried. And then there was that argument with her husband."

"What argument?"

"He accused her of having an affair with Mr. Wynton," she laughed. "As though she would do that."

"Was Mrs. Harrison anti-telepath?" asked Darcy.

"Oh, no. It's not that he was a telepath. He was a client. She would never do that."

"She was a true professional," said Olivia.

"Yes, she was."

"Did she have problems with anyone in the office?"

"Not really," she said hesitantly.

Olivia looked at her, knowing the woman wanted to say more.

"Frank Adams, the new guy... It's not that she had problems with him, because his work was fine. He just didn't seem to fit in here."

"How long has he been here?"

"For six months, but he was still having problems fitting in. We all thought the world of Mrs. Harrison, but not him. It seemed like he couldn't stand her. I never understood why he chose to work here." She shook her head. "He's not here today."

"We'll check him out. Can you find his address for us? And we're going to need to look in Mrs. Harrison's office."

"I'm not sure ..."

"Help us prove Mr. Wynton didn't do it. Help us put the real killer away."

She shook her head again. Before the woman could continue, Darcy said, "She would want the right person to be punished, wouldn't she?"

The receptionist closed her eyes for a moment. "Yes, she would." She took a ring of keys from her desk drawer and stood up. "Follow me. The staff is meeting to try and figure out where we go from here."

They stopped at a conference room full of people eating pastries and speaking softly. "Everyone," Camille said, "meet Darcy and Olivia

Morrison. They are looking into our tragedy. They may have some questions for you, so please extend them every courtesy."

The group members looked up, and a few nodded before they went back to their food.

"Mrs. Harrison's office," she said as she unlocked the next door. "You can look, but you can't take anything out. Dial 0 if you need me. I've got to get back to my desk."

Camille pushed open the door and gasped. Papers covered every surface of the room. Clearly, someone had already been there, looking for something, leaving a mess behind.

Olivia pulled her phone from her bag and began taking photos.

"What did she keep in here?" asked Darcy.

Camille looked dazed. "Everything that was sensitive: papers, files, notes. In this business, sometimes you have to deal with unsavory things, so anything really damaging was in the safe."

"Can you open it?" asked Olivia.

"Yes. But ..."

"Once the police get here, they'll open the safe, with or without your help. Then we'll have to wait until they are done before we can see everything."

Darcy interrupted. "The bottom line is that we'll see everything sooner or later, and if we're going to help Mr. Wynton, sooner would be better."

Camille closed her eyes for a moment and sighed. "Okay, let me find the combination. It's in my desk, somewhere."

She returned a few moments later. "I've got it. If you could respect our clients' confidentiality?"

"We'll do our best. But if there's evidence of a crime, we'll have to act on it—" said Darcy.

"Our first priority is to find who did this horrible thing to Mrs. Harrison," interrupted Olivia.

The receptionist smiled at Olivia and opened the safe. She paused. "The business belongs to Mr. Harrison now, and I really think he would be upset if he knew you were looking at all these files."

"I really think Mr. Harrison wants us to find who killed his wife, don't you?" said Darcy.

"Yes, I suppose he would." She leaned in, conspiratorially. "Unless you think he did it?"

Darcy shook her head. "He's got an alibi. He was in Texas at the time of the murder."

"Still, things were rocky between them. And I think he hit her."

"We're looking into his alibi, but so far it looks solid," said Olivia.

Darcy took the files from Camille's hands. "Thank you. We'll work in here. Please make sure we aren't disturbed."

The sisters sat across from one another at the desk and got to work. A half hour and zero suspicious files later, they heard a loud commotion outside. Before they could get to the door, a short, red-faced man looked into the office and began yelling at them, even as Camille was trying to explain why they were there.

"You! What are you doing in my wife's office? Get out of there right now." He looked Olivia over and smiled. "I don't recognize you, you must be new. It doesn't really matter. You're fired, just like everyone else."

"Mr. Harrison?" asked Darcy.

"Of course. Pack your things and get out of here. You have five minutes."

Darcy stood and looked him straight in the

eye. "We are conducting an investigation into Mrs. Harrison's murder, and no one is to leave the office until I've had time to question them."

Harrison spluttered. "I'm not paying them to sit around here and wait for you to get around to talking to them."

"No. Your wife is."

"The hell she is. This business is mine now that she's dead, and I'm not paying these people one more cent. The business is closed, effective immediately, and I'll be selling everything off next week."

Olivia hated people like this, people who put profit above everything else. The man didn't even seem to be grieving. "No, you won't. Nothing happens until we're done here and the case is solved, if that takes a day, a week, or a year." She let her voice rise so the employees in the conference room could hear her. "You will keep this office open for the employees, and pay them, for two weeks."

"So it's in your best interest to cooperate with us, isn't it?" said Darcy.

"I'm not about to let two little girls tell me—"

Broadbent strode down the hall, his face as red as Harrison's. "What's all this, now?"

Harrison turned around. "I'm closing down the business, and these two," he pointed to Darcy and Olivia, "think they can keep me open. This business is closed, as of now."

Broadbent pulled out his badge and flashed it at Harrison. "No one goes anywhere until I say so, including you."

Harrison began to sputter.

"I believe you were told to keep the office open for two weeks, and pay the employees. See that you do, or I will make sure this business is tied up with so many legal problems you'll never be able to sell."

Harrison glowered, but he nodded.

"Good. Go around to all these nice people and assure them they have two weeks to find a new position and that you will pay them and make the office available to them for that time."

Harrison slinked off toward the nearest desks.

Camille smiled at them. "Thank you. Here is Frank's address." She handed Darcy a piece of paper before running off after Mr. Harrison.

Olivia opened the office door wider. "Broadbent," she began, before he pushed his way into the room and closed the door.

He did not speak loudly. He didn't have to. "I come down here to do one quick interview before I take the rest of the day off, and what do I find? My nieces acting as though they can tell a bereaved man what he can and can't do. If I ever catch you two impeding an investigation again, I swear that I'll have you uncertified before lunch."

"But—" began Darcy.

"No buts, young lady. You are a PI. You wait your turn. You investigate after the police. Is that clear?"

"Yes, sir," they answered in unison.

"Good. Since you've already started, fill me in on what you've found."

"She's got some notorious clients. What if she found out about something they didn't like, and they killed her to keep her quiet?" asked Darcy.

"Who did you have in mind?" asked Broadbent.

"This guy, J-Fre. He's been in the news a lot lately, all for violence."

"He has," Broadbent replied, "but that's the

nature of her work. It's public relations. She gets someone to say he did some horrible thing so he's arrested, and then they drop the charges. We haven't been able to prove it yet, but we're this close to arresting him for real, for wasting our time just to sell a few more albums."

"Why would he do that? He's been arrested. He's got a record now," said Olivia.

"A record is more of a selling tool than you realize. He isn't believable talking about life in the streets if he's got a comfortable life out in Newton. He's got to look like he's walking the walk and talking the talk."

She looked sad. "Oh. I guess I never thought of that."

Darcy looked up from her files. "Look at these threatening letters. And some of them are incredibly detailed."

Olivia took the top letter from the file and read it. "Damn! I can't believe she told Camille not to worry about the letters."

"The next one isn't much better."

"We're going to have to run down each of these people for alibis," Olivia sighed.

"I don't think so," said Broadbent as he took the file from her. "Fraser and I will take care of these. You two have no business near violent people."

Olivia was about to say something before she caught the steely determination in his eyes. "Fine. We've got other leads. Let's go, Darcy."

Chapter 9

Dan exited the car Hill had sent and walked into The Oak Bar. It had been refurbished since the last time he was there. He noticed the dark wood trim and gold upholstery and thought the place now looked like a nineteenth-century British officer's club. Waiters in crisp uniforms stood at attention, monitoring their tables.

He found Senator Hill holding court at a corner table, lecturing to a half-dozen younger men. As Dan approached, they all became silent. Hill waved off his companions with an airy gesture. They stood and moved to a table across the room.

Dan shook Hill's hand. "It's nice to meet you in person, Senator Hill."

"My pleasure." He pointed to the chair across from him. "Have a seat. What's your drink?"

"Scotch, neat," he told the waiter standing behind the senator. Turning to Hill, he said, "What can I do for you, sir?"

"I'd like to talk to you about your future."

"My future?"

"Yes." Hill finished his drink and set the glass on the table. "I've taken the time to check you out, Stevens, and I think you're a good man. You've got a solid head on your shoulders, and, quite frankly, you wouldn't be where you are if Gray and Shalek didn't have faith in you, too."

The waiter arrived with Dan's scotch.

"A toast to your bright future," said Hill.

"Thank you, sir." *What the hell is Hill leading up to?*

"I'd like to offer you some advice and a boost in your career."

Dan looked in Hill's cold, calculating eyes. *Advice from a snake.*

"This telepath case. It's troubling me."

"Sir, I've already said I can't talk about an open case."

"I know you can't. But I can. We're just two men, sitting in a bar. Nothing to worry about." He gestured to the waiter, who brought him another glass of beer. "To be blunt, if the telepath wins the case, it's going to be very bad for human beings like us."

"How so?"

"It doesn't take a telepath to know that he killed her in some sort of fit of passion," Hill answered loudly. "Hell, maybe the telepath's gone crazy. Always seems to happen, sooner or later."

Dan couldn't believe Hill had said that out loud. Sure, lots of people thought that way, but not many were bold enough to shout it in a bar. He looked around, but Hill hadn't drawn anyone's attention.

Hill continued. "If he gets away with it, well, we could have a telepath revolution on our hands. It wouldn't be long before we'd be under the yoke of the telepaths, forced to do their bidding, and we would lose our God-given rights to these … freaks."

Dan, leery of the direction the conversation was going, asked, "Just what do you think I can do?"

"Well, son, what I'm about to say can never be repeated. Do I have your word?"

Dan hesitated, but he decided that if whatever Hill said was worth reporting, he'd break his word. He nodded.

"You don't have to do your absolute best for him. Of course, you can't be incompetent, but you can be just slack enough to make sure he's convicted."

Dan sipped his scotch. "Regardless of my own personal feelings about telepaths, I can't throw the case," Dan said.

"No, of course not. You can't *purposely* throw it. But you're a young attorney. You might make a few mistakes, just enough to let the prosecution get the upper hand. You're a smart man. You can make that happen."

Dan finished his scotch in one swallow to hide his indecision. He enjoyed the warmth of the liquor on his throat as he considered his options. On one hand, he completely believed Wynton belonged in jail, or worse, because he was a telepath. On the other hand, he could never be seen doing anything but his best for Wynton. He was honor-bound to provide the best defense he could for his client.

"I have friends. Friends who can make sure your career turns into everything you want. Junior partner in a year, senior partner in another ten. Everything you want, handed to you on a silver platter, all for the price of letting the prosecution get the upper hand."

"I don't like the idea of framing a potentially innocent man."

Hill laughed. "You're an attorney, not the judge or jury. You provide the best defense you can, or almost the best defense you can, and let others worry about guilt. And even if, for some strange reason, he's not guilty of this particular crime, he must be guilty of something. He's a telepath. He belongs in jail. You know it and I know it."

Dan stood. It was time to end this conversation before anyone overheard it. "I'm not sure I can help you, sir. Thanks for the drink."

Dan strode out of the bar and waited for Hill's driver. He wanted Wynton to be found guilty, but hearing Hill's blatant disregard for ethics made him question his plan. Was he ready to completely abandon his own ethics? No matter what happened, or what he planned to do, one thing was certain. He had to look like he was doing his best for Wynton. Wasn't he already trying to look diligent, hiring the girls to investigate for him, knowing there was no way they'd get to the bottom of it all before the end of the trial? Hell, they found lost-dog cases difficult. He was already paving the way for Wynton to be convicted, because Hill was right. Wynton was a telepath, and he had to be guilty of something.

He nodded to the driver and said, "Back to the office." His new secretary was at her desk. *Miracles never cease. I might actually keep this one for a while.* She hadn't gone wandering off on a social tour as soon as his back was turned, and she was decent to look at. Not as beautiful as Olivia, but she would do for now. Damned if he could remember her name, though. "Get me everything the firm has on Aaron Hill, would you?"

"Yes, sir. Anything else, sir?"

"Coffee."

She came back in fifteen minutes with a six-inch file and a mug of coffee.

"Anything else?"

"Hold my calls. I may need you for something else later."

Two hours later, he remembered her name.

"Emily," Dan said through the intercom.

"Yes, Mr. Stevens?"

"Come here," he said, exasperation in his tone. What did they teach at secretarial schools if not to come when called?

She opened the door, pen and notepad in hand.

"You won't need those. Put them on the desk."

She walked over to the desk, and he caught her by the waist. "You're so beautiful, Emily."

"Mr. Stevens, please stop."

"I'd rather not. And I'm sure you'd rather I didn't as well. I've seen how you look at me."

"But Miss Morrison ..."

"Miss Morrison need never know."

"But ..." Her protest faded out.

Dan leaned in and kissed her. She returned his kiss and put her arms around his neck.

I'm right. She's interested. He deepened his kiss and let his hand run down her back.

"Sir, I don't think ..."

"Shh, it's all right." He began to unbutton her blouse, hoping she wasn't the kind of woman who wore functional undergarments. He was rewarded for his trouble by the sight of a turquoise lace bra, her nipples straining against the fabric. He leaned over and took one in his mouth.

"Mr. Stevens. Please. Let me lock the door."

Shit. The door. He let her go. As she walked to the door, she removed her blouse and unzipped her skirt. Walking back to him, she stepped out of her skirt, showing him what little she had on underneath it.

"Come here," he rasped.

She walked to him, smiling. Her hands undid his belt and pants with practiced ease.

"No," he said to her. "Not here. Get dressed."

She looked confused. "But ..."

"Never in the office." He tossed a motel room key at her. "Meet me there in an hour."

She picked up the key and walked back to him, her face upturned for a kiss.

"Never in the office," he repeated.

She looked at the key.

"One hour. Don't be late. I have a dinner to get to."

#

Olivia looked at herself in the mirror. If things kept on the way they were going, she wouldn't fit in this dress for much longer. "No dessert," she admonished herself, "and more exercise." It wasn't as though she was fat, but last week's missing-dog chase had left her breathless and sore for two days. She needed to get into better shape if she was going to be an asset to the company.

She turned and looked again in the mirror behind her. *At least the seams aren't pulling. Yet.* Maybe Dan was right about her figure. She sighed and pulled her wrap from the closet. Last year, she would have just gone out and bought a new dress, thinking nothing of it. Maybe with this case their business would finally take off.

When she had explained to her parents that she was going to join Darcy in what they called "an ill-conceived, dangerous plan," they had cut her off, just as they had already done with Darcy.

One or two big cases were all they needed. Just

enough to get some people talking about what a great job they'd done, to make it plain that a woman's finesse was far superior to the blunt strength of a man. The sisters knew it was true; they had seen it even in the small cases they had taken. But to prove it to the rest of Boston would take a big, splashy headline.

She sat at the vanity and fixed her eye shadow. The idea of dinner with Dan's boss jangled her nerves. She'd met Stirling Phillips during the Pescado case, and he had treated her as nothing more than an inconvenient lackey. She hoped she'd make a better impression on him tonight. The buzzer for the security door rang. She rushed to the intercom and said, "Yes?"

A strange voice answered. "Mr. Stevens for Miss Morrison."

"You aren't Mr. Stevens."

"No, ma'am. I will be your driver for the evening."

Driver? This will be different. Dan loved driving his little red Porsche, even though it was very cliché. He relished zipping in and out of traffic, beating other people off a red light, and making her gasp when he took corners at high speed.

She smiled. At least tonight she wouldn't fear for her life on the drive to dinner. She pushed the button. "I'll be down in a moment."

She left a note for Darcy, telling her she was out with Dan and not to wait up. Darcy would wait up anyway; she always did. Sometimes the way she took her responsibilities to her "younger" sister made it seem like Darcy was the older sister by several years, not several minutes. Olivia recognized the protective care for what it was: love.

Outside her building, the driver stood under a large umbrella, keeping the sleet off. He opened the door for her. "Miss Morrison?"

"Yes."

He led her to the limo parked on the street. She climbed in and was surprised to see she was alone. "Where is Mr. Stevens?"

"He will meet you at our destination."

Olivia felt nervous. She had just gotten into a car with a strange man. "He's left you a note on the seat."

She relaxed when she saw Dan's familiar handwriting on the outside of the envelope.

"Fine. Thank you," she said.

The limo pulled into the street toward the center of the city. She opened the envelope and was surprised by the note.

> Dear Olivia, Tonight is very important to my career, so please be very careful with what you say to our hosts. You must win them over, with as few strikes as possible. Three strikes and we'll both be out. They are conservative and may not like your more liberal attitudes. I know you will do what is right. Love, Dan.

Important to his career? His career was already going well; everyone was still talking about last month's successful defense of Pescado. She settled back and thought about her attitudes. She didn't think it was liberal to want the same freedoms for all human beings; that was simply being a good American. She had told Dan as much when they had last argued about it. All he'd done was smile and tell her that someday her naïveté might get her into trouble.

She looked out the window, trying to figure out where the limo was going. They were headed into the city, away from the massive apartment buildings that ringed Boston and provided housing for all but the most wealthy. They drove into Back Bay, an upscale part of the city, and the limousine stopped on Marlborough Street in front of a well-tended building.

The doorman was out with his umbrella before the limo came to a complete stop. He held out his hand to assist her. "Watch the puddle, ma'am."

She smiled at him as she took his hand. "Thank you. I am not certain where I'm going from here."

"You'll be going to the penthouse, Miss Morrison."

She was not surprised he knew her name. "Thank you."

She walked into the building and went toward the elevator.

"Miss Morrison?" asked the elevator attendant.

"Yes. Penthouse, please." She realized how stupid that sounded. If he knew her name, he certainly knew where she was going. "Could you tell me if Mr. Stevens has arrived yet?"

The attendant grimaced. "Yes, he has."

Olivia sighed. Dan had a way of annoying anyone he thought he couldn't get anything from. "Are the Phillips's having a big party?"

"I really wouldn't know, ma'am." He softened when she smiled at him. "But I've only brought Mr. Stevens up this evening."

"Thank you, Mr ..." She looked for his nametag but couldn't find it.

"Davis."

"Thank you, Mr. Davis."

The doors opened, and Olivia found herself in the living room of the penthouse. She had expected an entryway and a moment to compose herself before she went in. Instead, she stood and smiled, waiting for someone to notice her. There was no one in the living room, but she heard laughter to her left.

A young woman was first to notice her. *The maid, no doubt, as no one else would dress in a dark skirt and top with that small white apron and ridiculous cap on her head.* "May I take your coat, madam?"

"Yes, thank you. Could you direct me to Mr. Stevens?"

"Mr. Phillips and his guest are through here. Please follow me."

As they walked down the hall, Olivia realized why there was no vestibule or front door. The penthouse took up the entire floor of the building. The maid led her to the most marvelous sitting room she had ever seen. Floor-to-ceiling windows lined three walls, providing a panoramic view of the city. Entranced with the beauty of nighttime Boston, she forgot she was a guest in someone else's home.

"Miss Morrison," the maid announced.

Dan turned away from Phillips and smiled at her. "Olivia. You look lovely."

She walked toward him, smiling. "Thank you, darling."

Before Dan could introduce her, Stirling Phillips held out his hand. "It's a pleasure to see you again, Miss Morrison."

"Mr. Phillips, a pleasure to see you again as well."

"Oh, now. None of that. A pretty girl like you

must call me Stirling." His wife nudged him. "And this is my wife, Mary."

"Mrs. Phillips," she held out her hand.

"Miss Morrison."

So it's to be like that, she thought. *Strike one.* "Please, call me Olivia, both of you."

Stirling smiled, but Mary scowled at her.

"You have a lovely home, Mrs. Phillips. I can't believe the beautiful view."

Mary didn't soften. "I hate it in here. With the lights on, everyone can see what we are doing. There's no privacy."

Damn, Olivia thought. *Strike two.*

"Would you like a drink?"

Would I ever ... "Yes, please." She glanced at Mary, who was drinking wine. "Chardonnay." Mary had nothing to say about that, so at least she wasn't at strike three yet.

"We were just discussing the latest news from the EU when you came in," said Dan.

Crap. News from the EU. She thought back, but the latest big news from the EU was too controversial for a dinner party.

"Do you know, I've been so busy lately that I seem to have missed the news. Please, fill me in."

"The EU has added telepathic status to all its identity documents," said Mary.

"Oh, yes, I had heard that," Olivia said. *Be diplomatic, and don't ruin Dan's career*, she thought.

"And what do you think?" asked Stirling.

"It's obviously a highly charged issue. On one hand, it's comforting to know there are no telepaths near you, but part of me wonders if it's anyone's business, similar to religion or sexual orientation. Perhaps some things should not be public information, and the potential for discrimination is enormous."

Stirling smiled. "Very good point. Have you ever considered a career in law?"

Olivia smiled up at Dan. "I leave that to Dan."

Dan put his arm around Olivia and jumped into the conversation. "It won't take long for someone to propose the same legislation here, though. And then what should we do?"

Olivia didn't dare to answer. There was no way she wanted to see this legislation introduced, but she couldn't say that here.

"I'll tell you what we should do." said Stirling, "We need to take this one step further and make them identify themselves as telepaths, so that even walking down the street we know who we're with. Or better yet, give them their own land so they can stay with their own kind. I'm sure they'd feel better that way."

Olivia sent Stirling a faint smile. She couldn't agree with him, but on the other hand, she couldn't disagree either, not with Dan's future riding on this dinner.

"Stirling, leave the poor girl alone," said Mary as she handed Olivia a glass of Chardonnay. "She's just gotten here, and you're going on about national policy. At least let her have some wine."

Maybe I'm not at strike two, after all.

"Why don't we leave the men to talk business and politics? I'm sure we can find something more interesting to talk about." Mary led her out of the glorious sitting room into a smaller, more private room with heavy curtains drawn over the window. Olivia noticed that Mary relaxed as soon as she left the sitting room.

"Much better now," she said. "Please, sit

down."

Olivia sat on the edge of a chair, not ready to relax with this woman quite yet.

"It's nice to have people over who share our sentiments about the telepath problem."

"Yes, it is nice to be with people who share the same convictions," Olivia waffled. "What I don't understand is how this all got to be such a big mess so quickly. It seems like when I was a child, there were no telepaths, and now there are thousands of them in every city across the world. How did it happen?"

"The prevailing theory is poor genetics," said Mary. "Certain families have weak genes and are producing mutations."

Olivia took a sip of wine to cover her surprise.

"The sad thing is, if they were farm animals, the mutants would be put down as a matter of course, and the whole breeding stock would be stronger for it. Sadly, we can't do that here; too many liberals to interfere."

Olivia bit back her response to the vile, hateful woman. She didn't dare say a word, afraid of what would come out of her mouth. Instead she smiled again. Mary continued on with her vicious diatribe for a few more minutes. Olivia was relieved to hear the maid announce dinner.

Back in the limo, Olivia relaxed against Dan and closed her eyes. "How did I do?"

Dan stroked her hair. "You were brilliant. Stirling said you were a great gal, and even Mary warmed up to you after a while."

"I'm glad."

"Come back to my place?" Dan asked.

"I can't. Darcy texted me and wants to meet at

the diner to go over some business matters. She said she had to get out of the apartment. We've got a really busy day tomorrow, so we're just heading home after that."

Dan sat up and took his arm away. "I really expected that after tonight you'd change your tune."

"What do you mean?"

"I mean, you need to decide. A life with me leads to a penthouse and anything you want. A life with Darcy leads to … well it leads to a shared, shabby apartment and eating in diners. You have to choose, and soon."

Olivia stared at him, shocked that he would force her to choose between the two people she loved most. "Just drop me at the diner. I've got work to do."

Chapter 10

The limo pulled up in front of Olivia's favorite diner, Bess's. Without waiting for the driver to open the door, Olivia leapt out of the car before the Dan could try to kiss her. She had nothing to say to him until he apologized. She slid onto a counter seat next to Darcy, who was reading through a copy of Harrison's threatening-letter file.

Darcy looked at the frown on her beautiful sister's face. "Hey, Liv. What's wrong?"

"Dan. I don't want to talk about it."

Darcy scowled. She could only imagine what he'd done this time. "You look great."

Olivia smiled weakly. "Thanks. How's the read-through going?"

Darcy sat back and grimaced. "She was a fool to ignore so many threats. Some of them are truly frightening and graphic. I had to get out of the apartment because I was getting too jumpy."

Olivia looked at her watch. 10:30. "Let's get out of here and get some rest."

\#

Back in the lobby of their apartment building, Olivia grabbed their mail. She began flipping through the envelopes and magazines as they climbed the stairs. "I don't even have the energy to go through this tonight." Reaching their floor, they stepped into the hallway.

"No kidding. We could—" Darcy abruptly stopped talking and stood still. The door to their apartment was ajar. *Damn*, she thought. *This is not how we need to end the day.* She strode to Mrs. Levine's door across the hall and knocked.

"Who's there?"

"Mrs. Levine, it's me, Darcy."

The door opened, and Mrs. Levine smiled. "Hello, girls. It's a bit late, but would you like to come in for some tea?"

"Yes. Thank you." Darcy tried to sound natural, but she didn't think she pulled it off.

Olivia slammed the door shut as soon as they were in the apartment and turned the three locks Mrs. Levine insisted on keeping bolted at all times.

"Did you notice anyone go into our apartment?" asked Darcy.

Mrs. Levine began heating water in the kitchen. "No, dear, but I haven't been looking. Is something wrong?"

"Our door is open, and we don't know if someone is still there."

"I'm keeping watch," said Olivia, her eye to the peephole, the can of mace she kept in her purse in hand. "Call 911."

Darcy pulled out her phone. "I'm calling Uncle Joe."

"No, don't. He'll get all over-protective. Call Fraser."

Darcy called Fraser's desk at the precinct, and he answered.

"Detective Fraser."

"It's Darcy Morrison. I need help."

"Where are you?"

"I'm in the apartment across from mine. Our apartment door was open when we got home, and we don't know if anyone is still in there."

"I'll send a car around. I'll be there in ten. Stay where you are. Do not follow if anyone leaves your apartment."

"But—"

"Darcy," he said in a voice that left no room for argument. "Don't."

"Fine. But you'd better have someone here soon."

"They're already en route."

Three minutes later, from Mrs. Levine's peephole, Olivia saw two uniformed officers go into the apartment and emerge moments later. They knocked on Mrs. Levine's door.

"Miss Morrison?"

"Yes," said Olivia as she opened the door.

"There is no one in your apartment. It's safe to go back in, but it's been torn up. It's a real mess. We'd like you to take a look around, see if anything is missing."

Inside the apartment, upholstery was torn and plants overturned. Several walls were spray-painted with the word BITCH. Olivia slid down an unmarked wall to the floor. "Who would do this?" One tear fell from the corner of her eye.

"Who knows why anything bad happens, dear," said Mrs. Levine.

Darcy slumped down next to her. "Why don't you go back to Mrs. Levine's? I'll take care of this."

"No, I can't let you …"

"Go and call Dan. You'll feel better."

Olivia hesitated. "After the drive home, I don't think—"

"He'll want to know. He wants to be your knight in shining armor."

Olivia stood up and took Mrs. Levine's arm.

"Come with me, dear. A little shot of something in your tea will calm your nerves."

When Olivia was gone, Darcy began to concentrate on the scene. "What the hell happened here?" she asked the officers.

Fraser tapped at the still-open apartment door. "Looks like someone is mad at you. You piss anyone off recently?" he asked.

"Who knows? Could be Shaughnessy," she said. *He's always pissed that we don't bring in enough money.* "Could be someone from a previous case. Could be the case we're working on now."

"Shaughnessy's not likely to do this, though, is he?"

"Seems like too much hard work to be his style. He's more the verbal-abuse type—that doesn't take any energy."

Fraser walked through the apartment and took a quick inventory of the damage. "Damn," he said. "I'm going to need a list of people you pissed off in previous cases."

Darcy nodded numbly, wondering how something as simple as a lost dog or fraudulent sick day could make someone do this to her.

"Who knows you're on the Wynton case?"

Darcy rubbed her cheeks. "Let's not be hasty here. We have no idea who could have done this. There's nothing to say it has to do with our current case. We haven't told anyone but you and Broadbent."

"And there's nothing to say it isn't related, either."

"Do you think someone who hates telepaths could have done this?"

"Detective, I've got something," an officer called from the bedroom. He held up two notes, in evidence bags. "One on each bed. Both threaten the women, by name. Darcy on the left and Olivia on the right."

"How could he know?" she gasped.

Fraser turned to her. "He got the beds right? Either you've got a stalker, or it's a telepath." He turned to the officers. "Check the room for cameras. Hell, check the whole apartment."

Darcy leaned up against the wall, needing its solidity to hold herself together. She wasn't ready to read the threats yet.

"Let's go out into the hall," said Fraser.

Outside the apartment, Darcy sat on the floor, head back, eyes closed, thinking about whether she knew anyone who could do this. No one came to mind. The worst kind of criminals they'd ever dealt with were people who used their sick days for vacation time. "Why do you think a telepath would do this? It doesn't make any sense, unless he's got enemies in his own people."

"Who else could get the beds right?"

She shook her head. The few people she and Olivia had in their apartment weren't capable of this.

"This has never happened to you before?"

"No, never."

"What exactly are you working on for Wynton?"

"We were hired to find anyone else who might want to kill Harrison. So far, we've only been to Harrison's office. We were side-tracked by her file of threatening letters. We haven't even started checking those people yet."

"Broadbent took that file from you. How — ?"

"The receptionist had copies. We can't let you two do our job for us."

"It looks like maybe you should." He chuckled. "Did you really threaten Harrison into keeping the office open for two weeks?"

She looked up at him and smiled weakly. "That was Olivia. He was being such a jerk— he deserved it. She never actually said who we were, though. He just assumed we were police when Broadbent showed up."

Fraser chuckled. "You're walking a very fine line, and you'd better make sure I never catch you crossing it."

"That file of threatening letters is really freaking me out." Darcy stood, knowing nothing would get better until she faced the apartment. "I'd like to go back in now, take a look around."

"Of course."

They walked back into the apartment, and she was unaccountably distressed to see it was still as trashed as it had been ten minutes ago. Somewhere in the back of her mind, she imagined the police cleaned up after intruders and that she would see them tidying up and vacuuming by now. She laughed at her foolish thought.

"What's so funny?"

"Oh, nothing," she sighed. "I need a drink."

"I'll get you some water. Why don't you look around?"

"There's vodka in the freezer. Don't bother with a mixer."

He looked at her, concern in his eyes. "I'm not sure that's such a good idea."

"Pour me a shot, and we'll call it a night."

He took a glass from the cabinet and poured her half a shot. She smiled as she took the glass. "Not one to follow orders, are you?"

"I'm trained to look after the well-being of the community. Drunk PIs are in no one's best interest."

"Salut," she said and drained the glass. She turned to the officer who had found the notes on their beds. "I'm ready to see the note from my pillow."

The uniformed officer handed her the note.

" 'Darcy Morrison. I know who you are. Leave him alone. He's mine'. Really? Not much of a threat. Not after what I've been reading today. Harrison's letters go into much more detail about the damage the writer wanted to inflict."

"Any new men in your life?" Fraser asked.

"Romantically?" she scoffed. "No. The only new man in our lives is Wynton, but we only met with him this morning. And the way he was talking about Harrison, I don't see him having another girlfriend."

Fraser sat next to her. "No one ever said telepaths were rational."

Darcy rolled her eyes. Fraser had seemed like such a nice guy. *Too bad he's a bigot, just like all the other men I meet.* "Hey now, that's enough of that. My client seemed completely lucid this morning."

"That's not to say he's always rational. I found him talking to a dead woman," Fraser said.

Darcy had no strength for the argument. She tossed the note on the coffee table and sank into the couch.

Dan burst into the apartment, frantically looking around. "Where is she?" he demanded.

"Take it easy, she's fine. She's with Mrs. Levine

across the hall." *And yes, I'm just fine*, she thought. *Thanks for asking.*

Dan rushed across the hall and knocked furiously on the door. Olivia opened it, and he pulled her toward him. "Are you all right? You're not hurt, are you?"

"No, I'm fine. We weren't home when it happened. Darcy noticed the door was open, and we came right here and called the police."

Olivia had never seen Dan look so worried. She tried to act calmer than she felt. The bourbon in her tea helped some.

Dan took her hand and started to lead her out of the apartment. "I've forgotten about everything you said earlier. I'll take you back to my apartment now."

"Not yet," she said. She couldn't leave Darcy to sort all this out on her own. She had already spent too much time hiding out in Mrs. Levine's apartment, not ready to deal with the invasion to her home. Someone had been in her bedroom. She didn't know if the intruder had gone through her belongings, but she imagined a stranger touching her clothing, trying on her shoes, and she shuddered. She would have to buy new things, things not violated by unknown hands. Involuntarily, one tear slid from her eye.

"*Now.* You can't take this kind of strain. Let me take you home and take care of you."

Olivia drew on what strength she had and looked Dan in the eye "No. Darcy has been dealing with all this on her own. I need to be with her. Once we're done here, we'll take a cab to your place."

Olivia walked past him into her own apartment. It was messier than she remembered, though on closer inspection it looked like things had just been pushed around. Kitchen drawers were not overturned, and cabinets were opened but not emptied. She hugged Darcy and then hesitantly stepped into their bedroom. "Can I touch anything?" she asked the officer taking photos.

"Not yet, ma'am. Do you need something right away?"

"No. I just wanted to know what the intruder had gone through."

"Everything was pulled out of your closet, but the bureau drawers were closed. I can open one up for you to inspect."

Olivia pointed to her top drawer. "This one, please." She hoped her panties were still neatly folded and in order. She didn't realize she had been holding her breath until she sighed at the sight of the drawer's contents, untouched, exactly as she had left them. "Thank you, officer."

Back in the living room, Dan was scowling at Darcy. Olivia doubted a telepath's power was required to realize how much he blamed Darcy for the invasion. "It's not her fault," she said. "And we'll get through this together."

Darcy smiled at her sister.

"Everything about this is her fault. If she hadn't talked you into this business, you'd be safe and happy, with me.

Fraser walked back into the living room. "We've got some paperwork to go through. If you could compile a list of missing items, we can get that list around to the pawn shops."

Darcy took the clipboard and turned to Olivia. "I can take care of this. You go home with Dan. I'll see you in the morning."

"No, I can wait. It will go faster with the both

of us. Let's go."

Dan followed the sisters, and his patience wore thin after they went through one room. He began tapping his foot. Five minutes later, he grumbled, "Olivia, it's getting late. We should go."

Olivia looked at him, surprised at how angry he was. "Dan—" she began.

"I'm going, and if you want a safe place to stay tonight, you need to come with me."

"Go ahead. It doesn't look like anything is missing. It'll only take me a few minutes to go through the rest of the apartment," said Darcy.

Olivia nodded and Dan practically dragged her from the apartment. Fraser took Darcy into the kitchen. "Look, you're having a hell of a night." He handed her a card. "If you need me, just call. You're not staying here, are you?"

"I was thinking about it."

"No good. We'll be here most of the night and you won't get any rest. Can you go with your sister?"

Darcy made a face. "I can, but ..."

"Look, I know him. He's an ass."

"I'm used to it by now. I despise him, he hates me. It's a comfortable relationship we've got going on." Darcy shrugged. "I'll go with her, make sure she's all right."

Fraser looked her in the eye. "You deserve better. Your parents nearby?"

"They are, but I won't tell them about this. We'd never hear the end of it." More than likely they'd use every trick in the book to reel the two of them back into suburban life and the great husband hunt. *Absolutely not what I want*, thought Darcy.

"I hate to seem, ah, inappropriate," Fraser said, "but I've got the night shift. I could give you the keys to my place. You could make yourself at home. My shift is over at noon, so you could just drop my keys back at the station." He blushed from neck to forehead and started to sweat.

"Detective Fraser, are you ..." she paused to think, "flirting with me?"

A look of horror crossed his face. "Miss Morrison, I hope you don't think that. It's just, well, I'm your uncle's partner and if he knew I left you stranded, he'd kill me."

Darcy looked at her watch. It was one in the morning already. "I doubt I'll get any sleep tonight, no matter where I am, so why don't I go through all this and make my decision when it's done?"

Fraser shook his head. "It can wait until tomorrow."

"I suppose it could, but if I wait until then, Liv is going to want to come back and deal with it, too, and she didn't look like she was up for it."

"Go to Dan's. Get some rest. That's an order. You won't get any sleep with us here." Fraser handed Darcy her bag and keys and walked her to the door. "Don't come back until after breakfast."

"But –," said Darcy.

Fraser stared into her eyes. "Do I need to bring you there myself?"

She took her bag and headed out of the building. She stood at her car, weighing her options. She could just wait for him to leave and then go back in. If she had any money, she could get a hotel room. Her phone rang and she answered. After she hung up, she said, "Damn him," and drove to Dan's apartment.

#

The knot between Olivia's shoulders didn't ease until after she was in Dan's fifteenth-floor apartment in his well-secured building. He locked all the doors and left instructions for no deliveries or disturbances.

She threw herself on the couch and closed her eyes. He sat next to her and pulled her close, stroking her hair. "You're safe here. It will be all right by tomorrow."

She stiffened. *How can it ever be all right there again?* "How can I ever walk into that apartment again, knowing that someone was going through my things, ruining my bathroom, handling my belongings?" She began to cry. "As far as I'm concerned, practically everything in there is tainted, and I'll just have to replace it all."

"Take a deep breath. No one is saying you have to go back, ever. As far as I'm concerned, you can stay here. Olivia …" He tilted her head until she was looking at him. "I want you to stay here. Move in—just abandon your old apartment and walk away. It will all be fine once we are together."

"Oh, Dan," she said, "Part of me would love to. But where would that leave Darcy? I can't abandon her to that apartment. She'd feel just as violated, and more vulnerable because she was alone. She's my sister. My twin." *Will he ever understand what it's like to love a sibling?*

"Fine," he sighed, "she can stay in the guest room until she finds a new place of her own."

"She won't stay here. There's no way she'd want to." She looked away. "I don't think she likes you very much."

Dan laughed. "I know she doesn't like me, but you want her here. The police probably wouldn't let her stay there tonight, anyway."

Olivia bit her lip. "I'll call her. But tomorrow, she and I have to go find a new apartment." She knew this wasn't the answer he wanted.

He stroked her cheek gently. "If that's what you think is best." He stood up and walked to the bar. "I'll make you a drink, and I'll call her. You go take a hot bath and try to relax. Let me take care of everything."

Take care of everything was his mantra. Let him do it all. Ordinarily, she would complain but tonight she was not up for anything else. "Dan?"

"Yes, darling?"

"Promise me that tomorrow you'll let me handle things."

He handed her a gin and tonic. "I promise."

Through the open door of the bathroom, she heard his one-sided conversation on the phone as she finished her wine.

"Darcy, it's Dan … Do you need anything? … Olivia would like you to come stay in the guest room tonight … Just for once, do what I say … I'm not arguing with you … Stay here. Think of your sister. She's out of her mind with worry about you … Fine. I'll see you when you're done."

She leaned back in the warm lilac-scented bubbles and closed her eyes.

"Good news. She'll be here once she finishes up the paperwork with the police."

"Thanks, Dan."

He turned to leave.

"Can you stay here? I don't want to be alone."

"I can stay for a few minutes, but then I need to get back to work. I'll just be out in the living room."

Work. Of course work. When isn't the man

working? "No, never mind. I'll be okay on my own."

"Great. That's my girl. Climb into bed, and try to get a good night's sleep. I'll be in around three o'clock, but I'll try not to wake you."

Chapter 11

Olivia woke up in the familiar bedroom, sun streaming across her face. On the antique cherry bedside table, the alarm clock read nine thirty. She reached across the bed, but Dan wasn't there. Of course he wasn't, he never slept past five. She knew he had come to bed, because his pillows were thrown to the floor. She rolled over; his side of the bed was cold. He must have been working for hours by now.

She got up, picked up his shirt from the bench at the foot of the bed, and threw it on. It smelled like his cologne, and him. She breathed deeply and tried to keep away thoughts of last night. It didn't work.

Coffee, she decided. She needed coffee to face the day. When she twisted the doorknob to the bedroom, she heard Darcy talking.

"It's up to her to decide, not you."

"Ha! She can't think logically about this. She would follow you anywhere, no matter the outcome. You have to be the one. You have to force her out so she can have some sort of normal life."

"You know what your problem is? You have no respect for her. Why she stays with you I'll never know. You treat her as if she can't make decisions for herself, and you are kind to her only when she agrees with you. One day soon she'll realize this, and she'll find a better man than you."

"There is no one better for her than me."

"What an ego!"

Oh, shit. They're going to start throwing punches if I don't get out there. Olivia pulled open the door and said "Good morning, everyone."

Dan smiled at her and pulled her into an embrace. "Did you sleep well?"

"Yes, I did. What's for breakfast?"

"Liv, I'm going to head back to the apartment and start getting it back in order. I'll grab something on my way," Darcy said.

"Oh, wait. I'll come with you," Olivia replied, surprising herself. Last night she'd felt that everything she owned had been violated, but now, in the light of day, it didn't seem so bad. *I can handle this.* She smiled. "We can get more done together."

Dan pulled her close to him. "I really think you should stay here. We have a lot to talk about, and you'll be safe here. I'm not sure your future is going in the right direction."

"What do you mean?" Olivia asked.

"I really think we need to talk about where you want to be next year and in five or twenty years from now, and make sure you're on that path."

He's all business school to the end. "I don't know where I want to be next year, never mind five or twenty years from now. But I know that today I want to go set my apartment back in order and get to work."

"What if the maniac comes back?"

Darcy jumped in. "Fraser said he'd post someone to keep watch while we were there. We'll be protected."

"I won't allow it. Olivia, you must stay here until Darcy knows for sure it's safe."

Olivia was stunned. How could he ever think she would use her own sister as bait? "No. Are you really such an only child that you can't understand how much I love my sister? She is not a tool to make sure I am safe. She doesn't go first to take the bullet for me. We are sisters, and we go together."

She wrenched herself out of his arms and marched into the bedroom. "Stupid jerk," she muttered to herself as she got dressed. When she emerged, there was an icy silence in the living room. She smiled at Darcy. "Are you ready?"

"Yes."

"Olivia, wait," said Dan. "Let me explain. What I said, it came out wrong. What I meant was—"

"I think you said exactly what you meant. Don't call me again, unless it's business."

Olivia took Darcy's hand, and they walked out of his apartment. Dan did not follow.

At the elevators, Darcy put her arm around Olivia. "Are you all right?"

Olivia sniffled. "No, I'm not. I think I just broke up with him." She brushed furiously at the tears she didn't want to shed for him.

"I know. It hurts."

"We had plans for our future; we wanted to spend it together. He was such a great guy when we met. Sure, he's not perfect, but I didn't realize..." *How can I spend any time with a man who thinks my sister is disposable?* "Will you forgive me? I had no idea how much he despises you. You must have put up with so much all this time, and I didn't even see."

"It's fine. He doesn't have to love me, but he does have to love you."

The elevator door opened. "Let's get out of here."

Out on the street, Darcy said, "Let's get some breakfast first. There's a lot of work to do, and there's no way I can face it all without at least coffee."

Olivia smiled. "Sounds good."

After dawdling over breakfast and coffee, they finally arrived at their apartment. Crime scene tape remained around the broken door without blocking their entrance.

"Are you sure you're ready for this?" asked Darcy.

"I won't be any more ready later on, so we ought to get this started."

Darcy opened the door. The spray paint was gone from the walls, and Fraser was washing dishes.

"Fraser?"

"Oh, hi. I didn't expect you back so early," he said.

"What the hell happened here?"

"I, uh … I hope you don't mind. I drew the short straw and spent the night watching the place. I figured rather than just sitting around, I could make myself useful."

Olivia walked around the miraculously reassembled living room. "You put everything back, and painted the walls, and now … you're washing our dishes?"

"You really didn't have to do that."

Fraser looked at Darcy. "I know, and ordinarily I wouldn't have. But I just felt like you two could use a break. I had to stay awake anyway, so the work helped me."

Darcy looked closely at the painted wall. "How'd you match the paint color so well?"

"That wasn't me. Your building manager was very helpful last night."

"He was?"

"Once I told him who I was, he couldn't help me fast enough. He's very impressed that you have police cleaning up your apartment for you."

Darcy had to smile. "I can't believe you did all this for us."

"Like I said, you needed a break. You'll have to buy a new couch, but at least you can walk around now, and it won't be so difficult to get the apartment back together."

Darcy walked into the bedroom. It was immaculate, except for the baskets of clothing in the corner.

"I didn't think you'd want me going through anything too personal, so I didn't wash all the clothes that were on the floor. I did your bed linens, though, so you can sleep here tonight. Your landlord promised me he'd have your door repaired today."

"That's just ... incredible. How can we thank you?"

He blushed. "Really, it was nothing. And please don't tell Broadbent. I'll never hear the end of it." His ringing cell phone saved him from more praise. "I'll be damned," he said. "You know a woman named Sue Ellis?"

Darcy shook her head. "Never heard of her."

"Her prints were all over." He dried his hands on paper towels Darcy knew hadn't been in the apartment last night. "I've got to go in and interview her."

"But you've been up all night," said Olivia. "You should go home and get some sleep."

"Can't. I know her. She's got troubles, and I've tried to keep an eye on her. You know, help her avoid the worst of it." He sighed. "She'll trust me more than anyone else."

Darcy grabbed her bag. "We're coming with you."

"No. If she sees you, you could set her off again."

"She doesn't have to see us," said Olivia. "We can just hide in the observation room."

As Fraser shook his head again, Darcy said, "Maybe we do know her, just not by name. We could shave hours off your investigation." He didn't look convinced until she said, "And then you could go home to sleep."

"Fine, but she can't see or hear you. Got it?"

The two women smiled and led him out of their apartment.

#

They walked into the precinct and were surprised to see their uncle. "Broadbent, you don't have to stay around for us. Why don't you start your vacation now?" asked Darcy.

"You think I'd leave town when you two were in trouble?" he asked. "Not likely. Your mother would kill me."

"But you had plans. Mom said you were going to Barbados," said Olivia.

"And it will still be there when this case is over."

Darcy asked her uncle, "What do you know about Sue Ellis?"

"Not much. She's Fraser's pet project," he said.

"I think she has some psychological problems. Says she hears voices, but she doesn't test out on the telepathic range." Fraser sat at his desk and pulled out a file. "I've got an unofficial file on her. I'm trying to keep her out of trouble."

"Why?" asked Darcy.

"She seems like a good person, just a little messed up, you know? I got her into counseling, but she said the therapist hated her. I got her into drug treatment, but she walked out."

"So she doesn't want your help?"

"The thing is, I think she does. She just needs … oh, hell, I don't know what she needs. Maybe I've been coddling her too long, and now she's escalating to real crime."

Darcy looked at Fraser and saw the regret in his eyes. "You did what you thought was best for her, didn't you?"

"I tried."

"Let's go see her," said Olivia.

"You stay in the observation room. If you're in any danger from her, I don't want her to see you."

The sisters sat in front of the one-way mirror and stared at Sue Ellis. She was young, maybe twenty years old, but her eyes looked as though they'd seen too much in her short life.

They watched Fraser walk in and place a sandwich and a can of soda on the table for her. "Sue," he said.

"Detective. What can I—" She looked at the mirror and screamed, "You let them in here?" She writhed and tried to break free from the handcuffs. "One of them wants to take him. You know she does. I'll kill her before I let her take my man!"

Fraser forced her to sit back down. "Stop, or you'll spend the day in a cell. I just want to ask you some questions. If you can't cooperate, I can't let you out."

Her eyes grew wide. "Not the cells—too many

bad people there. Too many scary minds. Please, don't do that. I'll behave, I promise."

"Tell me what you know about the Morrisons," he demanded.

She pointed with both hands to the mirror. "They're in there. Watching us."

Fraser stepped back. *How can she know that? She tested completely non-telepathic.* "What do you know about their apartment?"

Ellis smiled. "You saw my handiwork, did you? I made sure to leave enough fingerprints so that that you could find them."

"Why?"

"One of them wants to steal my man." She slammed her fists on the table. "He's my man! You hear that?" she screamed at the mirror.

"Sue," Fraser said in his calmest voice, "who is your man?"

"You've met him. George is my man," she smiled.

"George Wynton?"

"Of course George Wynton. I know it's old-fashioned, but when we get married, I'm going to change my name. Sue Wynton ... Sounds," she sighed, "perfect."

Fraser was sure she'd gone right off the deep end. He sat across the table from her and said very calmly, "Sue, has he ever met you?"

"It would be awfully hard for us to get married if we'd never met, don't you think? My mother is his secretary."

"And when will you be getting married?"

"Well, that part's a little tricky. Technically, he hasn't asked me, but now that the Harrison woman is out of the way I'm sure he'll come to his senses."

Fraser's instincts immediately clicked onto high alert. "What do you mean?"

"Now that she's dead, and once he's out of …" She waved her arms around. "All this mess, he'll be free to be with me." She sat forward, looking intently at him. "That's why I need you to help me. I need you to keep those two … man-stealers away from him. They're too beautiful. He'll forget me, even after everything I've done for him." She began to cry.

"It's all right, Sue. Let's take a little break. Why don't you eat your sandwich?"

She lifted the top slice of bread off the sandwich and sniffed. "I'm not hungry."

"You look hungry to me. Have you eaten today?"

"I think so. Or maybe it was yesterday."

Fraser looked at her, concern etched on his face. "Sue, we've talked about this. You have to eat every day, even if you don't feel hungry."

"But it's so hard," she whispered. "So many voices saying 'You're fat, you shouldn't eat' that I think I should listen to them."

"No one is thinking that now. Right now, I think you should eat to be healthy and strong. In fact, the stronger you are, the more you can help George."

"Is that true?"

"Eat the sandwich and find out."

She picked at the open sandwich, eating the lettuce and tomato. The food seemed to push her to realize she was hungry, and she then wolfed down the entire sandwich in six bites. She smiled up at Fraser. "That was good. I like turkey."

"You did a good job. I'm proud of you." He smiled at her. "I brought you dessert."

Sue's eyes brightened and started to water.

"My father used to bring me dessert. Mama never does."

He pulled a chocolate bar from a pocket and held it out. "First, I need a favor," he said.

She eyed him suspiciously. "What favor?"

"Tell me who killed Kathleen Harrison."

She closed her eyes and held her breath. Her index fingers began pointing in random directions and didn't stop until she opened her eyes and gasped for air. "I can see his face, but I don't know who it is."

He expected her to confess, not pull this charade. He decided to play along. "Did you see her being shot?"

"Yes, I just did, but I don't know who shot her."

"Were you there when she was shot?"

"Of course not. I wouldn't go anywhere with that fat ugly man. I only saw it now."

"Who is the fat ugly man?"

"I don't know. I've never seen him before."

"You don't know, or you don't want to tell me?"

"Honestly, I don't know."

He handed her the chocolate. "Sue, I hate to tell you this, but we're going to have to keep you here."

"No! Not here. I told the truth! Now you have to let me go!"

He shook his head. *Better to keep her here until she's straightened out. And maybe gotten whatever drugs she was on out of her system.* "Not this time. This time you've actually done something wrong. You shouldn't have broken into that apartment."

"But it was self-defense," she said.

"Finish your dessert, and then you can make

your phone call."

Chapter 12

Fraser walked into the observation room. "You see what I mean?"

"She seems ..." said Olivia.

"Is she a telepath?" interrupted Darcy.

Through the one-way mirror, they watched her being led out by a kind-faced matron. Before she left the room, Sue stared into the mirror and mouthed, "He's mine."

Fraser shook his head. "She tests negative on our tests, but she acts it."

"Maybe she pretends to be one because the man she loves is," suggested Olivia.

"And knowing we are here was just a lucky guess? I doubt it," said Darcy. "What was she talking about when she said she could see who killed Harrison?"

"I don't know. She's done that before, but it's never been much help."

Darcy stood up. "I think we need to see our client again."

"I'll bring him out." He jerked his head toward the interrogation room. "You three can talk in there."

The sisters moved into the unadorned room Ellis had just left. "I hate this room," said Darcy. "It's so bleak. I'd confess just to get out of here."

They waited only a couple of minutes before George was brought in to them. He walked in front of Fraser, handcuffed, his head hanging.

"Looks like he had a scuffle in the lockup. Broadbent took care of the guy who hit him," said Fraser.

Wynton looked up. His left eye was blackened and starting to swell. His lower lip had split, and there was a fist-sized bruise on his jaw.

"Mr. Wynton!" Olivia exclaimed.

He slumped into his chair and closed his good eye. "It's nothing."

When Fraser left the room, Darcy asked, "Police?"

He shook his head. "Not directly."

"What do you mean?"

"It was someone's idea of a joke to put me in a cell with a bigot. He was fine while he was passed out, but when he came to and recognized me, it was like Santa had left him a present on Christmas Day. I suppose that's what I get for wanting to be the public face of telepaths."

"What happened?" asked Olivia.

"It's pretty much written on my face. Didn't last long, though. An old officer broke us up and moved him to a different cell. Didn't keep him from yelling at me, but I just fell asleep."

Olivia put her hand on his. "You need to see a doctor."

He shook his head. "I'll be fine."

"Not from a legal perspective. We need to document this with a doctor's report. Once we're done here, we'll send one in to you."

"We just watched Fraser interview Sue Ellis," said Darcy.

Wynton opened his unswollen eye. "What's Sue got to do with this?"

"We don't know. She vandalized our

apartment last night because she thinks one of us will steal you away from her."

"She said that?"

Olivia nodded.

"I'm sorry. I never thought ..." He sighed. "She was a lonely kid, always awkward, so I paid her extra attention for my office manager's sake. Sue hasn't taken well to being a telepath or learned how to keep her mind separate."

"Fraser said she tested negative," said Olivia.

"Her mother taught her how to fake the test so she just seems crazy."

Darcy leaned forward and put her elbows on the table. "Is she dangerous?"

He closed his eyes and sat still for a minute. When he opened his eyes, he said, "It's all right now. I explained to her that you are working with my lawyer, trying to prove my innocence. She promised she'd leave you alone."

"You just –" Olivia started.

"Yes. She's close by and it's no more difficult to talk to her telepathically than it is for me to talk to you now."

"You're not worried about the Telepathic Corps?" asked Darcy.

Wynton shook his head. "They're not going to be able to get me in here."

"But what about when you leave?"

"It's a risk I have to take."

"And you're sure Sue will leave us alone?"

"She always does what I say, at least for a little while. But while you're here, I need to tell you about the Twenty."

"The Twenty what?" asked Olivia.

Don't panic. I have to tell you telepathically.

Darcy's jaw dropped as she realized she was hearing his voice in her head.

The Twenty are a group of vile, hateful bigots, determined to rid the country of telepaths by any measures necessary. If Steve's alibi really holds up, they're the only other ones who might have had such a grudge against Kathleen — due to the work we've been doing — that they would have killed her.

Olivia failed to hide the shock on her face. "I've never heard of them."

Wynton continued telepathically. *Well, you wouldn't have, would you? They don't affect you in any real way, and they are paranoid about secrecy. We only know about them because one of us works for one of them.*

Color drained from Darcy's face. "What are they doing now?"

I don't know. Our person on the inside has to be very careful and can't always get information out to us easily.

"Do you think Kathleen was killed by one of them?"

He leaned back and closed his eyes again. *No. These are powerful people. They'd never get their hands dirty or risk being caught. But I believe they could have put out a contract on her. That's more their style.*

"Great. So we've got twenty suspects now," Olivia said.

"Twenty suspects without names, except for the one George knows about," Darcy replied.

Wynton rubbed his temples. "There's a sniffer close by, and he's putting up interference. I can't tell you anymore. Talk to my assistant. She'll tell you what you need to know. She's also Sue's mother, but please let me tell her about Sue.

"We'll go see Joyce today."

"And while you're talking to her, tell her you need to know about the underground."

Underground what? Olivia thought.

Darcy stood up, ready to leave. "Other than a doctor, do you need anything?" she asked.

"To be out on bail."

"I'm sure Mr. Stevens is working on that right now. Anything else?"

"No. I just want to get out of here and find her murderer.

"Mr. Wynton, no one will let you out if you keep talking that way. Let us handle that part. We're the trained professionals." Olivia didn't like lying to him—they weren't really trained—but a lie to keep someone safe couldn't really be all that bad.

"But I could do it. Give me twelve hours and I can find the proof you need."

"Mr. Wynton!" she hissed. "You do yourself no good making threats like that. If the judge thought you were going to get out of here and start scanning people, you'd never make bail."

"I know. I'm pissed that I'm sitting around in here, not doing anything. She's dead." He pounded his fist on the table. "It's my fault, and there's nothing I can do about it."

"What do you mean, it's your fault?"

"There's no reason anyone would want to kill her, except for her association with me."

"How can you be so sure?"

"You would know if you'd met her. Either her husband killed her because she was going to leave him for me, or someone killed her because she was working to give me and all telepaths a better image."

Olivia put her hand on his shoulder. "Hang in there. Mr. Stevens is a brilliant attorney, and he'll have this all sorted out in no time."

"I wish I had your faith."

Olivia squeezed his shoulder, hoping to infuse him with some strength. "Just hang on to our faith, Mr. Wynton, for a little while longer. We'll get you out of this mess."

#

Darcy and Olivia pulled into their customary parking spot at the office.

"No Louie?" asked Darcy.

"Guess not. Maybe he's off getting some coffee."

Darcy held the door open. "I don't blame him. It's freezing out here."

They walked up the two flights to their office. When she reached the landing, Darcy held her hand up for Olivia to stop; their door was ajar. *Not again,* she thought. She slowly pushed the door open, cursing the squeaky hinges, and saw an incredible sight. Shaughnessey was sitting at his desk, working. *What the hell is going on here?*

"What are you doing here?" Olivia said.

"It's about time you two showed up. You're really slacking off here. I expect my girls to be on time, every day."

"Why are you here so early? Shouldn't you be sleeping it off somewhere?" asked Darcy.

He smiled an evil little grin. "I've got a case for you. My friend's lost his dog, and you need to find it."

Darcy sat on the couch and sighed. "Really? Another lost dog? Can't you just buy him another pet? Maybe a fish? They don't get lost."

"You got something better to do?" he asked. "We need the money."

"You're right. We've got nothing going on right now. Tell us about the dog," said Olivia.

Shaughnessy handed Olivia a file. She inspected it and remarked, "Guido Panzerelli lost his dog?"

"Yeah. He thinks someone may have borrowed it, on account of he owes this other businessman some money."

"Are you serious? You want us to find some gangster's dog? You trying to get us killed?" Darcy exclaimed. *That would be just like him, too. Well, not purposely to get us killed, but he certainly hasn't ever worried about our safety.*

"You two ought to be up to it now. You've done, what? Five or six lost dog cases? Time to move up to the big leagues."

"Doesn't he have guys who can take care of this for him? What does he need us for?" asked Olivia. She handed the file back to Shaughnessy. "We'll think about it."

Shaughnessey stood up but left the file on his desk. "No thinking required. He's put you two on retainer." He walked out the door, humming.

"Jesus!" Darcy said. "Retainer for the Panzer? We've got to stop this. But how...?"

Olivia picked up the phone. "I'll just call him and let him know we aren't taking the case."

"Do you think that's safe?"

"Dar, we can't let people push us around like that. What kind of PIs will we be if we can't make things go the way we want?"

She checked the file and dialed the Panzer's cell phone. "Mr. Panzerelli? This is Olivia Morrison from Morrison Investigations. I'm calling to tell you that, unfortunately, we have no room in our schedule for your case. We wish you the best of luck finding ..." She checked the file. "Brutus. Thank you for thinking of us, and again, I am sorry we can't help you."

She hung up and pressed her shaking hands

against the desk.

"What did he say?"

"I didn't give him a chance to say anything after he said his name." She sat back and took a sip of coffee. "I've never been so afraid of a phone conversation in my life."

Darcy stood up and grabbed her bag, willing her heart rate to slow. "Maybe we should get out of here, just in case he decides to stop by and convince us we should find Brutus."

"Right. I'm sure Dan has an office we can use. We are still working for him, after all."

I doubt he'll find space, Darcy thought. *Not if he knows we're both going to be there.*

"Let me call him and see." Olivia dialed Dan's number and asked her question.

"You interrupted me for that?" Dan asked. "No, I don't have an office you can use. I'm really sick of you picking fights with me and then calling the minute you need a favor. You walked out on me this morning, and, frankly, that hurt. You've got your own office. Work from there."

"Well, we would, except there's one little problem," said Olivia.

"Infestation? Rats? Building been condemned? Wouldn't surprise me in the least."

"No. We had to turn down a job for a scary guy."

"I hardly think you are in a position to turn down any work. Who was the client?"

"Well, ah … His name is Panzerelli."

"Guido Panzerelli?"

"Yes."

"Why the hell would he want to hire you two?"

"Apparently he's a friend of Shaughnessey."

"No surprise there," he scoffed. "You finding dead bodies for him?"

"It's a lost dog."

Darcy could hear his laughter through the phone. "Give me the phone," she said. She hit the speakerphone button while he was still snickering. "Stop laughing. We could be in trouble here. We need an office to work in today. If you're not going to help us, then just shut up, and we'll find one somewhere else."

"There's no need to take that tone with me. I'm your employer."

"Right. And we need a place to work today. Are you going to find us somewhere or not?" She tried playing on his affection for Olivia. "Liv really needs the quiet to work."

"Oh, no. She chose her path. She's with you. You keep her safe. You worry. As far as I'm concerned, you two are just low-level employees."

Darcy hung up the phone and turned to Olivia. "He doesn't know you heard that. He wouldn't be so cruel to you."

"But he has no problem being mean to you."

"He never has," Darcy sighed. "But I'm not worried about that."

Chapter 13

With no office to work from, they drove to the office of Wynton Signage, in Charlestown.

"No cars, no people," said Darcy.

"Let's just check the door."

Through the glass, they observed a gray-haired woman sitting at a desk. Olivia knocked to get her attention. Without looking up, the woman yelled, "We're closed."

"Joyce," Olivia called, "Mr. Wynton sent us to talk to you."

Joyce stood and opened the door but didn't let them in. "What?"

"I'm Olivia Morrison, and this is my sister Darcy, of Morrison Investigations. We work for Mr. Wynton. Well, technically, we work for his attorney. He sent us to talk to you. He thinks you can help us find who killed Kathleen Harrison."

Her expression softened. "In that case, come in. Can I get you coffee?"

"We'd love some. Last night was tough," said Olivia.

Joyce handed them steaming mugs and motioned for them to sit down next to her desk. "What can I do for you?"

"We were just talking to Mr. Wynton, and he says you have some information about a group called the Twenty. He wants you to tell us who the members are so we can check their alibis. But first, I suppose you should start with what kind of organization it is and what it does."

Joyce sat and took a deep breath. "Okay. Well, we don't really know much about them at all. No specifics, anyway. They're a group of people in Massachusetts who want to rid the world of all telepaths."

"That's about all Mr. Wynton was able to say."

"He was too exhausted to continue telepathically. He said he was being blocked by a sniffer," Darcy added.

Joyce sat back. "Sniffers. Didn't take them long to get here. The Twenty are some of the most evil people I've ever heard of. Right up there with the Klan and the Nazis."

"So who is in this group?" asked Olivia.

"We only know one member for sure. Francis Wallburton."

Darcy looked at Olivia, confusion etched on her face.

Joyce explained, "He runs NationalGrid in Massachusetts."

"So he runs the Twenty?" Darcy asked Joyce.

"Our person inside thinks he's somewhere in the middle of the pack, taking instructions from someone, then turning around and giving orders to others."

Olivia took a sip of her coffee. "Hard to believe such a powerful man isn't at the top. What kind of orders?"

"He set up last year's mass arrest of telepaths on New Year's Day," said Joyce

"I remember that." *And we're still afraid, even though there wasn't another raid this New Year's*, thought Darcy. The previous year, on New Year's Day, a city-wide sweep caught hundreds of known and suspected telepaths unaware. They were arrested and held for forty-eight hours, and the entire roster of city officials tried to find some reason, any reason, to hold each of them. *We were safe, but only because of the forethought of our parents. There is nothing, not a single scrap of paper or record in a school or hospital that alludes to our telepathic abilities. They saw this coming and did everything they could to protect us.* She'd felt guilty that day, still felt guilty, that she hadn't been able to help or protect the others. She was too afraid for herself, for Olivia.

"I'm surprised you do. Not many non-telepaths even noticed, and it hardly got covered in the news at all. You non-telepaths are so quick to shut your eyes and pretend we don't even exist or that we aren't about to be hunted to extinction."

"You're a telepath?" asked Darcy.

"Yes. I am. Mr. Wynton prefers to surround himself with telepaths. He says he feels safer, knowing he's with people who have the same basic survival needs he does."

"Interesting. His lawyer's not a telepath."

"I didn't have much choice there. I had to find him a good lawyer, with a good firm, more than I had to worry about his telepathic status."

"I see. So Wallburton set up the New Year's arrests. Were you caught up in that?"

"I was, because the sniffers caught Sue—my daughter—and she was too afraid to block them. Telepathy runs in families, so they naturally came after me. I was never so happy that I lead a boring, law-abiding life. I fooled them long enough that they had to let me go."

"How did you keep them from discovering

you're a telepath?"

She laughed. "It's not so difficult. I don't usually share that information with normals like you two. Let's just say they couldn't believe a nice old lady like me could possibly be a threat to them."

Darcy was impressed. "You fooled them? I had no idea that could be done." A shimmering hope sparked in her mind. *Perhaps the two of us will be all right, after all.*

"He also said we should talk to you about the underground," Olivia added.

Joyce shook her head. "I don't think so. We really don't know enough about you two girls to share secrets."

"But—"

"I'm going to talk to George this afternoon. If he can give me a good enough reason to bring you in on this, I'll call you."

Olivia handed her a card and said, "Thank you for your time. We'll look into Wallburton." She stood up and walked out of the office, leaving Darcy to trail behind her.

#

"What the hell was that?" Darcy asked as they drove back to the office.

"What do you mean?"

"I mean, why did you give up so quickly on her? We could have gotten her to talk."

Olivia took in a deep breath and sighed. "Yes, I suppose we could have, but why waste all that time when Wynton will do it for us?"

"He will?"

"Of course. He's her boss. Once he tells her we

can be trusted, she'll call. In the meantime, we can find out more about Wallburton."

"We'll have to go back to the office, though."

"I suppose so."

Darcy looked out the window at the gray, slush-covered streets of Boston. *How does Olivia always know how to deal with people? She has always had an innate sense of how to get people to do what she wants, and nine times out of ten they thank her.* "You didn't—"

"Of course not," Olivia said. "I don't trust her any more than she trusts me."

"Oh, good."

They pulled up outside their office building, where they saw two men flanking the door. Darcy looked at Olivia. "Panzer's men?"

"Most likely," Olivia replied. "We'd best get this over with now, instead of having them chase us all over town. Let me do the talking." She stepped out of her car and said, "Gentlemen, how may we help you?"

Darcy stepped out of her side of the car and did her best to look intimidating. From the smirk on the shorter goon's face, it seemed like she failed miserably. She walked to Olivia's side, determined to stick close to her sister.

The taller man, dressed in a cheap black suit said, "You can come with us. Mr. Panzerelli would like to speak to you."

"We're very busy right now. Can he call this evening?" asked Olivia.

"For the amount of money he's paid your associate, you can come with us right now."

Olivia smiled at the men. "I see the confusion. Mr. Shaughnessey, our associate, has taken this case." She checked her watch. "At this time of day, you're most likely to find him at Suffolk Downs."

He thought for a moment. "He said to go get the two Morrison women and bring them over to the club. He wants to know why you haven't started looking for Brutus yet."

"I recall Mr. Shaughnessy talking about Brutus. Yes, this is definitely his case."

"That's funny, because Shaughnessey said you was going to find the dog," said the shorter man.

"Oh, no. This was strictly his case. He took the money, didn't he?"

"Well …"

"I certainly haven't met Mr. Panzerelli, nor do I have any of the associated forms necessary to get started on his case."

"You need forms?" he asked.

"Yes." She started flipping through papers in her bag. "A contract spelling out exactly what Mr. Panzerelli is hiring us to do and how much he's willing to pay. A form for lost animals, sort of a specialty of ours, asserting he's the rightful owner of the animal." She looked up from her bag and into his eyes. "You'd be surprised how many people think they can dupe us into stealing someone else's animal for them. Of course, we check with local law enforcement on all cases before we begin."

If the thought of forms made him nervous, the mention of local law enforcement made him pale. He looked at his partner, who shook his head.

"I think you'll have to come with us and explain all this to Mr. P."

Darcy realized there was no way they were going to get out of this. "Let me call Mr. Shaughnessey as well. We'll pick him up on the way. I'm sure we'll get all this sorted out," said Darcy.

She pulled out her cell phone and angled it so Olivia could see the number she punched in. If there was ever a time for Fraser to be sitting at his desk, now was it.

"Fraser," he said.

"Hi, Miles. It's Darcy. I've got two associates of Mr. Panzerelli here at the office, and there seems to be a problem with our paperwork."

"What the hell did you get yourself tangled up in? Never mind. Don't tell me."

"Yes. They seem to think Olivia and I are working the case, but I told them we have no information. Since you took their money, you must be looking for Mr. Panzerelli's lost dog."

"Do they have guns?" he asked.

"I'm pretty sure. My idea was to pick you up at the track and then go to see Mr. Panzerelli." She turned to the shorter goon. "He's at the club?"

"Yeah. The Somerville Social Club."

She put the phone back to her ear. "We'll see Mr. Panzerelli at the Somerville Social Club."

"I don't like this. You should not be using yourself as bait. Keep them at the track until I get there.

"Great. We should be there in about a half an hour."

She put the phone back in her bag and smiled. She hoped Fraser would get this right, or they might not make it through the afternoon. He was a bright guy, she thought, a little new for this sort of thing, but that's why he was partnered with Uncle Joe. *Uncle Joe will sort it all out, and we'll be fine.*

She smiled at the goons. *Nothing to worry about. We're just a couple of women with a glitch in their paperwork.*

Olivia reached back into the car for her coat. "I presume we are taking your car?"

The taller goon nodded.

"Then if you would help me with my coat?"

He took her coat and held it out, hesitantly. "Uh, here you go."

Olivia beamed at both of the men. "Thank you," she said. "I'm sorry. I don't know your names."

"I'm Reggie," said the coat guy, "and this is Joey."

"It's a pleasure to meet you, gentlemen," she said. "Shall we go pick up Shaughnessy?"

"We should call the boss, let him know about the delay," said Joey.

"Do it in the car," replied Reggie.

Darcy and Olivia slid into the back seat of the Lexus sedan. "Nice car," Darcy said.

"Yeah, the boss doesn't like us to look cheap; it hurts his image."

And kidnapping women from offices does what to his image? Olivia thought.

They didn't speak during the entire drive to the track. Olivia had the jitters from the way Joey watched her every move and breath from the front seat. She felt as though she were a bug being examined under a magnifying glass. Although the sun was bright, the tinted windows kept the glare out of her eyes. She saw Darcy look out the window, fingering the clasp on her backpack.

Don't be stupid, Olivia thought. *If you pull your gun, we'll all die in here.* She wished she could talk to Darcy telepathically, but from earliest childhood she knew it was never safe to use telepathy. She'd only risked it once, when she was in a lot more danger.

Darcy looked at Olivia, then at her bag. Olivia

shook her head. Darcy frowned, but she put the bag down.

When they got to the track, Joey got out. "You stay here. I'll get Shaughnessey."

Shit. This is going too fast. "I've got to use the ladies room," Darcy said.

"You can wait until we get to the club. I don't think you want to use these."

"It's really an emergency."

"Sorry. No can do."

"Then can I at least get out of the car to stretch my legs?"

"No. We don't need anyone seeing you."

She laughed. "I'm sure I don't know anyone here."

"You'd be surprised at who comes here, even in the middle of the day."

Darcy sat back. She couldn't overpower him, and she'd never get to her gun before he became suspicious. She looked out the window but there was no sign of Fraser or Broadbent.

"So tell me, Reggie, have you worked for Mr. Panzerelli long?" asked Olivia.

He turned around in the driver's seat and smiled. "I've never worked for anyone else. I started with him when I was ten, sweeping up and running errands."

"He must be quite a man to command such loyalty."

His eyes lit up. "He's a good boss. Last year, when my mother took sick, he let me have all the time off I needed. He even paid her bills."

"That was generous. Is your mother well now?"

"Nah, she died. Cancer."

She reached forward to pat his hand that was resting on the center console. "I'm sorry to hear that."

"Thanks. Your parents still alive?"

"Yes. They're still alive."

"You spend any time with them?"

"Not much any more. They don't like my job. They don't approve; they think it's too dangerous for a woman."

Reggie laughed. "Women are tough. If I had my choice of going up against a man or a woman, I'd pick a man every time. Sure, men are stronger, but women," he tapped the side of his head, "they're devious, and they don't let anything go. Anyway, you should call your parents. Even if they don't like your job, they're still your parents and you're lucky to have them."

"Did your mother approve of your job?"

"No. But I was still there every Sunday for dinner, listening to her complain about Mr. Panzerelli." When Olivia looked confused, he continued. "Because she was my ma, and I was her son. She worried. It's how the world works."

Olivia felt shamed by this goon. *How can he, a kidnapper, be a better child to his parents than I am?* "You might be right. I should call my parents tonight. But tell me, how did you deal with the constant criticism?"

He wiped at his eyes. "I just thought about how she loved me. And she really did. She loved all of us kids and wanted what was best for us. She thought I'd be a good auto mechanic. I thought I'd be a good one, too, but when it came time to make money, Mr. Panzerelli offered a better-paying job."

"You had to start making money at ten?"

"Yeah. Ma couldn't make enough in her job, and none of us kids wanted to see her take another. We decided we'd all get jobs and help her."

"That was really ..." She searched for a word. "Mature of you and your siblings. She must have been very proud of you."

"She was, in some ways. Your parents must be proud of you, too."

"They don't show it."

"Sometimes you have to look hard, but it's there. You start going to Sunday dinners every week, and you'll see it start to come out."

The rear passenger-side door opened. Shaughnessey glared at Olivia. "I told you to make this case a priority. Now we're in trouble."

Olivia smiled at him. Better to keep her head down, make it seem like she just wasn't very good at the job, and hope Darcy's call for help worked. "Yes, boss."

Shaughnessey looked confused. She'd never before called him boss or agreed to anything he said. Once Olivia moved over, he sat in the back and smiled. *As long as he doesn't think I mean anything I'm saying*, she thought.

Another drive made in silence, although she smiled at Reggie, and he smiled back at her in the rearview mirror. Perhaps he would make sure nothing really bad happened to them.

At the club, he helped her out of the car. "You know, Reggie, I'm going to take your advice and call my parents. I think I'll have them over for dinner on Friday night. Maybe my sister and I can start to repair our relationship with them."

Shaughnessey scowled at her. "Any time you're done with all this touchy-feely crap, we can get to work."

Olivia looked around but saw no Fraser or police presence at all on the street. She took a deep breath, and the sisters followed Shaughnessey into the club.

Inside the building, Joey went to announce them to Mr. Panzerelli.

Darcy hissed at Olivia, "We're in serious trouble here, and you're taking family advice from our kidnapper?"

"I know it looks bad, but trust me, we'll be all right," she whispered.

Shaughnessey scowled at Olivia. "What kind of trouble have you gotten us into now?"

"Panzerelli isn't happy with our progress on his case."

"How far did you two idiots get?"

"Hey! You should treat the lady with more respect. What kind of man are you?" Reggie snarled.

Olivia beamed at Reggie until he turned back around.

"We haven't started the case."

"What? I told you to start immediately. This is a very important case, and his money could keep us afloat."

"Us?" Darcy scoffed. "All that money will do is keep you at the track. We haven't seen any of it. "

Olivia turned away from Shaughnessey and tapped Reggie on the shoulder. "Reggie, what's going to happen next?"

"You'll meet with Mr. Panzerelli."

"And after that?"

"I don't have any orders after that. We'll have to wait until he gives more."

Olivia looked up at Reggie. "Reggie, I'm

worried. I'm worried that our association with Shaughnessey is going to be bad for us. It's Shaughnessey who took the case, not me or my sister. He showed up, dumped it on our laps, and then took off for the track. He says Mr. Panzerelli put us on retainer but we haven't seen any of the money. I suspect Shaughnessey left it all at the track. He bets on anything that isn't dead yet."

"I'm not sure what I can do for you, Miss Morrison."

"Maybe you could put in a good word for us? Let Mr. Panzerelli know this falls on Shaughnessey's shoulders, not ours."

Shaughnessey lunged at her. "You backstabbing bitch!" His hands were around her throat, and then they heard the sound of Reggie cocking his gun.

In a low, quiet voice, Reggie said, "Take your hands off her."

The barrel of Reggie's gun touched Shaughnessey's neck and he complied. He stepped back and glowered at the gun Reggie kept trained on him.

Olivia shrank back and gasped for air. Darcy put her arm around her sister and glared at Shaughnessey. "If you ever—"

"Are you all right, Miss Morrison?" asked Reggie.

"I think so. I, it's just ..." her voice trailed off, and she began to cry. "I've never had anyone try to kill me before."

"I would think in your business you'd be used to it by now," said Reggie.

"In the past six months of lost pets and sick-day fraud, no one has even gotten angry at us. Well, no one but him."

"I'll keep him away from you, at least for now. After we meet with Mr. Panzerelli, I'm not sure if there's anything else I can do."

Reggie turned to Shaughnessey. "Every man in here is armed. I can trust you to behave now, right?"

Shaughnessey nodded.

"Good. Because we don't take kindly to men who try to kill beautiful young women."

Olivia smiled at Reggie. She had the feeling she could use the threat of Reggie to keep Shaughnessey in line long after she had talked their way out of this.

They entered a large dimly lit pool hall. A few men had cues in their hands and more men sat around, talking and laughing. In the corner, a large man sat alone at a desk. His slicked-back, graying hair suited his dark complexion and razor-sharp features. The group walked over to him.

The man extended his hand. "Ah, Shaughnessey. Good to see you."

Shaughnessey shook the hand. "Hey, Panzerelli. Good to see you, too. But why did you send men out for us? We would have come if you'd called."

"In this business, you never know. I thought Reggie and Joey here could make it easier on all of us." He turned to Olivia and Darcy. "And these are your associates?"

Olivia beamed at him. "Olivia Morrison. It's a pleasure to meet you, Mr. Panzerelli."

Panzerelli looked back at Shaughnessey. "She's the secretary, right?"

Olivia blushed. "No, sir. I'm one of the two investigators at Morrison Investigations."

"So what's he?" He gestured to Shaughnessey.

"He's our mentor. He's *supposed* to be training us to become better at the job."

"He doesn't?"

"No. He takes his half of all the money that comes in and goes to a bar, or the track, or the bar at the track."

Panzerelli looked at Shaughnessey. "This true?"

"I've trained them. I've gotten them cases, like yours."

"Is it true about the money?"

"Yes. It's in our contract. Half of all money comes to me."

"So, the ten Gs I gave you for a retainer. They only got five?"

Shaughnessey didn't say a word.

"We got none of that money," said Darcy.

Reggie stepped forward. "This is in line with what her sister told me earlier, sir. And we did pick him up at the track."

Panzerelli stood up and towered over Shaughnessey. "How are they supposed to find my dog if they have no resources? Give her the money now."

"I can't."

Panzerelli nodded to Joey, who calmly walked up to Shaughnessey and punched him in the gut. Every man in the room stopped what he was doing and looked toward Panzerelli.

Shaughnessey straightened up and took a deep breath. "I mean, it will take me some time to get it together. But they'll have it."

"See that they do. By tonight. In fact, I'm going to send Joey here to spend the day with you, to make sure you get the money."

Shaughnessey blanched. "Not necessary, I assure you. I'm a man of my word."

Around the room, several men laughed. It seemed to Olivia that everyone there understood what she and Darcy had to deal with every day.

Panzerelli turned to Olivia. "You still have to find Brutus, by tomorrow morning."

Olivia's heart sank. "I'm not sure we can do that."

Panzerelli glared at her. "Why not?"

"Sir, if I could talk to you privately?"

"No private audiences—too dangerous," said Reggie. "Not even for you."

"Then at least without him." She pointed to Shaughnessey.

"Joey, you go with him and find the money. Don't be afraid to lean on him if he doesn't cooperate."

Joey grabbed Shaughnessey by the arm and marched him out of the room.

"Thank you. You know he takes our money. We have bills to pay and we can't, so we took a case he doesn't know anything about. It's big, a murder case. And as much as your dog means to you, as much as I love all animals, we should be saving a man's life first."

"What man?"

"George Wynton. He's been accused of murder, but the police have the wrong man, and we need to find the right one."

"The telepath?"

"Yes."

"I saw that last night on the news. He didn't do it?"

She shook her head. "No murder weapon, no

gunshot residue on his hands, no motive. He was found at the scene, so they took him in and arrested him. Now it looks like they're going to railroad him to get a conviction."

Panzerelli looked disgusted. "I can't tell you how many times my people have been pinched for being in the wrong place at the wrong time. Added to that, people don't trust telepaths, and that's enough to get him hanged, whether he's guilty or innocent."

"Yes. I'm afraid for my client. I'm afraid the police aren't going to do a thorough job, and I'm afraid he'll waste the rest of his life in jail for a crime he didn't commit." *I'm afraid it will fracture the telepathic community and drive the normals further into the fear and panic Wynton was dedicated to removing.*

Panzerelli sat back and thought. "Brutus means everything to me. You must find him. On the other hand, this Wynton case is important. I've known a telepath or two in my day, and they helped me out of a couple of binds. They're good people, not like the crap you hear on the news and in the tabloids. If Wynton goes away for the murder, my friends are automatically in danger. So here's what I'll let you do. You can work on both cases at the same time. You work on one, and your sister can work on the other. And I need my dog back by the end of business tomorrow."

Olivia nodded. She knew it was the best deal she was likely to get. "Under the circumstances, that's very fair. Thank you."

"I'm going to call my telepath friends and tell them to lay low for a while. It might not be safe to be out of doors until the trial is over."

He picked up his cell phone and began to dial. The audience was over.

Reggie gently led Olivia and Darcy outside. "You can go now. I called a cab to come pick you up."

Fraser, dressed in civvies, started to cross the road, but Olivia shook her head. She took Reggie's hand to distract him from the nearby police officer. "Thank you, Reggie. That was very thoughtful."

Fraser continued to cross the road, ignoring Olivia and Reggie as he passed nearby.

"When do you think it will be here?"

"I called Yellow Cab when we got here, so it shouldn't be long."

Fraser slowed to hear Reggie's response. Then he picked up his pace and disappeared in the late afternoon crowd.

"Reggie, do you really think if we don't find Brutus by tomorrow …?" She let the question hang.

"I've worked for Mr. P for a long time, and he tries to be fair, but he's got to maintain his reputation. He won't kill you, if that's what you mean, but until you find Brutus, your life's going to be a lot more difficult."

Olivia looked away. "I thought as much. Reggie, you've been a good friend to me in the few hours we've known each other. I want you to know I appreciate you sticking up for me when Shaughnessey got out of line in the car, and when we were inside. If there's anything I can do for you, give me a call." She pulled out a business card and handed it to him. "I'll do my best for you as well."

Reggie took the card. "Thank you. It's a pleasure to do business with civilized people once in a while."

#

Darcy and Olivia climbed into the waiting cab. Reggie closed the door, and Olivia waved to him. He smiled back at her.

"Where to, ladies?" asked the cabbie.

Darcy gave him their office address and turned to Olivia. "Sweet Jesus. I thought we were screwed."

"Me, too," said Olivia.

"We still might not be out of it, but at least we live to fight another day."

Olivia nodded. "I think I should take the dog case and you should do the research for Wynton."

"I agree. You can get your new best friend to help you."

Olivia furrowed her brow. "What new best friend?"

Darcy laughed. "Reggie. He likes you."

"He's not a bad guy," she said, "but he doesn't like me."

Darcy laughed. "If it was obvious to me, it has to be true."

Olivia thought for a moment and then frowned. "You're right, but he could be a murderer. He seemed so kind, though."

"I know you don't want to think ill of anyone, but some people are actually capable of really bad stuff."

Olivia frowned. "I'm going to call Uncle Dean and see what he has to say about all this." She pulled out her phone and dialed.

"Uncle Dean? It's your favorite niece."

"Darcy?"

"No, your other favorite."

"Melinda?"

"Uncle Dean!" It was a never-ending routine they played out whenever they spoke on the phone.

"How are you, sweetheart? How's the new job?"

Olivia sighed. "That's what I wanted to talk to you about."

"Sounds bad. Want to have dinner? Bad news is always improved over food."

She was relieved. A face-to-face meeting would make this much easier. "Yes."

"Okay. I don't have a lot of time today, so meet me at the hot dog vendor outside the Superior Court in an hour."

"That's dinner?"

"More often than I'd like, kiddo. See you then."

The hot dog vendor was starting to pack up for the day when Olivia waved and called to her uncle. "Uncle Dean!"

He smiled and excused himself from the very serious-looking woman he had been talking to. "Livvy, you're a ray of sunshine. You look wonderful."

She blushed. He always said the same thing, and she knew he always meant it. "Thank you." She gave him an appraising look. "You look like you've been having too many chili cheese dogs."

"Perils of middle age, my dear, and not having a wife to look after me."

"You really ought to get one of those. I hear they come in quite handy."

He held up his arm and called out, "Two loaded. One no hots."

The vendor handed Dean his hot dogs and said, "No charge. I was about to throw them out anyway."

"Thanks, Max."

He led her to a bench by a fountain. "Tell me what's wrong."

"Can't a girl have dinner with her favorite uncle without something being wrong?"

"A girl can, but you look worried about something."

She sighed. "It's work. Shaughnessey somehow got us involved with Panzerelli."

At the name, her uncle looked up from his dog. "Guido?"

Olivia nodded.

"Get out of it. Whatever it takes, run far and fast from him."

"Shaughnessey already took his money."

"Give it back."

"Can't. He kept the money; we do the work."

"How does that work?"

"Really badly. Usually he keeps half the money, but this time he kept it all."

"And what does Panzerelli want you to do?"

"He's lost his dog. Apparently we're now the lost-dog experts. Shaughnessey has a laugh over that every single day."

"Lost his dog? Seriously? Who would be crazy enough to take his dog? It's a death sentence."

"No idea. Haven't started looking into it. We've got this other case, though. It's a good one. George Wynton."

Dean's eyes widened. "Who's his lawyer?"

"Dan's lead defense counsel. He wants us to find other suspects."

"Damn. That's a career-making case for him — and you."

"Exactly why we can't be worrying about Panzerelli's dog."

"I can't help you with either case."

"Why not?"

"Conflict of interest. My office has a case against the Panzer coming up soon, and I'm prosecuting Wynton."

"You are? Dan didn't tell me that."

"He might not have known. I just got the case an hour ago. I haven't even started to look at it."

"Can you give me any advice about Panzerelli?"

Dean leaned back against the bench and thought for a moment. "He likes to think he's fair, and he doesn't like violence against women, not unless they're in the racket. Women like you and Darcy helping him find his dog should be safe, assuming you find the dog. If you ever cross him, though, you should leave town."

"What if we can't find his dog?"

He shook his head. "The problem is, he's a moody bastard. It's hard to tell how he'd take that."

"So I should be my charming self no matter what. Act like a lady. Be as absolutely nonthreatening as I can."

"Right."

"Anything you can tell me about your case against Wynton?"

"Nope. Not a thing."

"I'm afraid he's going to be railroaded into a conviction because he's a telepath."

"That won't wash with me, or the judge. I had the same concern, but he's got Judge Alward, and he's fair. He's not easy, but he's fair."

"Uncle Dean, I'm surprised at your concern.

What about your conviction rate?" she teased.

"Conviction rate be damned. I'm not in this business to send innocent people to jail just to give the rabble a false sense of security."

She smiled at him, her hero. And Darcy's as well. Uncle Dean had always had an overdeveloped sense of fairness, and sometimes it had gotten him in trouble with the prosecutor's office. But he slept soundly at night, knowing he had done his best for justice.

"How's Dan?" he asked.

"He's doing well. He's moving up in the firm and is happy about it."

"I meant, how is your relationship with him?"

She paused to think. "It's rocky. I walked out on him this morning, and I think we won't be seeing much of each other anymore. He's under a lot of pressure right now, and you know how he reacts to that."

"He come to terms with your work yet?"

"He must have, hiring us like this."

Dean looked at his watch. "I've got to get back in and review some notes. Be careful, and don't be afraid to get help, professional help, to keep yourself safe."

"I love you, too." She walked away from the courthouse, smiling. Even though he hadn't been able to help her, dinner with Uncle Dean always left her feeling better, stronger, more capable. He was one of the only people, aside from Darcy, who admired her for exactly who she was, and she loved him for it.

Chapter 14

First thing in the morning, Olivia and Darcy pulled into the parking garage of Frank Adams's apartment building. A guard stopped them at the gate and Darcy rolled down her window.

"Good morning. Who are you visiting?" he asked as he wrote down their license plate number.

"Frank Adams. Apartment 238."

He checked a list on his clipboard. "Elevator is toward the rear of the garage. Have a nice day."

They parked and rode the elevator to the second floor. It opened onto a lobby that looked like a living room. Four chairs were grouped around a table, and a couch rested in front of a crackling gas fireplace. A security desk, unoccupied, was to their right. Darcy hustled Olivia down the hall before they might have to explain their presence to anyone.

"Nice place. I wonder how he affords it."

"Not on his salary at Harrison's, that's for sure. Maybe he's got a roommate?"

Olivia knocked on door 238. "Mr. Adams?" There was no answer. Darcy took out her lock pick kit and smiled as she inserted the tools, worked her magic and the lock clicked. She opened the door.

"You've been practicing," said Olivia.

Darcy replied, "I never use the key to our apartment anymore, and this is the same type of lock."

Inside the apartment, they looked around. A

large television hung over a gas fireplace in the living room. Two leather couches and a wingback chair clustered around a glass and wood coffee table. "Mr. Adams? Are you here?"

There was no answer. "You get the bathroom, I'll get the bedroom." Darcy moved toward the bedroom, which was tastefully decorated with gender-neutral furnishings. The sleigh bed had been stripped of all bedding; she discovered that the bureau was empty, and the closet held only a few wire hangers. She got down on her hands and knees and looked under the bed, where she found a receipt for an Indian restaurant and one lone sock.

"You find anything?" asked Olivia.

"Not sure. One sock and a restaurant receipt. Anything in the bathroom?"

"Not even a hair in the drain."

Darcy opened the bedside table drawer, which was empty as well.

"Looks like he's out of here for good."

Darcy smoothed out the receipt. "Indian food, delivered last night."

"Where did he go?"

Darcy pulled a clipboard out of her backpack. "I'm going to check in with the neighbors." She entered the hallway and knocked on the door to apartment 236.

An elderly woman answered. She peered at Darcy. "You're not from the pharmacy."

"No, ma'am, I'm not. I'm looking for your neighbor, Mr. Adams. I have a delivery for him to sign for, and he indicated he would be available this morning to accept the package."

"Oh, no. That can't be. Mr. Adams moved out last night. Noisy as all get out, they were. We have rules here: no moving in or out after 7 PM or on Sundays, you know. I had to threaten to call the super before they quieted down."

Darcy looked back at her clipboard. "That's odd. Did he say where he was going?"

"All he said to me was, 'Yes, ma'am. I'll tell the guys to be quieter.' "

"Do you know much about him?"

"I know he worked for that woman who was murdered—Harrison. When news got out she was dead, I heard him yelling at someone. I think he was on the phone, because no one was talking back to him. These walls aren't nearly as soundproof as we might like."

Darcy nodded, hoping she would continue.

"What is it you are delivering, dear?"

"Tropical fish."

"Maybe you could ask the super. He might have a forwarding address."

"Thank you for your help. I'm sure he'll call the shop and arrange for a new delivery."

There was no ne home in the next four apartments she knocked on. Back in Adams's apartment, Darcy said, "That was a bust."

"I'm sure Fraser will be looking for him, too. I bet if you met him for dinner somewhere, he might be willing to share what he's got."

Darcy frowned. "You're the one who gets people talking, not me."

"Not in this case. I can tell by his body language, Fraser likes you."

Darcy rolled her eyes. She did not need this complication, her uncle's partner falling for her. "Let's just get out of here."

As Darcy pulled out of the parking garage, a

black Lexus sedan followed. Three blocks later, Darcy observed, "Panzerelli's goons are following us."

Olivia turned around to look. "It's just Reggie. He's not going to be a problem."

Darcy snorted. "Ha! He could be a murderer for all we know."

Olivia waved at Reggie. "Pull over. I'll talk to him."

Reggie followed them into a grocery store parking lot and parked next to them.

Rolling down her window, Olivia said, "Hi, Reggie. Are you going to follow us all day?"

Reggie looked sheepish. "I'm sorry, Miss Morrison. I've got to stay with you until you find Brutus."

"That's all right. We all have our jobs to do. I know we told your boss we would split up, but right now, we have to find a murderer. But as soon as we find the murderer, we'll find Brutus. I promise. At any rate, it doesn't make any sense for you to follow us around, pretending we don't see you."

"I have to make sure you follow orders."

"Orders or not, right now we're going back to the office and we'll be ordering lunch in a little while. Do you like Indian food?"

"Never had any."

"You're in for a treat, my friend. We'll all go back to the office. You can watch us work from our couch, so you won't have to sit in a cold, boring car all day."

Reggie smiled. "That's very thoughtful of you. I really wasn't looking forward to a day in my car."

"All right, then. We'll see you at the office."

Olivia rolled her window up, and Darcy drove off, saying, "Are you kidding me? We can't have a goon sitting around in our office."

"I don't see why not. If he's not in the office, he'll be outside waiting for us to go somewhere. It's really cold out. He was good to me. I can return the favor."

"Maybe he'd get too cold and he'd leave us alone."

"I doubt it. Think about this: he's the one who's going to report back to Panzerelli about our progress. Doesn't it make sense to have him happy with us? If we're nice to him, maybe he'll cut us some slack when we need it."

"Just don't expect me to be all friendly with him. I don't trust any of those guys."

At the office, Reggie arrived at the door first. "Let me check it out, make sure it's safe."

"Reggie, I'm sure we'll be fine."

"You never know in this business, and I'm supposed to keep you safe as well as focused on Brutus."

"All right, go ahead."

They crept up the stairs as silently as the creaky wooden steps underfoot allowed. Reggie tried the doorknob; it was locked. Olivia handed him her key. He unlocked the door and burst into the room in one smooth motion. Gun out, he searched the few potential hiding places in the office and then called out, "Come on in."

Olivia smiled. "Thank you, Reggie. Can I take your coat?"

"Uh, sure. Just let me … I mean, I'm sure I won't need it … but just in case …" He tucked his gun into the back of his waistband.

Poor Reggie, Olivia thought. *He's completely baffled by this treatment. How many people are genuinely nice to him in the course of a day?* "Don't worry, we'll be fine here."

Darcy sat at the desk. "If you two are through becoming best friends, can we get some work done?"

Olivia scowled at Darcy. "Fine. You look into Adams." She turned back to Reggie. "Tell me about Brutus — when you last saw him, who would want to take him, even what he looks like would be helpful. The photo Mr. Panzerelli gave us wasn't all that good; it could have been almost any Doberman in that shot." She took a notebook from the desk, sat down on the couch and patted the cushion next to her.

Reggie sat down and furrowed his brow. "Mr. Panzerelli, he doesn't take the dog out much. Brutus is old and he doesn't move so well anymore. He got so bad that he needed some sort of a harness around his body that she had Joey hold to help him walk."

"She?"

"Mrs. Panzerelli. She's the only person who isn't sad Brutus is gone."

"Really? Why is that?"

"She never really liked Brutus. Said he scared her. But Mr. Panzerelli, he insisted on a guard dog. You know, with business being what it is."

Olivia nodded. "Completely understandable. Everyone wants to protect his family."

"Anyway, being afraid of Brutus didn't help her when she had to be so close to him and take care of him."

"So she was most likely the last person to see Brutus?"

"Yes, but she says she doesn't know where he is. She let him sit outside in the fresh air, and when she went back to get him, he was gone."

"So that's why he suspects kidnapping. Where

was the dog sitting?"

"In the back yard."

"That doesn't make any sense. Who would go into the back yard to kidnap a dog? The house has other guards, right? It would be very dangerous to break in just for a dog."

"Yeah, but you can't tell Mr. Panzerelli that maybe his wife was lying to him. He'd shoot you for even thinking that."

"Do you think we can go talk to her?"

"I can bring you there, but I don't know that she'd tell you anything different."

#

The Panzerelli house was a giant monstrosity straight out of the movies. Because the house was in the middle of Somerville, iron grating covered the windows and doors, and a wrought iron fence surrounded the property. Olivia smiled at the ridiculous ostentation of it all.

Reggie rang the bell, and Joey answered. "Hey, Reggie. Thought you were off doing a special job for the boss."

Reggie shook Joey's hand. It amused Olivia that they pretended to be civilized. "I am. I thought you were with Shaughnessey for the day."

Joey grimaced. "He spewed in my car. I dropped him off at the club to sober up. I'm going back in a few hours and if he doesn't have the cash, I'm going to start breaking one of his fingers for every hour he keeps me waiting. What are you doing here?"

"Miss Morrison would like to talk to Mrs. P about Brutus."

"I don't think so. She's busy this afternoon."

Joey began to close the door, but Reggie held it open with one beefy hand. "Go ask her. We'll wait inside."

Joey, clearly the junior partner in the relationship, complied and returned. "She'll see you in the den."

He turned to lead them in, but Reggie stopped him. "You can stay here." Turning to Olivia, he said, "This way, Miss Morrison."

Olivia didn't have to guess or measure or estimate—it was clear that her entire apartment would fit in the den. Mrs. Panzerelli stood by the crackling fireplace—real wood, not the fake gas fireplaces so common these days—holding a glass of what looked like whiskey. As she walked toward them, she stumbled over the rug and caught herself without spilling her drink. "Reggie! How lovely to see you again."

He smiled at her. Olivia observed the sadness in his eyes. "Wouldn't you like to sit?" he asked.

Mrs. Panzerelli patted his cheek. "You know me so well," she said. "You should sit as well. Miss Morrison, is it? Can I get you a drink?"

Olivia opened her mouth to decline when Reggie said, "I'll take care of that. Why don't you two get to know each other?" He moved to the bar and began pouring.

"Well, ah, Mrs. Panzerelli," Olivia began. "I'm sure you know my firm has been hired to locate Brutus. You were the last one to see him, so I'd like to know what you remember about that day."

Mrs. Panzerelli sat back and closed her eyes. "Let's not talk about him right now. Brutus was old and was going to die soon anyway." She opened her eyes and stared at Olivia with red, glassy eyes. "So what if he's gone a little earlier than we expected? No

one cared about that stupid dog except me, anyway."
She slumped back into the deep cushions of the couch
and sniffled. "Nobody, no one shingle pershon," she
paused and tried again, "single person loved that dog
like I did."

Olivia moved from the chair where she was
sitting to the couch, next to Mrs. Panzerelli, and tried
not to wrinkle her nose at the woman's bourbon
breath. "I know how hard it is when a pet runs
away," she said. "It's a terrible feeling, not knowing if
he is safe."

The older woman nodded and blinked back a
tear.

Olivia continued. "Particularly when one has
been the sole caregiver for a beloved pet. It's a
difficult burden to bear, and I just want you to know
that I am here for you, if you want to talk about
Brutus or, really, anything at all."

Joey, who had been listening at the threshold,
strode in and said, "I think that's all for today. Mrs.
Panzerelli has had a difficult few days and needs her
rest now."

"I'm sure—"

"No, he's right," slurred Mrs. Panzerelli. "It's
been so tough, not knowing where my beloved
Brutus is. Perhaps we can talk tomorrow."

Olivia looked to Reggie but he did not come to
her defense.

"That's all, Miss Morrison. Perhaps you can
come back on another day, when she's feeling better."

Chapter 15

Darcy closed her eyes and put her feet up on the desk. She'd been able to find out a lot about Adams without having to call Fraser. Frank Adams had apparently only existed in the public record for five years. It smelled like undercover work to her. *But why would someone go undercover at a PR firm?* Her reverie was interrupted by the phone.

"Morrison Investigations."

There was a pause, and then Joyce came on the line. "Miss Morrison? It's Joyce, from Wynton Signage."

"Yes, Joyce. What can I do for you?"

"I need your help. The police are only letting me see George once a day and I can't get hold of his mind."

"You can't what?"

"I can't find him, telepathically. I'm worried. Worse, some of the more radical telepaths aren't listening to me anymore. They're planning to storm the precinct and break George out."

"And what do you need from me?"

"I need you to talk to him and get him to start communicating with the other telepaths or else this is going to get out of hand."

"I'm sorry. That's not possible. I'm up to my ears trying to prove he's innocent, and I can't stop work because you can't get a few telepaths to listen to you."

"It's not just a few people. There are over a thousand telepaths in the Boston underground."

Holy shit, Darcy thought. *There are a thousand telepaths in Boston? And they're organized?*

"You must be exaggerating."

"No. We're the largest underground in the country. Telepaths have been moving to Boston specifically to join our organization. It's one of the things Kathleen was working on—larger numbers for political strength. I can't hang on to them all without some help."

Darcy sighed. "I'll head down there in a few minutes and I'll call you once I'm done."

#

On the drive back to the office, Olivia suddenly clutched her head and began moaning.

Reggie, startled, looked over at her, and the car hit a patch of black ice. The Lexus slid sideways down the hill. He struggled for control but could not avoid the telephone pole at the bottom.

Olivia looked up in time to watch the pole smash her door in. Her head slammed against the doorframe, and she passed out.

She woke to the wail of a loud siren and slowly opened her eyes. She was strapped to a backboard, unable to move. An EMT flashed a penlight in her eyes; she couldn't see well enough to determine whether the person was a man or woman.

"It looks like you have a concussion, miss," said the deep-voiced man. "Can you remember what happened?"

She tried to nod, but her head was immobile. "Reggie? Is he okay?"

"Your driver is banged up, too. He's being transported in another ambulance. Do you remember what happened?"

"He was driving, and then suddenly we were fishtailing, and then we slid out of control."

"Did he say or do anything just before the accident?"

"What do you mean?"

"Did he complain of a headache, or possibly an illness?"

She fought to keep her face neutral. *Sniffers must be in town, hunting telepaths.* She'd been almost certain of it when her head began to throb before the car slid and hit the pole; now she knew. She had to warn Darcy and Joyce. "No, he seemed fine. He swore a lot when we were sliding down the hill, though. Is that what you mean?"

The EMT relaxed. "No. That's just fine. The government is searching for some very dangerous people in town, but you don't need to worry about that."

"Telepaths?" she asked.

"I'm not allowed to talk about it. But I suggest staying away from crowds for a few days, just in case."

Olivia closed her eyes to think. The Telepathic Corps were in town to stir the pot while Wynton was in jail. If the sniffers could provoke the telepaths into some sort of action, they would pull as many off the streets as possible. "I'd like to call my sister to let her know what happened."

"We've already called your office. A woman named Darcy will meet us at the hospital."

"Am I all right? Why am I strapped to this board?"

"It's just a precaution, miss. The car hit that pole hard, and we want to take some x-rays to make sure there's no damage."

She wiggled her toes but couldn't see if they were actually moving or not. She tried her fingers and felt them moving against her leg. "I'm moving my fingers and toes. Can you see them move?" she asked.

The EMT smiled. "Yes, your feet are moving, and so are your fingers. That's a good sign."

After a short drive, the ambulance stopped. She was wheeled out into the hall of an emergency wing, still strapped to the backboard on a gurney. "I'll give your paperwork to the nurses, and then I have to go. It's a busy afternoon. You rest, and get well soon." He patted her on the arm and took off. She lay there, alone, unable to move, for what seemed like forever. Realistically she knew it was probably only five minutes, but she had never dealt well with feeling abandoned. Her mouth was very dry, and she called out for a nurse. Her raspy voice sounded foreign to her, but it brought an orderly over promptly.

"Yes?" he said.

"Could I have some water?"

He shook his head. "I'll have to check with the nurses first." He checked at the foot of her gurney. "Where's your file?"

"The EMT said he gave it to a nurse. Please, I'm very thirsty."

The orderly grunted. "Great, now I'll have to figure out who you are. I hate it when they do that."

"I'm Olivia Morrison."

He walked off without saying anything else. She didn't even know if he heard her name. After another interminable length of time, a nurse approached. "Olivia Morrison?"

"Yes. I've been waiting for some water."

"Soon." She flashed another annoying penlight in Olivia's eyes. "You've suffered a concussion. We're going to wheel you into x-ray and take a look at your spine. Once the doctor gives you a clean bill of health, you can have anything you want to drink."

"Okay," she whispered.

Olivia closed her eyes. She realized she must have fallen asleep, because when the nurse woke her, she was in a hospital room. "Miss Morrison?" said the nurse.

"Yes?"

"I am Grace, your nurse for the night. The doctor has admitted you for a twenty-four hour watch, and it's my job to wake you up every hour to check on you."

Olivia realized she wasn't strapped down anymore and could move her arms and legs. "My spine?"

"Your x-rays came out just fine. No spinal damage. All we—"

"I had x-rays? I don't remember them."

"You passed out during them and haven't woken up until now. We will be monitoring you all night to make sure you don't pass out again and that your brain swelling goes down over night, you should be good to go tomorrow afternoon."

Olivia pushed the button to sit up in bed. As the bed rose she felt more pressure in her head. "Ow!" She stopped the bed. "My head hurts."

"Yes, it's bound to hurt for a while. As the swelling goes down, you'll start to feel better. Are you feeling nauseous?"

She didn't dare shake her head. "No."

"Good. I'll bring you some ginger ale."

Olivia used her time alone to survey her surroundings. She was on the window side of the room, and the divider curtain was drawn so she could not see the other half. The name GRACE and a smiley face were written on a whiteboard on the equally white wall. She could not see her clothes, shoes, or bag. Thinking back, she didn't recall her bag being with her in the ambulance or the ER.

Grace returned and pulled the divider curtain back. "There, now you won't feel claustrophobic." She handed Olivia a can of ginger ale with a bendy straw already inserted.

"Thanks." She took a sip and coughed when the carbonation hit her dry throat.

Grace helped her sit up and reminded her to breathe normally.

"I'm okay," Olivia croaked, and she took another sip.

"Good. Try to get some rest. I'll see you in an hour."

"Wait. What happened to my driver? Is he all right?"

"I don't know. I can try to find out. What's his name?"

"Reggie."

"Last name?"

She was embarrassed to realize she didn't know his last name. "I don't know," she whispered.

"I'll see what I can do. I'll let you know when I wake you up again."

Olivia put the can down and fell asleep as soon as her eyes closed.

She dreamed about Darcy being caught by the sniffers. She tried to wake herself up but couldn't. She dreamed about Darcy being taken to a lab, where giant stainless steel rods took samples from her brain. She woke, screaming, in darkness and continued to panic. "Darcy! Where are you?"

Lights snapped on, and the painful glare forced Olivia to screw her eyes shut.

"Olivia," she heard Grace say as she settled her back down in the bed. "You're having a nightmare. Take a deep breath. Everything is fine."

Olivia opened her eyes. "I need to see my sister."

"Of course," Grace said. She released her grip on Olivia's arms and stood back. "She was here earlier but she looked so bad I sent her to the cafeteria to get something to eat. She should be back soon."

Olivia sat up, wincing at the pain in her head. *Is it the concussion or the sniffers?* She didn't care. She threw the blankets off her legs. "Bring me down there. I need to see her, right away."

Grace adopted her most calm nursing tone and said, "We'll send for her. You don't want to be out in your johnnie, flapping in the breeze, do you?"

Olivia tried to stand, but her legs felt so weak she wasn't sure she'd be able to make it out of the room. "You have three minutes, or I'm going to find her myself."

She was sure more than three minutes passed, but Olivia was in no shape to argue by the time Darcy arrived.

"Liv! You're awake." Darcy cried as she ran into the room.

"I can only let you visit for five minutes, and then you'll have to go. I shouldn't have let you in earlier at all, but she was unconscious, so I didn't think it would hurt. The doctor doesn't want her disturbed," said Grace as she went to stand by the door.

"I'm fine; just a bump on the head. Reggie, though—how's he?"

Darcy sat and put her arm around Olivia. "He's here. He's not doing so great. The nurse said this wasn't the first time his head has been smacked around, and he's still unconscious. You were only out for about fifteen minutes. She gave Olivia's arm a squeeze. "You're fine now, so don't worry. And I'm sure Reggie will wake up soon."

"Can I see him?"

"You have to stay here and take care of yourself," said Grace.

Darcy stood. "I'd like a few minutes alone with my sister, nurse."

Grace frowned but nodded and left the room.

Olivia grabbed Darcy's hand. "Sniffers!" she hissed.

Darcy nodded. "I know."

"I don't feel safe here," said Olivia. "I want to go home."

Darcy looked at Olivia, concern in her eyes. "Are you sure you're well enough? You look terrible."

"I feel shaky, but I think I'll be fine." She stood up slowly and began to walk toward the tiny closet by the door. "Help me find my stuff."

Darcy pulled Olivia's clothing out of the closet. She noticed the nurse approaching and closed the door to the room.

Olivia slowly got dressed as Grace knocked, then banged, on the door.

"Miss Morrison," Grace called through the door.

Darcy held the door shut until Olivia finished dressing. Olivia opened the door to a very angry Grace and announced, "I'm going home. I don't need to stay here."

"That's not a good idea. Let me get the doctor."

"No. I am going home to sleep in my own bed. My sister can wake me up as well as you can."

Grace put her arm out, preventing Olivia from moving forward. "You'll have to sign forms then. We won't be held responsible if you leave before you are discharged."

Darcy quickly stepped next to Olivia, stopping inches from Grace. "Move your arm, nurse, before I break it," she growled.

Grace dropped her arm, reluctantly.

"You have until we reach my car to bring her the forms to sign," said Darcy.

Darcy put her arm around Olivia and helped her walk slowly down the corridor. Olivia scrawled her name on the forms a nervous hospital administrator brought her and they left the hospital.

Chapter 16

Joyce locked the door to Wynton Signage behind her. She'd thought she would never make it through the day. The phones had been ringing nonstop; with no one else in the office, she had to field every call herself. The calls from the media weren't so bad; she had a prepared statement, and once they realized they couldn't pry anything more out of her they stopped calling.

The other telepaths had made her day very difficult. It seemed like every single telepath in the United States had called today, wanting to know the battle plan. There was no battle plan, outside of the one George's attorney was formulating, she'd told them. George had a very good lawyer, she'd explained over and over, and his innocence would be proven in open court. He would walk out of court a free man. Any rash actions before then would only hurt his case.

It was not the answer most of them wanted to hear. One of their own was in danger, and they were frustrated at their inability to do anything to help. Immediate action was the only course of action they wanted. Joyce understood the feeling; she was living with it herself. But she suspected Jose Delgado was behind a lot of the unrest.

Jose was George's second in command and foreman of the print shop. He was a good man, but young and rash. Joyce didn't want to deal with him tonight. She had waited as long as she could for Darcy's call; she couldn't put it off any longer. She knew morning would be too late. She drove directly to the meeting location, but parked two blocks away to make sure sniffers weren't following her.

She still didn't understand why Jose insisted they meet at the print shop instead of the quieter office. She'd suggested dinner, hoping a public meeting place would keep his temper under control, but he wouldn't agree. She walked the two blocks, considering her arguments. George knew what needed to be done, and his instructions were clear: keep people calm, do charitable works, and maintain the good reputation of telepaths. Any violence would only hurt his defense and ruin the hard-won respect he'd already achieved with Kathleen.

The print shop was crowded with people waiting, interspersed among the machinery. *I should have known he would pull this kind of stunt.* "Where is Jose?" she asked the woman closest to the door.

"He's toward the back, near the stage."

Stage? There was no stage in the print shop.

The woman pointed toward the back of the large room, where Jose stood next to a platform, speaking to a group of men.

He must have built that today. Damn him. He clearly wanted a rally or a debate. She wanted a quiet meeting where the two of them could come to an agreement. It appeared she would have to be the voice of reason to the hundred people who were there, and for the telepaths who weren't.

Jose's arms waved wildly as his voice rose. The group cheered, but Jose looked a bit sheepish when he turned around and noticed her.

"Jose. We need to speak privately."

"No. Anything you have to say to me needs to be said in front of everyone here. We need to decide our course of action together. The two of us can't dictate policy."

"How the hell do I have a chance at getting these people to consider what I have to say? You've already riled them up."

Jose turned and walked onto the stage. "Now that we're all here," he yelled, "let's begin the debate."

The crowd quieted, and all eyes turned to the stage. Joyce took a deep breath, climbed the steps, and looked out at the assembled telepaths, hoping to see some calm faces. She found precious few.

"My mentor," Jose began, "George Wynton, taught me that we need to present a unified front as telepaths. I believe this is true. But he also thought we should go through the world with a quiet, calm demeanor to keep the normals from fearing us." The crowd began to murmur. "I say now is not the time for quiet. Now is the time to make our voices heard, to demand the release of our leader. Now is not the time for calmness. Now is the time to let the normals see what we can do. Let them fear us."

The crowd erupted in cheers. Joyce felt as though she had already lost the debate. Gathering her will, she projected the word *quiet* into each person's mind. The crowd became silent immediately. She felt their awe as her power flowed through the room.

"Now that I have your attention, I would like to point out the flaws in my colleague's plan. First and foremost, his plan is in direct opposition to the instructions George has given me, which I have been relaying to you all day. You should all know by now that he does not approve of using fear or violence as negotiating tactics." She paused and slowly looked across the room, trying to make brief eye contact with every person there. "You know this. Every single one of you knows this."

No one spoke, but many looked around at their neighbors, uncertainty on their faces.

"He wants trust between telepaths and normals. This problem is just a temporary setback. He did not kill Kathleen Harrison, and we need to have faith that our justice system will set this right. That is what he wants."

She turned to Jose. "Tell me, what was your plan? Were you going to storm the jail, free him by force? How many people would be killed in that little stunt? Possibly even George. And then what? Were you going to go on the run, living like fugitives? Behaving like the criminals the normals think we are?"

She looked out at the assembled crowd. "How many of you would be willing to do that? Give up everything you have and everyone you love?"

Murmurs rose from the crowd.

"Jose has no wife, no children, nothing that ties him here. Sure, it would be easy for him to leave and never look back. But you, Sean—would you leave your wife and new baby for this crazy plan?"

Sean shook his head. "I didn't think it would come to that."

"*Didn't think.* That's what this all boils down to. You aren't thinking clearly. Go home, kiss your husbands and wives, hug your children. This sacrifice isn't needed."

Jose strode toward the steps.

"Not you," Joyce said.

He turned to her, anger blazing in his eyes.

"You might be able to control this crowd of sheep, but you can't tell me what to do."

"No, I suppose I can't tell you what to do. But I can make sure you don't cause any trouble tonight." She gestured toward Sean and his brother William. "Make sure he doesn't go anywhere but home tonight. Stay with him; keep him out of trouble."

"You're as bad as the blind humans," Jose shouted. "I'm being imprisoned for something I did not do. I'm a victim, just like George."

Joyce sighed. "No, Jose, you're not. You're more like a man being put in the drunk tank to sleep it off until morning, to keep yourself and others safe."

William and Sean marched him out of the building. Joyce knew they would keep him out of trouble for the night. Before morning, she would have to come up with a more permanent solution to the Jose problem.

She looked out over the slowly dispersing crowd. Once Jose was gone, the intense, kill-anything-that-gets-in-my-way rage left as well. Some people were still mad—*hell, I'm mad*—but no one would do anything rash tonight. Joyce sat on a step and closed her eyes. Without George beside her, it was all too much; too much to handle. He was the strong one, the one who made people see what was right. She needed him.

She heard a toddler babbling and opened her eyes. A young woman holding the hand of a small boy was looking at her.

"Thank you, Joyce."

"You're welcome. Uh, I'm sorry ...?"

"We haven't met. I'm Lucia." She paused. "Jose is my neighbor. He looks out for us, and if something happened to him, I don't know what I'd do."

"Maybe you can talk some sense into him. Get him to promise to hold off until after George goes to court. Once George is exonerated, Jose will calm down."

"I'll try."

"Good. You talk to him now and give him something to think about. I'll see him in the morning. Between the two of us, and Sean and William tonight, we may be able to get through to him."

Before Lucia could reply, the excruciating pain of the sniffers hit them, and both women grabbed their heads. The toddler collapsed, screaming.

Slowly Joyce beat back the pain from her own mind and began to spread soothing silence to the remaining telepaths around her.

Lucia bent down and picked up her son. "Shh, it's okay now," she said as she rocked the child back and forth. As the little boy calmed down, frightened telepaths staggered in from the parking lot.

Joyce walked onto the stage and held up her arms. She could not simultaneously shield the group and ask for silence telepathically, so she spoke. "Please, friends. Try to relax. Once they move on we can all go home."

She scanned the faces in the crowd, but the people were still panicking, and she could not calm them all. "All right, everyone. We need to hold hands, in a big circle." She stepped off the stage into the middle of the room. "That's right, form a circle as best you can around the equipment. It doesn't matter whose hand you hold. We're all connected here."

Once all the stragglers had joined the circle, she sent out a large push of mental energy to shield the group from the sniffers. With so many people in the room, she underestimated the toll it would take on her. Her knees buckled, and as she hit the floor.

Chapter 17

Darcy looked over at her alarm clock. 2:30. *Way too early to start the day; way too late to still be awake*. Olivia, banged up and bruised, was coherent every time Darcy woke her, easing Darcy's worries. The Wynton case kept churning around in her mind, and nothing was coming together. She sat up against the headboard.

Who killed Harrison? There were no suspects except her client. Steve Harrison's alibi was holding up so far; Broadbent hadn't found any credible threats in the hate mail. Could the Twenty be involved here? Her research on Wallburton had reached a dead end and she didn't know where else to look. Brutus was still missing, but Darcy hadn't asked about the case on her drive home with Olivia.

Next on her list of worries were the sniffers. She'd called Joyce to warn her, but Joyce had said the entire underground already knew. She had passed out after an attack last night, but reassured Darcy she felt fine today. Darcy was worried. She hadn't felt the sniffers yet, although she was sure it was only a matter of time until they reached her neighborhood, and if they were strong enough to make Joyce faint, what chance did she and Olivia have?

As with every bout of insomnia, her mind circled around to the ill-advised business of Morrison Investigations. How could she have thought it would support them? How could she have taken Olivia out of her comfortable life and pushed her into this small existence, grubbing for any work they could find? *Why did Olivia say yes so readily?*

It wasn't time to wake Olivia up again, but Darcy had to talk to her. "Liv, you awake?"

Olivia rolled over and opened her eyes. "Yes. Pi is 3.14159, my name is Olivia Morrison, you are my twin sister, Darcy, and I am at home, in my bed." She yawned. "Anything else you want to ask?"

"How are you feeling?"

"I'm fine. Not achy yet, but I expect by tomorrow I'll be really sore. Did you call the hospital?"

"Yes. Reggie is fine. He woke up and the nurse says he'll be going home in the morning."

Olivia yawned. "That's good. I was worried about him."

"Hey, Liv, I'm really sorry."

"It wasn't your fault. If I hadn't yelped when that sniffer hit me, Reggie wouldn't have swerved and we wouldn't have hit the pole."

"No, that's not what I mean. I'm sorry for dragging you into all this mess. Without me, you'd probably be engaged to Dan by now, living a happy life, with plenty of money and friends. You'd be planning the wedding of the decade."

Slowly, Olivia sat up. "Again? Really? Every time you can't sleep, your guilty conscience attacks you. How many times do I have to tell you that I would change nothing about my decisions?" She turned the small bedside lamp on and squinted. Once her eyes adjusted to the light, she looked into Darcy's eyes and said, "I wouldn't change anything. And planning the wedding of the decade isn't nearly as much fun as helping people."

Darcy smiled weakly. "You're right. It's an attack of guilt. It's just that I can't shake the feeling that Wynton's going to be locked away for this murder, and there's nothing we can do about it."

Olivia moved over to Darcy's bed. "I know. I have that same feeling, but we can't give up hope. At this point, we're all he has. Dan can do his best in court, but unless we find him something he can use, George will go to prison. We have to get up every day and attack the problem with all our energy, do everything we can, and then, at the end of the day, we need to sleep knowing we did all we could. And so far, that's exactly what we've done. We've done our best."

"I know. But I keep thinking if we knew more about our damn job, we could be better at it."

"That's true. But we have what we have, and that's all we can work with right now." Olivia stood up. "You need some chamomile tea. I'll be right back."

Darcy watched Olivia walk slowly into the kitchen. Olivia was such a nurturer, such a people person. Her sister knew that tea was what she needed, and then she could relax and go to sleep.

Olivia returned in a few moments with two mugs. She handed one to Darcy. "Drink this, and you'll sleep like a baby."

Darcy smiled at her and took the cup. "You must be feeling better. I still think the root of all our problems is—"

"I know. Shaughnessey. He is. No one will argue that point. The problem is we still don't have anyone to replace him."

"I've been thinking about that. We've been meeting more police, and maybe one of them would be willing."

"We need someone about to retire." She paused. "Uncle Joe is retiring soon, after his current cases are cleared up and he finds a good partner for Fraser. He would be able to mentor us, but would he be willing to make Mom angry?"

"I think that's something you should talk to him about. You're the one with all the people skills."

"You have people skills. You just don't use them," said Olivia.

Darcy looked sheepish. "I always feel like such a phony."

"That's because you concentrate on what you need from them, not what *they* need. I was able to get so much out of Reggie because he really needed someone to talk to. He's frustrated in his job but feels leaving the Panzer would be disloyal. I can understand those feelings, and I let that show. He was so relieved that I didn't judge him for his feelings that he wanted to tell me what I needed to know."

"To me, it looks like magic."

"It's not. You just need practice."

"So how would you approach Uncle Joe?"

"I'm not sure. I'm never sure until I start. I think I'd just ask him about his retirement plans. He says he's going off to a cabin in the woods to be alone and fish. Can you see that?"

"Can I see him fishing? Sure."

"I can't, not for more than a week or two. He's an inner-city cop; he's used to the noise, the hustle, people all around him. The quiet of the woods will drive him crazy, and he'll start coming back to the city."

"But if he just visits and goes back again?"

"He won't. Not if we give him an interesting

problem to deal with. Training us will be a full-time job for him, at least for a while."

"And he can talk himself into thinking it's just for a year or so before he can go back to the woods."

"See, now you're getting it."

"I promised Joyce I'd go see George last night, but ..." she trailed off. "I'll see him later this morning and you can talk to Uncle Joe."

"I'm frustrated that we haven't made any progress on the case yet."

"I know. But I can hardly think straight. A few hours of sleep, and we'll be able to come up with a new direction for the investigation."

Olivia moved back to her bed and turned off the light. "Try to get some rest."

"I will. And Liv?"

"Yes?"

"Thanks for being my sister."

"Any time."

Darcy smiled in the dark and fell asleep.

Chapter 18

Darcy rolled out of bed as her alarm went off. She shuffled into the kitchen and made a pot of coffee. After the pep talk and tea from Olivia in the night, she thought she at least ought to have coffee ready for her sister.

"Good morning," she said as Olivia entered the kitchen. She forced a smile. *Olivia will not like the way she looks.* Her lower lip was puffy, her right cheek scraped, and her right eye purplish gray.

"Have you looked in a mirror yet?"

"No," said Olivia. "How bad is it?"

"Makeup will cover most of it, but the swollen lip — I'm not sure about that. How are you feeling?"

"I'm feeling much better. I am definitely thinking more clearly. You're right about Uncle Joe. If we can persuade him, we'll be so much better off."

"Coffee?"

Olivia took the mug. "Thanks. I'm going to need a couple of these to jumpstart my morning. We should probably check in with Dan first thing. Let him know where we are and see if he's got anything for us. Now that we know Frank Adams didn't even exist before five years ago, I'm not sure where else to look for him. Maybe between the three of us, we can find a new lead."

"You want to talk to Dan after yesterday?"

Olivia grimaced. *"Want* is a strong word. I think we need to. We have to be professional."

"I suppose so. Does this mean I have to be nice to him?"

"Civil. You have to be civil, and if you tried not to say anything to piss him off, that would be good."

Darcy pulled out a frying pan. After last night, Olivia deserved her favorite breakfast. "French toast?"

"Sure!" Olivia smiled.

#

After breakfast, they drove to Dan's office in downtown Boston.

Olivia smiled at the lobby receptionist. "Olivia Morrison to see Mr. Stevens."

The woman looked up from her computer. "Do you have an appointment?"

"No." Olivia walked around the desk toward the elevator, but the receptionist was faster and blocked them.

"I'm sorry. No one gets in without an appointment. Mr. Stevens is very busy this morning, preparing for a case. His secretary called down and asked that he not be disturbed."

Olivia admired how she protected Dan, and she obviously didn't know who Olivia was, so she went easy on the receptionist. She pulled out her cell phone and dialed Dan's private number.

"Stevens."

"Hi, Dan, it's me. I'm downstairs. Your very efficient receptionist won't let me in."

"I'll send someone down."

One minute later, his secretary, wearing a sweater too tight for office wear, exited the elevator. "Miss Morrison?"

Olivia turned to her and said, "Yes."

The secretary looked horrified. "What happened to you?"

"Car accident," said Olivia.

"I'm not sure..." she hesitated and looked more closely at Olivia, "I'm sorry, Mr. Stevens is not available right now."

Before Olivia could say anything else, Darcy stepped forward. "He sent you to bring us up, not make judgments."

The secretary sniffed and walked back into the elevator. Darcy and Olivia followed.

Dan was waiting for them at his door. "What took so long?" he asked.

"She," Olivia gestured to the secretary, "tried to convince me you weren't available to see me."

Dan scowled at his secretary. "We'll talk later about this." He turned to Olivia. "Come in."

Darcy and Olivia sat in the comfortable leather chairs across from Dan's paper-strewn desk, while Dan sat on the corner, eyes glued to his secretary as she left the office.

"Busy today?" asked Olivia.

"It's this damned Wynton case. I can't seem to get a handle on it. The lack of gunshot residue can be explained away by the prosecution, and without that, there doesn't seem to be any way he didn't do it. And you two haven't been any help at all. I expected results from you by now."

"Aren't you even going to ask what happened?" asked Darcy.

He looked up from the file he was reading and handed it to Darcy. "I don't have time for all the drama your lives entail."

Olivia was hurt. Even though they had argued,

she thought he still cared for her.

"Fine," he sighed. "What happened?"

"I was in a car accident," she said.

Dan rolled his eyes. "Were you driving Darcy's deathtrap? I've told you a million times that car isn't—"

"No," Olivia interrupted. "I was in a Lexus. And before you ask, I wasn't driving."

"Does this have to do with Wynton's case?"

"Not at all."

"And the bruises will be gone in a week?"

"Of course."

"Fine. We won't go out until they are gone. I've chalked up your attitude yesterday to the stress of having your apartment broken into." He stood up and knelt in front of Olivia. "I am sorry I didn't take it easier on you. Will you forgive me?"

Olivia put her hand on his cheek. Before she could decide what to say, he took her hand and kissed her palm. "Please?" he asked.

"Let's just let it go and get back to work," she said.

Dan smiled at her. He stood and sat behind his desk. Olivia walked behind Dan's chair and began to massage his shoulders. "You're very tense for so early in the morning. You need to relax a bit, darling. Between the three of us, we'll find what we need to win this case."

Dan exhaled as his muscles began to relax. "You're awfully confident for a woman who brings nothing to the table."

"But we do have something. We're working on finding the proof right now."

"You do?"

"Yes. The police eliminated all the possible

suspects from Harrison's file of hate mail. Frank Adams, the new employee who went missing, didn't even exist five years ago. He's our prime suspect right now."

"It would help if you could get us back into Harrison's office. We really need to go through Adams's desk," said Darcy.

"I can't get you in. Her husband is blocking our attempts. Maybe your uncle can get you in."

"We'll find a way," said Darcy.

Dan took Olivia's hands and pulled her down gently so they were cheek to cheek. "Wouldn't you rather work for me? You'd have all the excitement of the office without any of the danger of your job."

Excitement of the office? Olivia snorted at the idea. "You really shouldn't fire this secretary, at least not yet. She was like a pit bull out there, protecting your time and solitude. And I'm sure you haven't gotten around to telling her who she should let in and who she should block."

"She should have noticed the photo on my desk and known."

Olivia smiled. "You expect her to read your mind? How could she know you would always accept a meeting with me, especially when I look like this?"

"She's a secretary. She should just know."

"That's incredibly unfair."

"And that's why I need you. You already know all those things. I wouldn't have to waste my time training you."

"Did you ever stop and think that if you spent a little time training them, your secretaries wouldn't let you down, and you'd have someone you could work well with?"

"No. Secretaries are a dime a dozen. They always seem to be leaving and starting families just as they get familiar with the place. Women aren't all that reliable."

Olivia pushed Dan's arms away from her. She knew he felt that way about some women, secretaries in particular, but to say all women weren't reliable ... "Dan!"

He smiled. "It's true. Take a look at the two of you. It's been more than twenty-four hours, and you've produced nothing I can use. Not a shred of proof, and just the barest whiff of reasonable doubt. All you've done is make sure other people won't be accused of the crime."

"Dan, that *is* progress. We'll keep digging deeper, and we'll get what you need."

He looked out the window, avoiding her gaze. "You have until the end of the day today, or else I'll have to fire you and look for another PI."

"The end of the day? Why? I thought you weren't going to court for weeks."

"I'm not. But if you can't handle the deadline, then I'll know you're not right for the case."

"Dan! I thought you would be able to keep our personal and professional lives separate. I know you're angry, but this made up deadline is ridiculous."

Darcy looked up from the folder containing Wynton's police report. "It's all right, Liv. We'll get a copy of this, and we'll have all that we need."

Darcy brought the folder out to the secretary. "Can I get a copy of this?"

"Yes, of course. And I'm really sorry. I'm new here. Today's my second day. I didn't realize I should have let you in."

Darcy smiled. "Don't worry. Olivia's already talked to him about not firing you. But if you ask me, the sooner you find a different boss, the better off you'll be. You'd have to be a telepath to know what he wants." She peered into the secretary's eyes. "You're not a telepath, are you?"

The poor girl blanched. Gray and Shalek had a strict no-telepath clause in their employment contracts. "No, of course not."

I shouldn't play with her like this. "Take it easy, I was just joking. But not about working for Dan. Really, find someone else. He's a jerk."

Again, the woman had no idea how to react. She looked down at the file in her hands. "I'll just go make a copy of this for you. I'll be back in a minute."

Darcy hesitated outside Dan's door. She didn't really want to go back in, but she felt like an idiot just standing there. She opened the door to an icy silence.

"She'll be back with the file in a minute."

"Good. The sooner we get out of here, the better."

Darcy looked at Olivia. Tears pooled in her eyes, but Darcy could see Olivia wouldn't shed them. The victory evident in Dan's face was ugly. He had brought her sister to tears, so he felt like he had the argument.

"We'll get back to you as soon as we have something," Darcy said to Dan in a clipped voice. She looked at Olivia. "I'm sure she's done copying, so let's go."

Olivia held her head high and marched out of the office without a word to Dan.

"What the hell happened in there?" asked Darcy.

"Not now. I'll tell you later."

Darcy put her arm around Olivia's shoulder as they waited for the secretary to make her way back to her desk.

"Here you are. And again, I'm sorry about the mix-up." The secretary looked at Olivia and handed her a tissue.

"Thank you," said Darcy. "Remember what I said."

Dan's secretary nodded, but without conviction.

Olivia stuffed the tissue in her coat pocket and was silent through the elevator ride. Not until they were back in her car did she pull out the tissue and release her tears.

"Why was he such a jerk to me?"

Darcy frowned. *Dan is always a jerk, but he's not usually this bad to Olivia.* "I don't know. Maybe he had a bad night, too."

"Could be. Or it could be the new secretary isn't working out, or just the pressure of the case." She blew her nose. "He'll be better once we get him what he needs."

Darcy was trying to not say only negative things about Dan, but she couldn't help herself. "Liv, you know I don't want to start an argument. But do you really think he'll be better? Or will he just be happy for a short time before he turns into a jerk again?"

"I don't even care right now. He said it was foolish for him to hire us, because it was obvious we couldn't handle the job. Obvious! As though he has any idea what we are capable of." Olivia turned to Darcy, fire in her eyes. "Now we have to find the real killer. We can't let him think we're incompetent. He'll tell all his friends, laughing at his little girlfriend and her 'job.' "

"Yes, he probably will. And it will ruin our chances for more high-profile cases. You're right. We'll have to find the actual killer. Not that Dan will acknowledge how great we are, but at least with a successful high-profile case under our belts, we'll be able to claim that right."

Olivia smiled. "We'll solve the case to stick it to Dan. Poor George. I bet he never thought he'd be a pawn."

"Office or jail first?"

"What did you find in the file?"

"Not much, actually. But I'd be damned if I'd let Dan know that. I'll have to go through it again to make sure I didn't miss anything. You two arguing was very distracting. We'll go see George. I've got to talk to him and then call Joyce with a message, and you can get to work on Uncle Joe."

#

By the time they were done with Wynton, it was lunchtime, and they knew their uncle wouldn't be at his desk. "Flannagan's?" asked Olivia.

"Most likely," said Darcy.

They were right. They found Uncle Joe holding court at the bar with a half-dozen younger cops, including Fraser, who smiled in their direction.

As they walked in, the men turned and watched them walk to their uncle. Olivia smiled and gave her uncle a kiss on the cheek. An officer from the precinct whom Darcy didn't recognize whistled.

"Give it a rest, Barnes. She's too young for you," said Joe.

Barnes looked sheepishly into his drink. "Sorry, didn't mean any disrespect."

Joe looked back at his nieces. "Jesus, Olivia! What the hell happened to you?"

"Car accident, but I'm fine now."

"What brings you two here?"

"We need to talk to you, and it's serious."

"Oh, serious, is it?" He led them to a table out of range of the bar. "What's wrong?"

Olivia took over, much to Darcy's relief. "It's Shaughnessey," she said.

Joe wrinkled his lip, like he'd just eaten something rotten. "Him again? I keep telling you I can probably find something to have him arrested for."

Olivia shook her head. "No. That would be very bad for us. We need to keep him around." She put her hand on his arm. "Until we can find someone to replace him."

He looked from Olivia to Darcy, warily.

"And that's where you come in."

"Oh, no. There's no way I'm helping out the two of you. Your mother would never speak to me again."

Olivia smiled at him. "Of course she would."

"She called me over a year ago to tell me exactly that. She said she would never forgive me if I helped the two of you in any way."

"Are you kidding me?" Darcy exploded. "How could she?"

Joe took a long drink and set his glass down before he continued. "It's hard for both your parents; they're worried. They want to see you fail, so you will return to your previous lives, Olivia to being a docent at the museum, and Darcy … well, they don't want you to go back to being a clerk in a store. They'd like to see you do more with your degree, maybe look for a programming job. In her own way, your mom thinks she's protecting you."

Darcy shook her head. "No way. Computer programming would make my brain shut down. It's so dull."

Olivia tried one more time. "What if we talked to them and got their blessing to bring you in after you retire?"

He frowned. "I don't think that would work. You could probably talk your father into it, but your mother is an entirely different story, and I don't want to do anything to draw her wrath."

Olivia knew what he meant. Her mother was one to hold a grudge, as the three sitting around the table knew too well.

"Have you had lunch? You want something here?" asked Joe.

"No, thanks. We've got more work to do."

The three of them stood, and Fraser approached Darcy. "Miss Morrison?"

She smiled at him. "After all you've done for us, really, you should call me Darcy."

"Yes, I … ah, I keep forgetting that. I'd like to talk to you later on. Can we meet?"

"Sure. How about Bess's Diner at eight?"

He smiled. "Sure. I'll see you then."

Once they were out of the bar, Olivia asked, "Did you just make a date with Fraser?"

Darcy scoffed. "Don't be ridiculous. He said he wanted to talk to me, that's all."

"But that's not how he looks at you," Olivia said.

"You keep saying that, and I still don't believe

you."

Olivia sighed. "Of course he does. He likes you. I think he likes you a lot. He wouldn't have done all that work in our apartment if he didn't."

"No, that can't be," said Darcy. "People do that sort of stuff for you all the time. He must like you."

Olivia shook her head. "He hardly even gives me the time of day when you're in the room. He didn't say a single word to me in there. He only wanted to talk to you."

"Really? I didn't notice."

They arrived at Darcy's car, and Olivia opened the passenger door with a laugh. "Yes, really."

Darcy settled into the driver's seat. "No way. I don't believe you." But she wondered, *Did I just make a date with Fraser?*

She drove to Wynton's house and, armed with a photo of their client, they began to question cabbies.

Olivia tapped on the glass of one cab. "Excuse me, sir? Have you driven this man lately?" She held up the photo.

"Hell, no. I don't take telepaths. You never know what they're going to do to you when you're not looking at them."

Darcy tried her luck with the next cab. "Mr. Wynton? Sure, I've taken him places. Not for the last few days, though."

Her heart soared. "Did you take him to Wilding Street a few days ago?"

He shook his head. "Wilding Street. I don't think so. Let me call my dispatcher. Maybe someone else did."

He picked up his handset and started talking. "Hey, Ed. Got a lady here wants to know if we brought someone to Wilding Street."

"What the hell? I can't look that up."

"It was 254 Wilding, and it was six nights ago, around seven."

"You get that, Ed? Just look it up for the lady."

"Thank you," said Darcy.

"Why do you need to know?" he asked.

"We're working for him, and we're looking for anyone who can give him an alibi."

The cabbie nodded thoughtfully. "He doesn't seem like a killer."

The radio crackled back to life. "Hey, Fred. None of our drivers went there that night."

"Damn," said Darcy.

"Thank you for checking," said Olivia.

"Good luck finding your cab."

They walked back to the sidewalk. "I had no idea they could check so easily. We could go to each dispatcher and ask them to look it up for us."

By the end of the evening, they had visited each of the seven cab companies in the Boston area with no luck, but one good piece of advice. *Don't forget the unlicensed cabs.*

Instead of going straight back to Wynton's neighborhood, they decided to hit the Indian restaurant Adams had ordered from the night before he moved.

Darcy looked through the steamy glass window of the Bombay Delight restaurant. "Not busy," she said.

Olivia opened the door and the sisters were surrounded by the warm fragrant air. The scents of cardamom, curry and tandoori made their mouths water as they seated themselves at the table in the picture window.

A young woman in the de-facto waitress uniform of black pants and a white shirt handed them menus. "Welcome to Bombay Delight. Can I get you something to drink?"

"I'd like a masala chai," said Darcy.

"One for me, too. And is it possible for us to talk to your delivery person?"

"I believe he is out right now, but when he returns I will ask him to speak to you."

"Thank you."

An older man returned with their drinks. "Good evening. I am Mr. Gupta, the owner of the restaurant. You have asked to speak to our driver? Is there a problem?"

"No," said Olivia. "We wanted to ask him about a delivery he made almost a week ago. The man he delivered to has disappeared."

"And you think he had something to do with this?"

"Oh no, I'm sure he didn't. We wanted to ask him if he remembered anything out of the ordinary that night, that's all."

"And you are with the police?"

"We are investigating the death of Kathleen Harrison. Perhaps you've heard about it on the news?" Darcy didn't enjoy misleading the man, but they really had to talk to the delivery guy.

The front door opened and Mr. Gupta waved the young man to their table. "This is Peter. Peter, these women want to talk to you."

A flash of guilt crossed Peter's eyes before he looked back at Mr. Gupta. "It's all right, they want to ask about a customer."

"You aren't in any trouble. We just want to ask about a delivery you made to Frank Adams six nights ago. He lives in Porter Square."

"I don't remember him," said Peter.

"He might have been packing to move, and he may have had more people in the apartment with him."

"Oh, that guy! Yeah, I remember him. He left me hanging, waiting for money. One of his buddies finally had to pay me."

"Cash or charge?"

"Cash. And a really lousy tip, too."

"Did you hear or see anything strange while you were there?" asked Olivia.

"Not really. There were three guys there, drinking beer and packing up the apartment. But one of them said something like 'it's a lot of work to move you two floors up'."

"In the same building?"

"I don't know. At that point, I got paid and left."

"Do you remember ever delivering to him in the past?"

"No. But I've only had the job for a few months."

Darcy pulled out a business card and handed it to him. "If you deliver to him again, would you give us a call?"

Peter looked skeptical.

"We're looking for a murderer," said Darcy.

"And if you find him, there's fifty bucks in it for you," said Olivia.

The thought of money made Peter smile. "I'll keep my eye out."

"Thank you," said Olivia.

A few minutes after Peter left, Mr. Gupta returned with appetizers. "Compliments of the house," he said. "I've known a few telepaths over the years and they're not so bad. I'm glad not everyone thinks George Wynton did it."

Darcy began to eat her samosa while Olivia was working on her phone. "What are you doing?" asked Darcy.

"Looking for a way to find our cabbie."

"How are we going to do that?"

"I've got this app that will call us an off-the-books cab. We go back to George's apartment, and keep calling until we find our guy."

"Seriously?"

"Amazing what a little research will get us."

"Eat something and we'll get out of here," said Darcy.

Olivia took a pakora and popped it in her mouth. "There, I've eaten. Let's go."

The owner and waitress were not in the dining room, so Darcy left twenty dollars on the table. "That should be enough, right?"

"Plenty. We'll have to come back here another time."

Darcy stomped her feet in the cold. "Are you sure this will work?"

"Not exactly, but it can't hurt." She pressed the hail button and put her hands back in her coat pockets.

Two minutes later, a car pulled up to them. "You looking for a ride?" asked the driver.

"We're looking for the cab that took someone from here to Wilding Street six nights ago," said Olivia.

"Are you kidding? Why are you wasting my time like this?"

"Five bucks to answer our questions," said Darcy.

"We're looking for the cab that took this man," she held up Wynton's photo. "You'd remember him because he gave you a fifty for a tip."

"Wish that was my fare – I never get the big tippers."

"Any idea who the driver might be?" asked Darcy.

"Nah." He looked at his phone. "Gotta go, real customer down the street. You got that five?"

Olivia reached through the open window and handed him the money and her card. "Keep your ear out for us?"

"Yeah, sure," he grunted as he drove off.

Olivia pulled her phone out and hit the button again. Another car pulled up within forty five seconds.

"You need a ride?"

Again, Olivia held up the photo. "We're looking for the cabbie that brought this man to Wilding Street."

"Let me see that," the driver said. He took the photo and turned his interior light on. "Yeah, I remember this guy. Gave me a big tip."

Olivia's heart began to race. *This is it. We've got his alibi.* "When did you drop him off?"

"Some time around seven, I think."

"Can you look it up? It's a matter of life and death."

"Nah. I don't keep any records, this is just to pick up a little extra cash."

"Can you at least tell us if you dropped him before or after seven?"

"Like I said, I don't know. It was close enough to seven that he gave me the fifty, but I don't remember."

Olivia's heart sank. "Can we get your name and phone number?"

"What for?"

"This man, the big tipper, is in jail for murdering the woman he went to see that night. We're working to find him an alibi."

"Like I said…"

"I know, but if we have any follow up questions it would be a lot easier to call you."

"For such a big tip, you could take a phone call for the guy," said Darcy.

"Fine." He scrawled his name and number on a paper napkin and handed it out the window.

"Thank you," said Olivia.

The driver pulled out from the curb and drove off.

"Well, that was a waste of time," said Darcy.

"Not necessarily. We'll get this to Dan – he's great at helping people remember things. Speaking of which, you've got to meet Fraser soon. Drop me off at home first?"

Chapter 19

Darcy waited in the back booth of the diner. She fidgeted, wondering if Fraser was really going to come. Although she knew his shift ended at seven, that didn't mean anything. If he got a call, he'd work until he was done.

After a terrible day spent chasing down the slimmest possible leads, they had absolutely no leads left. Everyone they checked had iron-clad alibis, except for their client.

There was still the problem of The Twenty. Darcy had spent most of the previous evening, while Olivia was sleeping, researching and came up with nothing. She filled Olivia in every hour when she woke her, and Olivia had agreed they were at a dead end. No names, no locations, no photos. Nothing to investigate.

In short, they had nothing. Dan's end-of-the-day ultimatum was almost over, and it looked like they were going to lose it all. Dan would make sure that no one he knew would ever hire them. He'd take every opportunity to remind Olivia of their failure. Olivia would leave the business and marry Dan. Darcy's nightmare was coming true before her eyes. The only bright spot in her day was when Fraser had said he needed to talk to her, outside of work.

"Can I get you anything, doll?"

"No thanks, Bess. I'm still waiting."

"Who's the damn fool who would stand you

up?"

Darcy smiled. "It's not like that. It's a business thing."

"I'll get you some more coffee." She squinted at Darcy. "Maybe a piece of pie? You haven't been eating enough lately."

After Darcy had demolished the pie and was on her third cup of coffee, Fraser rushed toward her booth. "I'm so sorry I'm late. I had a call, and I couldn't call you, so ..." He stopped for a deep breath. "Thanks for waiting."

Darcy smiled at him. "I already ate, but do you want something? The cherry pie is very good here."

He looked at his watch. "Nine o'clock. I'm going to need some dinner. I don't think I've eaten since noon."

"No breaks?"

"It's been a crazy shift. All minor stuff, but it's kept me going without stopping."

Darcy waved Bess over.

Bess stood before them with a smile. "You didn't tell me he was so handsome, doll. I'd have waited for him, too." Turning to Fraser, she said, "What can I get for you, darlin'?"

Fraser blushed. "Steak, potatoes, gravy."

"Coming right up. And coffee? You're likely to have a long night." Bess winked at Darcy and walked away.

"So, what did you want to talk about?" Darcy asked.

"I wanted to see how you were doing on the Wynton case. You know, just checking in."

"Did Uncle Joe put you up to this?"

Fraser laughed. "No. He's not exactly a genius at community relations."

"We've got nothing. Well, that's not true. We've got a client found at the scene of the crime, talking to the dead victim." Darcy paused to drink more coffee. "We ran down every lead we had. Nothing concrete. Adams is missing, so we can't even tell if he's a viable suspect."

"His apartment was cleaned out, he didn't leave anything at his desk in Harrison's office. We think we've got his prints, but there were a lot of prints in his apartment and it's going to take some time to go through them all."

Darcy rested her chin on her hand. "I hate this. From everything I've seen, our client is not a murderer, but if we fail, he's going to prison anyway."

"One of the hardest things I've had to learn in this job is that good people can do bad things. Sometimes the person you want to be innocent is guilty, and there's nothing you can do to change that — nothing legal, anyway."

Darcy looked at him. He sounded sad, like he'd had to put away someone he cared for. "What happened?" she asked gently.

"My uncle. As a kid, I never realized what he was up to, and of course my mother wouldn't ever say anything bad about her brother. After my dad left he gave us money every week so she could make ends meet. Every Sunday afternoon he was over for dinner and coffee. They would talk and laugh, and he would always give her an envelope. She would refuse it, but in the end, she'd take it because she needed it. My uncle kept us from going hungry, or being homeless, or any of a million bad things that could have happened.

"It wasn't until I was much older that I realized

he also kept anyone from bothering us. Men didn't hassle my mother, like they did all the other moms on the street. When we needed anything fixed, someone was always there to take care of it but never charged her more than a few dollars. It was all because of my uncle. He's the reason I became a cop. I wanted to take care of people, like he took care of us." He sat back and closed his eyes.

"But ..." Darcy prompted.

"During my first year on the force, we came upon a robbery in progress. Two guys were knocking over a store—small stuff. We knew they'd be out on bail by the morning. But it was my uncle who bailed them out. I asked him why, and all he said was 'I'm doing what I've always done, taking care of my people.' " Fraser looked away. "Turns out his people were the very people I swore to put away. I haven't spoken to him since."

"Oh, Fraser." Darcy didn't know what else to say. She reached out and gave his hand a squeeze. He looked up at her and tried to smile.

Bess stopped at their table. "Not to interrupt this touching moment, dolls, but here's your steak."

Darcy took her hand away quickly, embarrassed by the emotion she had shown.

"That looks good," she said.

"I'm starving," he answered, sounding as normal as if they had been discussing the weather.

"So, ah, where's your uncle now?"

"A few years after that, I had to arrest him. Broadbent said he'd do it for me, but I couldn't let him. I'd be safe from the Panzer if I arrested him, but Broadbent wouldn't."

"Your uncle works for the Panzer?"

"Always has, and I feel like such a fool for not

ever seeing it." He cut his steak with more force than Darcy thought necessary. "So anyway, the whole point of this story is sometimes the guilty are not the ones we want to arrest."

"But I really don't think Wynton did it. It's too convenient. It's not like him, either."

"You're right about that. We had him under surveillance for a year, ever since he started his PR campaign. He's never done anything we could arrest him for. In fact, he seems like a real stand-up guy. Of course we knew about the affair with the victim, but if we arrested every person who had an affair, there'd be hardly anyone left out on the streets."

"Did you have him under surveillance that night?"

"No. We finally had to pull the teams because they weren't justified. He wasn't doing anything wrong."

"Any idea who would have done it? Anything not in the records? I'm desperate here. I'll take anything you've got."

"I'm still not sure what I can tell you." He sat back, chewing thoughtfully for a moment. "He looks guilty. He was the only one there. He was practically incoherent when I found him, and there's no evidence anyone else had been there."

"You sure the husband was in Houston?"

"Absolutely. Now that guy, he's a piece of work. He checked in with the head of airport security when he got his flight home, to confirm his identity. He's got written notes for alibis and photos confirming where he was and when. Basically, as soon as he got the call, he started accumulating witnesses."

"Sounds like he's guilty of something," Darcy

said.

"Yeah, but not this."

"Do you think he hired someone to do it?"

"There's nothing in his bank records, and we searched them all. Plus, he had just met with a lawyer to draw up divorce papers."

"So?"

"Men who go to the trouble of divorce don't generally kill their wives first."

"But what if he thought divorce would leave him with less money than he wanted? A funeral has to be cheaper than alimony."

Fraser shook his head. "It didn't read like that. I think he's a guy used to covering his ass."

"But for what?"

"Don't know. It's not part of this investigation. There is one odd thing, though."

"What?"

"Camille Johnson disappeared two days after Harrison's murder."

Darcy leaned forward. "The receptionist at Harrison's PR firm? Did you find her?"

Fraser smiled. "No. That's what vanished means," he teased.

Darcy blushed. "I thought you might have found her later," she said. "We met her. She was really broken up over Harrison's death. Nice woman, though."

"Came into work the day after the murder, everything seemed normal, and then ... gone."

"Interesting."

"Well, it would be, if we didn't know where she was at the time of the murder. She was having dinner at Legal Sea Foods. The mayor was there, so we've got photos of her in the background. No one has come forward to list Camille as a missing person, so she's on the back burner for now."

How horrible. No one seems to care where she is. "No one has missed her?"

Fraser shook his head. "We can't find any family, and her apartment is completely cleaned out."

Just like Frank Adams. "And there's nothing you can do?"

He shook his head again. "But maybe you can? If you had time, as sort of a favor to the department, you could look into her?" He slid a thin folder to her. "It's all I've got on her, plus a couple of photos. Everyone's working on the Wynton case, and no one has time for one unreported lost woman."

Darcy paged through the file. There wasn't much to go on, but she could do some checking. "I'll see what I can find."

Fraser's face lit up with a smile. "I knew it. I knew under your gruff exterior you really care about people and will do whatever it takes to protect them."

"What? Quit grinning at me like that."

He tried to stop smiling but couldn't. "You know I can't pay you for it, right?"

Darcy sighed. "I figured as much, but some good PR with the police can't hurt."

#

What is that noise? Olivia thought. She struggled to open her eyes and wake up. *Phone. Where is my phone?* She reached for the bedside table in the dark and punched the speaker button. "What?"

"Hey there, baby." *Oh God, it's Shaughnessey. I really don't want to deal with him.* She looked at the clock. *Damn. Three thirty.*

"Go home and sober up. I'll see you in the morning."

"Can't do that, luv. Need you to come down to bail me out."

"Are you kidding? I'll come down after breakfast."

"It's got to be now, darlin'. I can't spend the night in a cell. Do you know the kind of people who are left in here? Only the worst of the worst don't get bailed out, and I can't stay with that sort."

She sat up and rubbed her eyes, forcing herself to wake up. "Who knew you had standards? What's your bail?"

"Five thousand."

Shit, she thought. *The business doesn't have it.*

"How am I going to get that? You've already cleaned out the business account."

"I'm sure you'll think of a way."

In the next bed, Darcy sat up. "Who's that?"

"Shaughnessey needs to be bailed out. Five grand."

"Are you kidding?"

"You need to sober up and get the money yourself in the morning," said Olivia.

"I will not spend the night in here. You will come get me, or I'll close your business so fast you won't know what happened," he threatened.

"All right, all right. Calm down. Let me get dressed. I'll be there as soon as I can."

"Don't spend too much time getting dressed. Maybe we can … you know."

Olivia shuddered. "Just shut up." She hung up.

"I can't believe you're going down there!" Darcy exclaimed.

"It's the same threat as always. He'll close the

business, he'll ruin us, and he'll make sure we never work again."

"One of these days we'll have to call his bluff."

"But not today."

Darcy looked uneasy. "Where are we going to get the money?"

"I'll have to put it on the emergency credit card."

"What if he skips?"

"I don't know. I can't imagine he'll go too far. He'll want his share of the money coming into the business."

"All right, give me a few to get dressed."

"No, you go back to sleep. One of us should be well-rested tomorrow."

"No chance. I'm not letting you out this late to be alone with him."

"Really, I'll be fine."

"No."

"If you insist," Olivia said, relieved. *If there's another sniffer attack, I'll feel better if neither of us is alone.*

#

The precinct was quiet for four in the morning. The sisters walked up to the desk and had to ring a bell insistently before someone finally came out to help them.

"We're here to bail out Miles Shaughnessey," said Olivia.

The officer looked them up and down. "You family?"

"No, coworkers."

He leered at them. "Right. Fill out these forms. How will you be paying?"

Olivia took out her only-for-emergencies credit card, which her father usually paid without questioning her. A charge like this, though, he would question. She was sure of it.

Fifteen minutes later, Shaughnessey was led out and consigned into their care.

"I knew I could count on you, baby." He leaned in to kiss Olivia.

She recoiled backward. "Don't touch me, you pig," she whispered angrily. "You're still stinking drunk."

He sniffed the air. "Not stinking, but definitely still drunk. Had to drink until Joey passed out. Once he started talking about breaking fingers, I knew I had to get out of there. Gotta avoid him until I can win that money back." He turned to the officer. "What do you think about these two? Nice work situation I've got. See these two every day, and now at night, too. Think I'll have to spend some time at their place, so they can keep an eye on me. I've been a very naughty boy."

The officer scowled. "Do you need help getting him out to your car? Or maybe I could ..." He gestured back toward the cells.

"That won't be necessary, thank you. I think we can take it from here."

He pulled out a card and wrote a number on the back. "If you insist, but if he gives you any trouble, call me, and I'll haul him back here for you."

Olivia smiled. "Thank you, officer ..." She looked at the card. "Tremblay. I appreciate it."

Darcy grabbed Shaughnessey before he fell over, twisted his arm behind him, and marched him out of the precinct. "Let's go, you drunken SOB."

"I love it when they get rough with me."

Shaughnessey winked at the officer and then walked out cooperatively.

Darcy dumped him in the back of the car. "Where do you live?"

"Don't want to go home. Too lonely there. Take me back to your place."

"No chance. What's your address?"

"He lives in Revere. I've got the address here, on the forms," Olivia said. She punched his address into her GPS and started driving.

"Hey, I know this great after-hours place. You like naked women, right?"

"Shut up."

"I'm just feeling a little dry, that's all."

Darcy rounded on him. "You stupid bastard. You're lucky we don't dump you on the street and walk away. You deserve nothing—nothing that we give you, yet you still take and take." She would have continued on to demand the money he owed them from the Panzerelli case, but he had already passed out.

#

Miles Shaughnessey sat back in the limo and smiled. It was a good thing the girls had insisted on bringing him back to his apartment last night, or he would have missed the most important call of his life.

He hadn't thought his little scam with the girls would lead to anything more than a few extra bucks, but the call from Senator Hill changed his mind. Sure, the girls came from money and knew the right people, but they certainly wouldn't have set this up for him. They hated him. So why had the senator insisted on a face-to-face meeting? He wasn't in any trouble; that much was certain. Those kinds of meetings don't happen at country clubs over lunch. No, Shaughnessey was poised to make a big leap, but to what, he didn't know.

The limo driver opened his door. Shaughnessey got out and tried to tip him, but the driver would not hold out his hand. Instead he looked vaguely embarrassed and said, "There's no need for that, sir."

Shaughnessey felt like an idiot. How the hell was he supposed to know he shouldn't tip the driver? He stood there, wanting to say something to save face, but he could think of nothing.

"Sir? Senator Hill is waiting," the driver prompted.

Shaughnessey nodded and entered the club. He ignored the doorman and stood in the center of the lobby, looking for the bar. Men and women walked past him, holding quiet but urgent conversations. *Where the hell is the bar?*

"May I help you, sir?"

Shaughnessey looked at the woman standing before him. Her name tag read MARIA. He didn't bother to look up at her face; he was enjoying the view down her sweater. "Yeah, babe. I have a meeting at the bar."

"Of course, sir. To the left and up the stairs."

Reluctantly, he looked up. "Thanks, babe."

He bounded up the stairs two at a time and almost knocked an elderly woman down. "Watch out," he said as her companion steadied her.

In the bar, he saw Hill sitting alone at a table. He recognized him from his photo in the *Globe* last week. "Senator Hill, it's a pleasure to meet you."

Hill stood. "Mr. Shaughnessey, good of you to

come on such short notice." He gestured to the chair across from him. "Have a seat."

Shaughnessey sat, and a waiter brought him a menu. "My name is Jack, and I'll be your waiter this afternoon. Would you care for a drink?"

Shaughnessey took a good look at Jack. Jack's crisp white shirt and navy pants were expensive, better than Shaughnessey's best suit. "Get me a beer, Jack. On tap." *Little shit is probably working here just to be able to tell Mumsy and Daddy he has a real job.*

Jack waited for specifics, but Shaughnessey ignored him and focused on Hill.

"So, Senator, what can I do for you?"

Hill leaned back and took a good look at his lunch companion. Shaughnessey was not what Hill had in mind when he'd conceived this plan. Realizing Jack was still waiting, Hill said, "Bud will be fine for Mr. Shaughnessey." Hill picked up his own glass of scotch. *Budweiser is probably what the man likes.* He took a thoughtful sip. *Should I go through with it? Is this really a man I can trust to be on the payroll?*

"I have a business proposition for you."

Shaughnessey smiled. "Go on."

"I find myself in need of an investigator, in an on-call capacity. One with experience and the will to do whatever it takes to get a job done."

Shaughnessey nodded.

"I have heard you are that kind of man."

"I have an excellent track record."

"Yes. But there are some problems with your current position."

"Problems?"

"Yes. Your protégés are working for a known telepath."

"Panzerelli is a telepath?"

"No. George Wynton."

"They aren't working for Wynton. Right now they're looking for Panzerelli's lost dog."

Hill shook his head. "Perhaps I should reconsider my offer. If I know more about what is going on in your office than you do, I doubt your abilities as an investigator."

Shaughnessey sat back and took a sip of his beer. "They don't have it in them to take a case without me."

"I have it on good authority they have," Hill said.

"I'll have to look into that."

"They'll have to drop the case. It would be a clear conflict of interest."

"What do you mean?"

Hill grimaced. Surely this man knew something about him. "I can't have an employee working against my interests, not even indirectly."

"Oh, I see. The telepath thing."

"Yes. In fact, it might be best if you left them completely."

Shaughnessey's eyes glinted. "Leave my girls? I'm not sure I could. They need me; they're not really very good at what they do yet."

"I'm afraid it's not negotiable. Your salary with me, however, is." Hill let that sink in before he continued. "How much money do you make with Morrison Investigations?"

Without hesitation, Shaughnessey answered, "Ten thousand a month."

Hill knew it for the lie it was. "I can double that, with a significantly lower workload."

Shaughnessey took another sip of his beer.

"How much lower?"

"I don't expect to call on you more than two or three times a year."

"Triple it and we've got a deal."

Hill stretched out his hand. "Welcome to the firm. You'll be working strictly out of the legal office, not the political one. Stop by the office tomorrow and get all the paperwork squared away with my secretary. Bring proof you've left Morrison Investigations."

Shaughnessey stood up. "Yes, sir." He managed to turn away before the huge grin appeared on his face.

Chapter 20

A loud knock on the office door startled Darcy. "Come in," she said.

A bike messenger opened the door and said, "Letter for Morrison Investigations." He held out a PDA and said, "Sign here."

Darcy signed with the pen he gave her and accepted the letter.

"Have a good day," he said sarcastically when he realized they weren't going to tip him.

Darcy opened the letter and scanned it. She thrust it to Olivia. "I can't believe it."

"What? More bills?" Olivia looked up and saw the shock on Darcy's face. She took the paper and read it, sinking heavily into her chair. "Oh, my God."

Darcy put her head in her hands. "That's it. We're done."

"Not necessarily."

"Of course we are. No Shaughnessey, no business."

"I know that's what is supposed to happen, but until he gets around to filing the papers, we can still work. He'll 'officially' still be with us."

"And how long will he let that happen? How long do you think his new employer will let him be associated with women trying to prove a telepath is innocent?"

Olivia sighed. "That bigot Hill? Not long."

The two sat, not looking at each other, for

several long minutes. Darcy looked up, tears pooling in her eyes. "The thing is, I really love this job. Even the stupid lost dog cases. I like feeling like I'm helping people. And now he's taking it all away from us."

"Rat bastard."

Darcy laughed. Hearing Olivia swear, such as it was, always made her laugh because her sister was so proper about it.

"Maybe there's something we can do, legally. I'll call Dan and see what he says," Olivia offered.

"Don't call. Go see him in person. I'll stay here so he won't be annoyed."

"For the millionth time, if you tried a little harder the two of you would get along."

"Just go see him. I'll stay here and, I don't know, do some filing, write up the notes I've neglected all week."

#

Olivia drove to Dan's office, rehearsing the conversation she wanted to have, imagining his comments and preparing a response for each one. She imagined a positive response that would put their future in a good light.

"Olivia Morrison for Mr. Stevens," she told the receptionist.

She barely had time to sit before Dan's secretary exited the elevator. The secretary smiled as she walked to Olivia. "Miss Morrison. May I thank you for speaking to Mr. Stevens on my behalf? I was certain he was going to fire me, but I'm still here."

"I'm glad." Olivia leaned in conspiratorially. "Sometimes I think he's a bit harsh on his employees."

The secretary nodded but said nothing more during the ride to the seventeenth floor. She knocked and entered Dan's office. "Miss Morrison to see you."

Olivia walked in and sat down. "I have some wonderful news."

"You know who killed Kathleen Harrison. Terrific! I didn't think you could—"

"No. We don't know that yet." *He doesn't think we can? Oh really?* "The news I have is that Shaughnessey has finally moved on to a different job."

Dan stared at her. "How is this good news?"

"We don't have a leech taking half our money anymore. We can pay our bills, buy some advertising, really start to make something of ourselves."

"That's great, except you're no longer allowed to work as PIs."

"Technically, until he files with the board and we get a certified letter telling us to stop working, we can continue."

"And how long will that be?"

"Enough time for you to find a loophole that lets us keep working."

Dan stood, anger flashing across his face. "I have enough to do without having to fix your problems as well. Do you know how important this case is to me, to my career? I don't have time to do free legal work for you, particularly not now that I have to find myself new investigators."

Olivia's tone matched his anger. "This case is no more important to your career than mine. Remember, if you lose this case, you'll get another, and another. Your paycheck keeps coming in. If I lose this case, I look incompetent and no one hires me. I

get no money — nothing. And neither does Darcy. If
we lose our license, it will kill her. She loves this job,
and so do I. The only difference is that the job is all
she has. At least I still have you."

Dan said nothing.

"I do still have you, don't I?"

"Yes," he snapped.

"Then find a paralegal to figure out how I can
keep my job."

"I suppose I could do that, although I'm not
sure it's in my best interest. If I get this worked out,
you won't ever leave her."

"She's my sister. You make it sound like we're
having some sordid affair."

Dan walked around to the front of his desk and
sat in front of her. "Darling, you know that someday
you will have to leave her." He took a deep breath.
"For me, and for our future."

*For our future? I don't think I can live in the future
he has planned for us anymore.* "Our future?"

"Yes, our future together — our family."

She furrowed her brow, confused. "Are you
asking me to marry you?"

"No ... ah, not exactly," he flustered. "I'm
saying there's that possibility, and to make it happen
you're going to have to conform to fit in a little
better."

"A what?" she almost yelled.

"I can't have my wife parading around town,
putting herself in danger or making a fool of herself.
What will people say?"

Olivia was shocked, but she did her best to
remain calm. "What do they say now?"

"You're young, this is just a phase, you'll settle
down in a while and get serious about me and having

a family. I tell them finding lost dogs is not so bad. I haven't dared tell anyone you're on the Wynton case."

"I embarrass you?"

"Not embarrassed about you. But sometimes your job ..." he hesitated. "And your sister."

"You're embarrassed about my sister? She's my twin, the other half of my heart and soul. To be embarrassed about her is to be embarrassed about me."

"Olivia, please. Sit. And for God's sake, lower your voice. The secretary can hear you." Olivia hadn't realized she'd jumped up in anger.

"You're blowing this all out of context. I love you. You know that. I want—that is, I think I want—to spend my life with you. But for a wife of a lawyer in this firm, well, there are certain proprieties that have to be adhered to. You've met Mary Stirling. Wives of the partners never work. With the connections I've been making, I'll be partner sooner than we expected. You'd have to give up your job at that point anyway. Why bother to build a career you'd have to abandon?"

She looked at him. He looked like the man she had fallen in love with, but his attitude seemed so different. "Why haven't you brought this up before?"

"I thought I had. I tried to be kind and guide you in the right direction. Before you started this crazy business with Darcy, you were the perfect woman for me."

Her voice was icy with rage. "And now?"

"Darling, you are still the perfect woman for me. It's just that you've gotten off the path we were travelling together. Come back to the path we were on, and I swear to you our life together will be perfect." He put his arms around her, tentatively. When she didn't push him away, he held her close.

He held her until her shoulders began to shake. "What is it?"

"I don't think I'm the woman for you," she whispered.

He looked down at her; she had been crying into his shirt. "Of course you are. We just need to make some adjustments."

"We?"

"You have to remember that people are watching you all the time. It's a harsh, judgmental world out there, and embarrassing yourself will only harm us both."

With a sinking feeling, Olivia understood deep in her heart that he was not a man she could spend her life with. To him, she was just a possession, a wife to be trotted out, admired, and then put aside when the men were talking.

"I've got to go."

"Will I see you tonight?"

"No. I've got a lot to think about." She didn't have the time or energy to deal with a prolonged breakup right now and she knew Dan wouldn't make it easy on her when she did.

Olivia flew out of his office before he could see her cry anymore. "Have a good afternoon, Miss Morrison," called the secretary. Olivia ignored her and ran into the open elevator before she could be escorted out.

#

Aaron Hill paced in his home office. Unlike the masculine office he enjoyed at work, this office had been decorated by his wife "to maintain the integrity of their home decor." It was far too light and airy for his taste; he'd always felt cigar smoke clashed with floral fabrics. Aggravation over his office increased his mounting stress levels.

Things were not moving quickly enough. He had already begun second-guessing his choice to hire Shaughnessey. It wouldn't be enough. He had to remove those two busybodies, permanently. They could ruin everything if they could prove Wynton's innocence. Already they had the lack of gunshot residue—a small twist of doubt, but not if the prosecutor stuck with the idea that the damned telepath made someone else do it. Problem was there weren't any documented cases of telepaths forcing people to do their will, probably because they were also controlling the minds of the people looking for the evidence. But until there was proof, the jury might disregard that theory.

He poured himself a scotch and forced himself to calm down. After several calming breaths, he looked down at his glass. The scotch was gone, and there was only a trace of burning down his throat. He poured another one and downed it just as quickly. *No more*, he thought. His wife would be furious if he came to dinner drunk. She'd demand to know what was wrong, and he'd have to make up some stupid story he'd have to remember for years because there was no way he could tell her the truth. She was too soft, too full of love for all living creatures, to deal with the harsh realities of his life.

"Focus," he told himself. *Back to the question at hand: how to derail the investigation into Wynton.*

He could take his issue to the chief of police, but he'd have to give a rationalization, and that would bring him too far into the light for comfort.

Young women, he realized, had all sorts of secrets. Promiscuities, experimentations with drugs, a few too many drinks one night, a few photos taken that they'd rather not see out on the Internet. But discrediting the sisters would not be enough. There was no way around it, they'd have to be eliminated. That could work. He'd have to go through an intermediary, a trusted intermediary. Someone from the Twenty? He considered the members he had recently met. *Who can help?*

No one came to mind. He sat at his desk; the chair felt more comfortable than he remembered. He dialed Smith, his first contact with the Twenty.

"Smith residence."

"Senator Aaron Hill for the judge."

"One moment, sir."

He heard a series of clicks, and then he was on hold, listening to instrumental music. *The Beatles*, he thought. He was trying to place the song when Smith answered.

"Hill, what can I do for you?"

"I'm in need of a person to do some dirty work for me. I wondered if you knew anyone from our mutual associates who could help me?"

"It all depends. What sort of work do you need done, and how much are you willing to pay?"

"I need to eliminate a couple of busybodies trying to prove Wynton's innocence."

"I see. Meet my associate in three hours at the Public Garden, near the ducks. He's Mr. Black, you're Mr. White."

He had one more phone call to make and then his problem would be solved. Three hours, and he could go back to worrying about the simple problems of the upcoming election season.

#

Reggie woke up in the hospital a few hours after Olivia had checked herself out. He had no one to care for him at home, so he stayed the night, but left first thing in the morning. Panzerelli told him to rest up at home for a day or two before coming back to work. He spent the time puttering around his apartment and working in the little garden he kept on his patio. He was considering what to have for dinner when his boss called.

"Reggie, I've got a job for you. A very important man has a friend who needs two women taken care of."

"But –"

"He's important enough that we've got to take the job. Meet him at the ducks, over at Boston Common in three hours.

"But boss, two women?"

"I don't like it either, but I owe him too much to say no. He insisted on code names," Panzerelli laughed. "You're Mr. Black, and he's Mr. White."

At six thirty Reggie pulled up to Boston Common. The bronze duck statues were a famous landmark, easily visible from the road. He saw a man lounging against a tree, smoking, obviously waiting for someone. *Amateur,* he thought. *This could go badly.*

The man threw his cigarette on the ground and stomped it out. "You Mr. Black?"

Reggie nodded. "You White? Our mutual acquaintance sent me here to talk about your problem."

"Good. I've got two women I need to get rid of."

Reggie nodded. "I can take care of that for you. You got names and pictures?"

"It's all in here."

Reggie pulled out a photo of Olivia and Darcy in front of their office building, and he stiffened. "Fine-looking women. Shame to off them. How are they trouble to you?"

"The bitches are too nosy for their own good. They're PIs, looking into the Wynton case. We can't let him get away with murder."

"Ten grand. Each."

"Twenty grand? I heard you were reasonable."

"I am. PIs get offed and police start investigating. Hits a little too close to home for them."

"Fine." He handed the envelope over. "I need it done as soon as possible."

Reggie took the envelope and flipped through the bills. "You're a little light here."

"Half now, half when I read about them in the paper."

Reggie nodded. "You want anything specific done to them first?"

Mr. White thought for a moment. "My boss didn't specify, but if there isn't any extra charge, making them look like drug-addled whores would put a smile on his face."

"Shouldn't be much of a problem. Give me a day or two and then start reading the papers."

White turned and walked away without another word. Reggie watched as he climbed into his red Mercedes. *Amateur,* he thought again as he watched the car drive away.

Reggie walked away, tucking the cash into his

pocket. There was no way he could take this case, and Panzerelli would be pissed when he saw who the targets were.

He climbed into his car and called his boss. As expected, Panzerelli was furious that someone would try to kill his employees, even though they were only temporarily working for him.

His orders were to protect the women and get them back to finding Brutus. He would turn the job down in the morning and put out word that no one was to touch the Morrison sisters.

Reggie knew not everyone would heed Panzerelli's warning to leave the sisters alone, not for twenty grand, and he'd have to be vigilant.

He pulled out into traffic and started driving. At the next red light, he took the photo out of the envelope. Cars honked all around him as he stared at the photo. He didn't notice. *Had they found what they needed to prove Wynton was innocent?* The last time he was with them, they hadn't. He finally heard the horns and gunned his car down the street. He drove directly to their office, trying to figure out who they could have pissed off so much. He looked up, hoping they were still there, but the light was off. *So much for that.*

He sat in his car and emptied the envelope. He had hoped for some other information, but Mr. White had included nothing beside their home address and vehicle information. He'd never taken a job that he wanted to back out on. He'd never been asked to kill women, though. Once he had a personal connection with someone, he couldn't kill them. Sure, he could hurt them, but not kill.

He pulled out his phone and the business card Olivia had given him. He hesitated, only briefly, and called her.

"Olivia Morrison," she answered.

"Miss Morrison, it's Reggie. I hope you remember me."

"Of course I do, Reggie. It's nice to hear from you. Are you out of the hospital?"

"Yeah. Got out yesterday morning. Feel like a million bucks."

"I'm glad to hear it. Are you just checking to make sure I'm safe?"

"Ah, no. Can we meet somewhere? I have to talk to you."

"Sure. How about the diner near my office? I can be there in ten minutes."

"I'll see you there. And you might want to bring your sister, too."

"All right."

He walked the two blocks to the diner, the cold February air sharpening his mind and his resolve. No one would get to them, not on his watch.

He took the back booth and ordered three coffees before the women slid in across from him.

Olivia smiled. "Hi, Reggie. What's up?"

He looked from one woman to the other and frowned. "I've got some serious news for you two."

"How serious?"

"Deadly. Earlier this evening, I was hired to kill you."

Darcy started, but Olivia held her arm. "By who?"

"I don't know. I think I just met with an intermediary. He said his boss needed the job done."

"Are you …?" asked Olivia.

"Of course not. I never take jobs on people I know."

Olivia breathed a sigh of relief. "Thank you."

"And Panzerelli is furious that someone wants to kill his employees."

Darcy took a sip of her coffee. "We aren't really his employees."

"You're close enough and he's putting out word that no one should take the job. The guy I met with said it has to do with the Wynton case."

Olivia's face paled. "Are you sure?"

The waitress approached, but she veered off when Reggie scowled at her.

"Yes."

"Makes sense," Olivia nodded. "Telepath rights are such a hot topic right now, and people on all sides of the argument have gotten irrationally angry."

"But we haven't found anything worth killing us for. All we've found is the cabbie who drove George, and he can't even establish exactly when he got there. That's not much for evidence, and it certainly doesn't prove Wynton's innocence," said Darcy.

"No, but we may be on the right path. Maybe the real killer is getting nervous."

"Reggie, could you describe the man to us?"

"Not much to say. Medium height, medium build, red glasses, suit."

"Not much to go on, except maybe the glasses," said Darcy. "And you've never seen him before?"

"No. But he was a referral."

"You have a referral system?" asked Darcy.

Olivia nudged her.

"It's all right. You don't understand the business I'm in. Using a referral means they're not just yanking my chain or will change their minds when it's too late. It's protection for me."

Olivia nodded. "It's the same for us, only, well …" She trailed off.

"Don't worry. Mr. P told me to protect you until you find Brutus. He says you can have until tonight, on account of the accident."

Darcy laughed. "Shaughnessey would spit nails if he knew this job was keeping us safe." She turned to Reggie. "Where can we go that we can still work but not get hurt?"

"We can't go back to our apartment. It's already been broken into once this week," said Olivia.

"There's no telling if I'm the only one he hired, so I was thinking we could go back to the club," Reggie suggested. "We can stay there for the night. With all the guys there, you'll be completely safe."

"And where, exactly, will we sleep?"

"There are a few couches in the building. It won't be like the Ritz, but you'll be surrounded by guys who will take a bullet for you, if Mr. P tells them to."

Olivia grimaced. "Like our own Secret Service detail."

Darcy turned to her sister. "We don't have any other option."

Chapter 21

The next morning, after Panzerelli put out the word that he wouldn't take the job, Olivia arranged to meet Dan at the police station.

The sisters, Dan, Broadbent, Fraser, and Reggie then gathered around Fraser's desk. Darcy explained the situation, and then Dan roared, "You stayed where?"

"We were perfectly safe. Reggie was true to his word. No one bothered us, and I learned how to shoot a pretty good game of pool."

"I won't—" began Dan.

"Shut up, Stevens. It doesn't matter where she slept or what you won't put up with. Someone is trying to kill them," said Broadbent.

"I was going to say, I won't rest until we find who wants to kill Olivia."

Broadbent snorted. "Let the professionals take care of that, son." He turned to Reggie. "When are you returning the money?"

"Ten. The Public Garden, by the ducks."

Fraser looked at his watch. "We've got time to set up."

"I've got to be the only person this guy sees," said Reggie. "You two look like cops, and he's going to be real suspicious." Reggie turned to Olivia and Darcy. "As for you two, stay in the car, heads down."

"Oh, no," said Fraser. "There's no way we're bringing these two into danger. They stay here."

"I agree," said Dan.

Reggie looked at Dan. "Why are you even here?"

"I'm here to protect Olivia and make sure she stays safe."

"If you don't mind me saying so, you've done a lousy job at that," said Reggie.

"I'm not the one who crashed her into a telephone pole," Dan growled.

"That couldn't be helped," Reggie said. "They have to come with me." When Fraser started to object, he cut him off. "They have to stay with me. I'm their bodyguard until further notice."

"Their what?" asked Dan. "I'm not paying them enough to hire a bodyguard."

"My employer, Mr. Panzerelli, is paying for my time. You don't need to worry."

Dan looked from Reggie to Olivia to Joe. "Why aren't you arresting him? He must have some sort of warrant out on him."

Olivia had heard enough. Four men were arguing over what she should be doing. But before she could get a word in edgewise, Darcy slammed her hand on Fraser's desk.

"Enough! Dan, you don't even need to be here. Just go to your office. We'll call you when we have news."

"There's nothing you can do from here," Olivia said to ease the sting of Darcy's outburst.

He stood and glared at Reggie. "Make sure you do a better job protecting her this time. I'm holding you personally responsible for her safety."

Reggie nodded at Dan's receding back. "All right. Now that we've got the blowhard out of here, let's get a move on. I've got some of Panzerelli's men staking out the scene already. You two," he nodded to Fraser and Broadbent, "take one unmarked car, and I expect you two," he pointed at Darcy and Olivia, "to stay in my car."

Olivia and Darcy stood. "Right. Let's go." They were out the door before anyone could say another word.

Reggie trailed behind them, but he insisted on checking the street before they left the building. He trotted over to his orange Camaro, and they all drove to the meeting site.

#

Olivia held Darcy's hand. She was nervous, but they had talked through the plan in painstaking detail last night. She had been surprised how helpful Reggie's … coworkers had been. They knew a lot about tailing, avoiding tails, and getting information out of people. They'd been too graphic about interrogation techniques, but if she ever needed information that badly, she knew who to call.

Even Panzerelli had been helpful. He loaned them men and cars "at no immediate charge," he said. Olivia knew she'd have to do him a favor someday, but he promised it wouldn't be an illegal one. Not because he was incapable of asking, he said, but because she would be lousy at carrying it out.

#

Reggie leaned against a tree and waited. Mr. White arrived fifteen minutes late. "Took you long enough."

"Had to make sure no one was here with you. I don't like impromptu meetings."

Reggie handed him the envelope with the ten thousand dollars and an audio bug the size of a pencil eraser. "Here. Tell your boss thanks, but no thanks. These girls owe a debt to my regular employer, so you can see the conflict of interest I have going on here."

The man looked at him suspiciously. "Never knew a killer with a moral compass before."

Reggie looked at the man, equally suspiciously. "Never knew a toady who had any manners, either." He turned and walked away.

He didn't look back at the man until he was in the Camaro with Darcy and Olivia.

Darcy set the binoculars down and said, "Bug works great. He called his boss, says you're a problem as well, and now the three of us have to be eliminated."

Reggie slammed his fist on the dashboard. "No honor among thieves, I guess."

Mr. White's red Mercedes pulled out into traffic, headed toward Government Center. Reggie pulled out three cars behind it.

Darcy's cell phone rang. "Yes?"

"We'll take it from here," said Fraser.

"Hang on. They said they'll take it from here," Darcy told Reggie.

"No way. They're planning to hit me, too. I've got to see this through, take the fight to them. Tell Broadbent to hold back. He doesn't want to get involved in this."

Darcy understood. "Reggie says no. They're going to come after him now, too, and he's going to take care of the situation himself."

Fraser hung up the phone and threw his light on top of his unmarked car.

"What the hell is he doing?" asked Reggie.

The car pulled up alongside them, and Broadbent motioned for them to pull over. Reggie shook his head and continued to follow the man with the money.

Four blocks later, Reggie's car was blocked in and stopped. Police with guns emerged from each car that surrounded the Camaro.

"Shit!" Reggie swore. He unlocked the doors and raised his hands.

Broadbent opened the rear passenger door and motioned for Darcy and Olivia to get out. "We've got other cars following the Mercedes. We'll take it from here."

Fraser pulled Reggie out of the car and threw him against the hood. "You got any weapons on you?"

Olivia saw Reggie smirk. "Yeah. Knife inside my sleeve, gun in an ankle holster. I got a permit for that, so don't get all worked up."

Fraser took a step back as a burly patrolman retrieved the weapons and frisked Reggie.

"That's all there is," said Reggie. "You don't need to get so personal."

"I ought to arrest you," said Fraser. He pulled Reggie off the car and said, "Get out of here."

Darcy and Olivia were shocked that Fraser was so angry. Darcy stepped forward and then slid back into Reggie's car. She looked sheepishly at Broadbent and said, "He's got the transmitter, so he's our best chance to find Harrison's killer. We've got to go."

Olivia kissed her uncle and climbed into Reggie's front seat. With a curt nod from Joe, Reggie was allowed to drive off.

"No idea which way he went," said Reggie. He

pulled out his phone and dialed. "You got him?" He paused for a moment and said, "Call me when you do. I want to handle this matter personally."

"What happened?"

"He ditched his car and ran down into Park Street Station. We've got one guy still on him. He'll call when he can. And Mr. P says your clock is still ticking."

Darcy sighed. "Seriously? He expects us to worry about his damned dog?"

"Yes."

Olivia glared at him. "Well, we can't. Not when someone's trying to kill us."

Reggie said nothing as he kept driving. After a minute, Darcy said, "Where are we going?"

"I'm taking you somewhere safe and we're killing two birds with one stone."

As Reggie pulled into the Panzerelli driveway, Olivia scowled. "I thought we might be going back to the club, not here."

"Trust me," Reggie said, "no one is going to come after you here, and we need to talk to Mrs. P again. She'll be easier to talk to this morning. She's probably only had one drink."

Darcy rolled her eyes. "She's a drunk? How can we believe anything she says?"

Olivia turned to face Darcy in the back seat. "She's lonely and needs a friend. I think if I talk to her alone, she'll open up to me."

"Great. I guess I'll just sit in the car and twiddle my thumbs," Darcy replied.

"You might hear something on the bug." Reggie turned the car off and put the key in his pocket. "I'll set you up in the kitchen," he said to Darcy. "If you're lucky, Gretchen will have something coming out of the oven." He smiled. "She's a great cook. I'll keep everyone else from bothering Olivia. We should be in and out in half an hour, tops. Then you can get back to your own case."

The unlikely trio walked into the Panzerelli home without event.

"Where's Joey?" Olivia asked the door guard.

"Called in sick. What's it to you?"

"Nothing. I didn't realize people … uh … that he got sick days."

The guard squinted at her. "People like us? Sure, we get days off, and health benefits, and even a pension plan if we live long enough to draw from it."

Olivia looked sheepish. "I'm sorry. I just never thought—"

Before she could put her foot further into her mouth, Darcy said, "We'd like to see Mrs. Panzerelli."

The guard shook his head. "Sorry. She's not accepting visitors right now."

"C'mon, Len. She didn't say that. You know she wants someone to talk to."

Len shrugged. "Don't matter. I got orders from Joey. No visitors while he's away."

Reggie smiled at Len. "You're new here, so you don't understand. Joey doesn't give orders; he takes them. And he takes them from me. So stand aside and guard the door against any actual threats."

Len squinted at Reggie and finally stepped away and let them pass.

"Kitchen's down the hall at the back of the house," Reggie told Olivia. "Come find us when you're done."

Olivia walked to the huge den and found Mrs. Panzerelli staring out the picture window. "Excuse me," she said.

Mrs. Panzerelli turned around and smiled. "Miss ... how nice to see you again," she slurred. "I think, I think I might be a little tipsy. Join me in a cocktail?"

A little? How is she even standing up? Olivia thought. She walked to the bar and said, "I think I will."

"Excellent. I never did like drinking alone, but none of the men my husband hires will drink with me."

Olivia poured herself a soda and sat on the couch in front of the fireplace. "Come sit with me," she patted the couch, "and we'll have a nice long talk."

"I will, but you have to tell me your name."

"I'm Olivia Morrison. We met a few days ago."

"That's right," she said. "You're Reggie's friend. And you must call me Lizzy. No, wait. Elizabeth. Lizzy is a name for silly girls." She walked to the bar to freshen her drink. "He's a good boy, that Reggie. I'm not sure what he's doing working for my snake of a husband."

"What makes you say that?"

"Because he's always kind to me. Reggie doesn't pity me, like the rest of them do. They think I don't see it, but I know. I know they all hate me."

"It must have been better for you when you had Brutus."

"My poor puppy." She looked at Olivia. "You know he's dead, right?"

"I thought I heard something like that. What happened to him?"

She looked alarmed. "I'm not supposed to tell."

"That's all right; it's just between friends."

"Joey said not to, and he's about the closest thing I've got to a friend here."

"I see." Olivia rattled the ice in her glass and got up to refill her drink. "And is Joey here now, when you're so lonely and need a friend?"

"He isn't." She looked sad.

Olivia sat back down and put her hand on Elizabeth's arm. "No, he isn't. But I am. I'm here, and I'm your friend, Elizabeth."

Elizabeth looked into Olivia's eyes and began to cry. "He's not … not … not here," she stuttered. "He said he wouldn't leave me, but he did."

Olivia shook her head. "Sometimes you just can't trust a man. Believe me, I know." She put her arm around Elizabeth and hugged her. The two women sat without talking for a few minutes.

Elizabeth sighed and said, "It's good to have a friend like you, Olivia."

Olivia felt a stab of guilt and pity. This woman had everything she could want in life, everything but friends and love.

"I'm glad to be your friend," she said.

"And friends tell secrets to each other, don't they?" asked Elizabeth. "Tell me a secret, and I'll tell you one, too."

Olivia thought. There was no way she could tell her the big secret of her life, but a smaller one would suffice. "I am not in love with my boyfriend."

Elizabeth looked up. "Then quit wasting your time with him. Find a man you can love for the rest of your life—whether he goes bald, or gets fat, or loses his job."

Olivia smiled. "I think I will. No use wasting my time on this one."

"My secret is a big one." Elizabeth whispered,

"I killed Brutus."

Olivia sat back, shock evident on her face. "You did?"

Elizabeth nodded. "I fed him all the pills the vet gave us and he just laid down, fell asleep and never woke up. Joey buried him for me."

"But why?"

"He was in too much pain, and Guido wouldn't let the vet put him out of his misery." She began to cry again. "I had to. It wasn't right, letting an animal suffer like that."

Olivia nodded. "You have to tell Guido."

"I can't. He'll be mad at me."

"Maybe I—"

"You can't either," she said. "Promise me you won't tell Guido."

"I won't tell him, but sooner or later it's going to come out, and it would be better if you told him the truth."

She shook her head violently. "No. It won't come out. Brutus is missing, and that's all he needs to know."

Olivia moved her arm off Elizabeth's shoulder and turned to face her. "Listen to me."

Elizabeth looked startled by the firmness in Olivia's voice.

"I was hired to find Brutus. If I don't find him, Guido'll be a lot more than mad at me. I have," she looked at her watch, "about four hours left to tell him what happened to Brutus. If I don't have anything to tell him, he's going to hurt me."

Elizabeth's eyes widened.

"That's right. Hurt me very badly. You've got to tell him."

"I can't. I can't face him."

"We can go together. I'll be there for you, because I am your friend."

Elizabeth picked up her empty glass and frowned.

"No more drinking. Let's get you dressed and ready to go. Maybe some food, too."

"You promise you'll be with me?"

"I promise."

#

Reggie burst into the kitchen and saw Darcy staring fixedly at the microphone. "Mrs. P did it," he announced.

"What?" Darcy asked.

"She killed the dog."

"Oh. Good. Now we can get out of here," Darcy said distractedly. "Is there any way to track where this microphone is? I can't hear anything anymore."

"That's what the guys out in the field are supposed to be doing. We've got to head back out to the club and get this whole dog situation settled. Then you two can track the money all you want."

Olivia and Elizabeth walked into the kitchen. "Gretchen, can we have some coffee, please?" Olivia asked.

"Yes, ma'am."

"Black, three sugars," said Olivia, "and nothing else."

Elizabeth gave her a sour look. "Coffee won't taste right without a little kick to it."

"No. You've got to be as sober as we can make you by the time we get there."

Elizabeth reached for the cup Gretchen handed

her, took a sip and sputtered. "Jesus! That's horrible. Who drinks it like that?"

"We all do," said Reggie. "Except some people like cream in it, too."

Elizabeth winced. "No cream. I can't get fat."

While Elizabeth was drinking the coffee, Olivia turned to Darcy. "Did you hear anything?"

"Nothing useful. He was on a train, but I couldn't hear any of the station names. Then he got off, walked for ..." She consulted her notes. "Three minutes, entered a building, and then everything went silent. We had to find the most unfriendly person to bug. He didn't say a single word to anyone."

"Damn," said Reggie.

Olivia looked in Elizabeth's empty mug. "Time to go," she said.

#

Joey opened the door to the Somerville Social Club for the delegation headed by Darcy and Olivia.

"I thought this was your day off," said Darcy.

"Yeah, well," he looked sheepish, "Once Mr. P figured out I wasn't sick, just hung over, he made me come in. Didn't think I'd see you back again so soon. You find the bastard who's after you?"

"Not yet. We might have that rematch sooner than you expected. You ready to lose to a girl again?" Darcy winked at him.

Joey smiled. "I been practicing. Got me a new set of darts, too."

"New darts won't help your aim," she said.

"You wanna make it interesting? How much per point?"

Darcy shook her head. "No way. Just bragging rights."

Joey frowned. "Not much bragging rights in beating a woman," he said.

"Can you two talk inside? It's damn cold out here," said Olivia.

Joey looked at Elizabeth. "Mrs. P, why are *you* here?"

"I'm not sure I should be here," said Elizabeth.

"It's time for the truth, before anyone gets hurt," said Reggie.

Joey flinched, but let them pass.

Olivia took Elizabeth's hand and gently led her inside. "You know this is the right thing to do."

Inside the main room, Panzerelli was standing over a man with a freshly broken nose. Blood still dripped down the man's shirt. "You won't be short next week, will you?" he asked.

"No, boss. I'll make it up to you, I swear."

Panzerelli took a handkerchief and wiped blood off his knuckles. As he turned, he saw Elizabeth; he was not happy.

"Reggie. You know better than this," he said. "Yes, boss. I know. But Mrs. Panzerelli has something important to tell you."

Panzerelli smirked. "Does she, now? I can't imagine what is so important at home that my wife has to come down here, to my place of employment, and bother me."

Elizabeth shrank back.

"Courage," Olivia whispered to her.

Mrs. P looked at Olivia and nodded. "As a matter of fact, I do have something important to tell you. But before I do, you have to promise not to be mad at me. Or Joey, because it wasn't his fault. He just did what I said."

Panzerelli sighed. "How much trouble could you get into at home? Did you spend more than your allowance again? Do I have to rehire all the staff? Just tell me. I've got real work to do here."

"Okay, but remember, you promised." She took a deep breath and said, "I did it."

Panzerelli looked at his watch. "I've got another appointment in five minutes. What, exactly, did you do?"

"I killed Brutus."

He took three long strides toward her, and she immediately hid behind Reggie. "You promised," she said meekly.

With evident difficulty, he stopped and forced his fists to open up. "How?" he growled.

She peeked out from behind Reggie. "The pills from the vet. I couldn't take it anymore. He was in so much pain, and you didn't care. But I couldn't live with it anymore."

"Where is he now?"

"Joey buried him out in the woods, I don't know where. Once Brutus stopped breathing, he said he'd take care of him. He felt bad for Brutus, too. By then, we all—everyone in the house—wanted Brutus to go peacefully."

Panzerelli began to pace. When he reached the wall, he punched a hole in it. Elizabeth began to cry.

"You," he roared at Joey. "I expect better from family. I thought my sister raised a loyal son. Get out of here, and don't ever come back."

Joey opened his mouth to protest, but Reggie cut him off. "Just go," he said.

"As for you two," he said to Darcy and Olivia, "get out of here. You're done with this job. Tell

Shaughnessey I never want to see his ugly mug again."

Olivia nodded, and the sisters left as quickly as possible.

Chapter 22

Reggie let them keep the receiver, but it didn't make a sound for the rest of the day. Dan had called and officially fired them, but Olivia didn't care. She walked out of her office, a smile on her lips. They were close to cracking the case and, client or not, she was determined to see it through to the end. She had finally found Camille Johnson. She'd run off to Vegas to get married. When Olivia had tracked her down in her hotel, Camille said it was Harrison's death that prompted her to re-evaluate her life.

Darcy was busy checking a couple of things with Joyce, and they'd work it all out tonight.

Once she left the building, she looked to the side to wave good night to Louie.

He waved back. "See you in the morning," he called.

A man was walking by the lot, apparently having an argument with himself.

She stood under a streetlight and rummaged through her purse to find her keys. Before she could even understand what was going on, she was lying face up on the ground, a hand covering her mouth.

She heard Louie yelling from his corner of the building. "Hey! Let her go."

The man pulled a gun out of his waistband and waved it at Louie. "Get lost, old man." He turned his head back to Olivia, his eyes full of hate. "Scream and I'll kill you, you whore."

She tried to nod, to show she understood, but he held her head down. She stared at him, taking in his frayed hoodie, blue eyes and large nose, searing the memory into her brain so that once she got out of this mess she could hunt him down.

Louie was trying to run across the parking lot to save her, but he fell and hit his head on the pavement.

"I should kill you anyway."

She looked at him, trying to ask him why with only her frightened eyes.

He pulled out a roll of duct tape from his coat pocket and taped her mouth shut. "Get up, and give me your keys."

He kept a strong hold on her left arm as she found her keys. He walked her to her car and said, "I will shoot you if you try anything." He shoved her in the trunk of the car and drove off. Tears stung her eyes as she ripped the duct tape off her mouth. *Louie! How long would he lay there before someone found him?* She forced herself to breath calmly and concentrate on her situation. *Not a very bright one, this guy.* He didn't even bother to bind her hands. She dredged up everything she had learned in college about self-defense. She knocked the tail light out and looked around. They were heading toward Somerville.

She reached around and found the trunk latch. She waited until the car slowed to a stop, and then she pulled the trunk release and sprang out, screaming for help.

People turned their heads away, not wanting to get involved. She ran into a bodega and pushed the customers in line aside.

"You've got to help me! There's a man. He kidnapped me."

The cashier looked at her warily.

"Please. Hide me. He could come in here any minute."

The cashier reached under the counter, but whether for a gun or a panic button, Olivia didn't know. It didn't matter. Either way, she would be safer in the crowd.

Her assailant burst through the door, wild-eyed. "There you are. Come with me."

To his credit, the cashier whipped out a sawed-off shotgun faster than Olivia thought was humanly possible. "Not so fast. We'll just wait until the police get here."

Olivia's kidnapper tried to back toward the door, but a large man blocked his way. "We'll all just stay right here. You can explain to the cops why you were chasing this woman."

Olivia had never been more grateful for the kindness of strangers.

A police car pulled up, sirens flashing, and two very young cops jumped out. They rushed through the door, pushing the kidnapper aside, forcing the cashier to put down his gun. Before her would-be abductor could run out of the building, the large man resumed his post in front of the door, his arms crossed.

"You officers should be asking this one here," he pointed to the assailant, "why he came running in after this young lady. She was scared out of her mind, and it looks like she was lucky to escape him."

The kidnapper pulled his gun and grabbed an elderly woman standing next to him. "Everyone stand still. I don't want to have to shoot Granny."

His captive looked at the would-be kidnapper, disgust in her eyes, and said, "Don't you worry about me, officers. If he shoots me now I only lose a few weeks of my life. You just catch him, and make sure he pays for what he's done." At that, she stomped on the instep of his foot, turned in his loosened grasp, and hit him in the nose for all she was worth.

He reached up to protect his face, and she twisted the gun out of his hand. "Officers, I believe you want this." She unloaded the gun and handed it to the nearest officer. His partner threw the assailant on the floor and handcuffed him roughly.

Sheepishly, he accepted the gun. "Thank you, ma'am."

"Don't mention it. You don't live your whole life in this city without knowing how to defend yourself."

After the man was led out to the cruiser, Olivia began to relax. She looked at the old woman and said, "You shouldn't have done that! He could have killed you."

"No, I don't think he would have. Sometimes," she winked, "you just get a feel for these things."

Was the woman trying to tell Olivia she was a telepath? Or did she just have a lot of life experience to draw on? Either way, Olivia let it drop, and she hugged the woman. "Thank you for saving my life. Can I repay you in any way?"

"You can make sure you don't waste this chance you've been given. Don't waste your time with that boyfriend of yours. Find yourself a man who respects you and will make your life easier, not harder."

Olivia was shocked. The woman must have just done a deep scan on her. Olivia didn't say anything. She moved on to thank the rest of the people in the store for helping to keep her safe.

The cop by the door waited for her to finish before he said, "You'll need to make a statement."

"Yes, of course."

"We'll start here. Which car were you in?"

She pointed out her car and described how he'd forced her into the trunk. She told him everything he'd said.

"Is that all?"

"Yes. It was a short interaction. I'd really like to go home now."

"We'll have someone drive you home and check out your place."

"Detective Fraser can do it. He was there after our recent home invasion."

The cop looked up from his notes. "Your what, now?"

"Oh, it was just a misunderstanding. A woman thought my sister and I were trying to steal her boyfriend from her, so she broke into our house, threw a bunch of stuff around, and tore up the furniture."

"That's a lot of damage for a misunderstanding."

"She's a passionate woman, that one. But it's fine now."

"I'll get Fraser to go over and take a look."

"All right. Can you ask him to also check on Louie? He fell in the parking lot, trying to save me."

"Who is Louie?"

"He's the homeless man who watches our building."

"Here." The officer handed her his cell phone. "Maybe you should tell him all this yourself."

While she was on the phone with Fraser, Dan showed up in his red car, screeching around the corner.

How did he know where to find me? She thought.

He jumped out of his car and ran toward her. "Damn it all to hell, Olivia. I don't have time to keep coming to rescue you."

The officer stood between Dan and Olivia. "Your name, sir?"

"Dan Stevens. I'm Miss Morrison's former employer."

"Sir, take a step back."

Dan complied, but he shot an angry look at her.

"You know this man?"

Olivia heaved a sigh. "Yes. He's okay."

The officer stepped out of the way, and Dan awkwardly embraced Olivia. After a heartbeat, she put her arms around him as well.

"How did you know?"

"I've got someone listening for your name on the police band."

"Really?" She was confused. He claimed not to have time to deal with her work emergencies, yet he had raced to her when she was in trouble. Did he love her or not? More importantly, did she love him? And was this the kind of behavior she could put up with?

"Yes. I hired him when you started working with Darcy. I never know what kind of trouble you're going to be in."

"This was not my fault. I was kidnapped, right in front of my office."

"I've told you time and time again, it's not a safe neighborhood."

"I know. And Louie is hurt."

"Louie?"

"He's the homeless man who keeps watch over

our building." Dan had nothing to say, so Olivia continued. "I asked Fraser to make sure he's all right."

"The homeless guy? What's he to you?"

"I told you, he watches our building. Last month he saved Dr. Pak from a couple of kids breaking in, looking for drugs."

"Whatever. I've got to get back to work. I will drop you off at my apartment, where you will stay until all this is over."

"No. I've got work to do. Now I've got to figure out who hired that guy and where he was taking me."

Dan grabbed her arm. "I can't allow that."

"Let go of me." She wrenched her arm free. "I've got work to do. The longer we stand around here, the longer before I'm done."

The officer next to her didn't even bother to cover his smile. "That's right. She's going to have to come down to the station and fill out a report. We'll take it from there."

Dan handed him his card. "Call me when you're done with her, and I'll come pick her up."

That's just about enough, she thought. "No. When I'm done, I'll go home. Fraser will have checked out the apartment, and it will be safe. I'll be fine on my own."

And she would be. She knew she would make it through this, and anything else life threw her way. She'd be fine. She turned and walked with the cop to his cruiser.

On the drive, he kept looking at her. "What is it?"

"I'm trying to figure out why you put up with him."

"Who? Dan? He means well, but he's not used to me being in danger. I told him that my job would be mostly paperwork, running things down on the Internet, stuff like that. And now, between the home invasion and the kidnapping—well, he's worried for me."

"What do you do?"

"My sister and I are PIs. Morrison Investigations."

He nodded. "You a new outfit?"

"Yes. After six months, this is the first case that has had any element of danger at all." She shook her head. "He hasn't worked out how to deal with it. Are you married?"

"No. Have a girlfriend, though. But she knew what she was getting into when we started dating. I think she'd like to see me doing something less dangerous, like being a CPA, but on the other hand, she's proud that I keep people safe."

"Do you tell her about what happens in your day? How will she deal with you being in an armed standoff?"

"I minimize a lot of it. I don't want her to worry needlessly, and if I come home at night, then everything worked out in the end."

"I like that. But I don't think that will work with Dan."

"Because he's got someone listening for your name on the police scanner?"

She turned to face him. "I can't believe he's doing that. It's like he's got someone watching me all the time."

"Doesn't sound like he's the guy for you, not if you're going to continue in this line of work."

She turned away. He was right; the old woman

was right. Dan had seemed so perfect for her when they met. They had similar values, similar interests, and almost identical backgrounds. It would have been a perfect match.

She sighed. "You're probably right."

Her cell phone rang, and Fraser's name appeared on the screen.

"Hi, Fraser."

"I've found Louie. He's got a bump on his forehead but says he's fine. I did a quick check for concussion and he's okay. He's worried about you, though."

"Can I talk to him?"

The next voice on the phone was Louie's. "Miss Liv? You safe now?"

"Yes. I managed to escape and the police have the kidnapper."

"Good to hear. I'm so sorry, Miss Liv. I wanted to save you, but by the time I got back up, your car was already gone."

"You were great, Louie. You distracted him enough that he didn't even bind my hands and feet and that's what let me get away." Her hands began to shake as she realized how true this was. "I might not have made it without you."

"But you did and that's all that matters. You take care and I'll see you tomorrow."

Fraser came back on the line. "Your apartment checks out. No one's been around, and no one's been in. You're good to go home. Ask the officer you're with to take a look around when you get there, just to be on the safe side."

"I will. Thanks, Fraser." She closed the cell phone and turned to the officer. "My apartment is safe, and my friend is as well."

He nodded.

"Can I listen to the interrogation?"

"We don't usually let civilians listen in, but I think in this case it will be all right. He might say something you will pick up on that we have no idea is important."

"Thanks."

#

Good old Interrogation Room Two, Olivia thought as they brought her kidnapper in.

"Name," said Fraser.

"Harold Milliken."

"Mr. Milliken, why did you kidnap Miss Morrison?"

"I didn't. She's crazy. I just went into that bodega for a pack of smokes."

"All right, then. Why did you hold a gun to the head of the old lady?"

"I had to. She wasn't going to let me out alive."

"Who? Miss Morrison couldn't have harmed you."

"No, not her. The woman in my brain."

Fraser rolled his eyes. "You hear voices often?"

"Just lately. She won't leave me alone, either. All day, all night, she tells me, 'Morrison PI, go get them. They can't be allowed to live.' " He put his head in his hands and began to cry. "What else could I do? She wouldn't let me sleep, wouldn't let me eat until it was done."

"You wait here. I'll get a doctor."

Fraser entered the observation room and summoned the on-call therapist.

"Well, that was a waste of time," he said. "He's

a nut."

Olivia put her hand on the one-way mirror. "I'm not so sure. Why would he have picked us for a delusion? Why not someone more prominent?"

Fraser sat in front of the recording machines and sighed. "Doc will figure it out and let us know."

"I hate to say this, but what if he's being controlled? And if he is, Doc won't figure it out." She turned to Fraser, compassion in her eyes. "I know you have a soft spot for her, but it sounds like Sue. If she's behind this, there's no way the doctor will know what's going on."

He shook his head. "There's no way Sue could do this. She's just a messed up kid."

"We talked to her mother. She said Sue hasn't been right since her telepathic powers got to be too strong for her."

"I don't believe it. She tests negative."

Milliken walked up to the one-way mirror and stared at the spot Olivia was standing in. "She has a message for you, too. She won't warn you again. Leave her man alone or she'll force me to kill you." His shoulders slumped and he began to cry. "Please, lady. Don't make her hurt me anymore. Just do what she says."

Olivia focused on Milliken and tried to sense anyone else trying to communicate with him, but she heard nothing. She was about to give up when Darcy burst in.

"Liv, thank God you're all right." She looked Olivia up and down. "You are all right, aren't you?"

Olivia nodded. "What's wrong?"

"We've got to go."

"But –"

Darcy grabbed her sister's hand and said,

"Can't talk now. We've got to leave." As they were passing through the main office, Darcy's phone rang. "Yeah?" she said.

"It's Reggie. Got some information for you about –"

"Can you text it to me? I'm on my way to stop a riot."

"Uh, sure. But it's real important, so make sure you read it right away."

#

Out in the parking lot, Olivia refused to get in the car until Darcy explained herself.

"It's Joyce. I was just at her office and she says she can barely hold onto the telepaths. They're preparing to storm the precinct and get George out. We've got to get to the print shop and talk some sense into them."

Just then, three Wynton Signage vans pulled up in front of the police station. Olivia counted fifteen men, a few with not-well-hidden handguns, exiting.

Darcy strode up to the group of men and asked, "Which one of you is Jose?"

A man no taller than Darcy turned to her and said, "I am. You *normals* should get out of here."

"Don't be a fool. You'll get yourselves *and* George killed. Then no one will ever care if he was innocent. All they'll remember are the brutal telepaths, shooting their way out, killing innocent people."

Jose paced back and forth, agitation coursing through his muscles. "I know. Sean and Michael had me calmed down, and I was going to wait it out. But this morning I woke up, and it was like my brain was on fire. I had to do something. I had to get him out. Action was the only thing I could think of, and I haven't been able to stop moving yet."

Olivia put her hand on his shoulder. "Sniffers are in town. Maybe they've found a way to affect you?"

He shrugged his shoulder and continued pacing. "They've never bothered me like this before, and so what if they are now? They're right. I've got to get George out."

"There's no way you'll be able to reach him. The sniffers gave him really horrible headaches, so bad they had to put him in solitary. He's all right now, but they're leaving him in solitary," said Darcy.

"I don't understand. Did the sniffers give up on him?"

Darcy hesitated. She didn't want to give Jose any clues that would lead him to think she was a telepath. "He said he pushed them away." She mimicked forceful breaths. "He did this to help."

Jose stopped walking and ran his hand through his long hair. "He can do that?"

"It took him about ten minutes, but he did."

Olivia didn't know if it would work, but she tried to project calming thoughts toward him as she walked forward. "Sit back in your car and give it a try. I'll sit with you."

"How is that going to help?"

"I'll keep a lookout and make sure no one comes near you while you're concentrating. Hand me your gun, and I'll protect you."

"Why should I trust you?"

"Because George does."

Jose looked deeply into her eyes, handed her the gun, and sat in his van.

Olivia slid into the passenger's seat and said, "Good. Now, close your eyes and focus on the anger. Push it away. Keep pushing until it's a tiny spot on the horizon."

Jose sat still, but the sweat beading on his forehead betrayed his calm exterior.

"Can't get them far enough away," he said.

I have to hold his hand to help him. Can I trust that he'll keep our secret?

Olivia reached out and put her hand on Jose's. "Breathe deeply and relax. I'll help you."

Jose turned and looked at her, shock in his eyes. "You're ...?"

She nodded and thought, *It's a secret. Let's get rid of the sniffers.*

Together, they sat in silence for twenty minutes while Darcy and the other telepaths looked on. Finally, after his shoulders relaxed and his jaw unclenched, Olivia removed her hand from his. "How do you feel now?"

Jose blinked. "Much better. I can't believe I was going to rush in to get George. Why? I'd have been shot."

"It's the sniffers. They were trying to tell you what to do, and they almost succeeded. Part of you really wants to rush in and save him, and they amplified those feelings until you could see nothing else."

"What if they try it again?"

"I don't think they will. They know you can ignore this command now. They'll look for someone else to manipulate."

"I've got to warn everyone else."

"Yes. Keep them safely inside their homes. Once we wrap up this case and prove Wynton's innocence, they'll move on to another town.

Darcy joined in. "I'm going to warn Fraser to keep an eye out for people wanting to break into the precinct."

"How can you do that and not tell him the truth?" asked Olivia.

"I'll tell him my telepathic source warned me. You should stay with Jose. Tell the telepaths what George wants them to do. Help them block the sniffers."

Olivia shook her head. "I don't like it. Today is not a day we should be separated."

"We'll be fine. I'll be in the precinct. You'll be protected with all the other telepaths around you."

"Come back as soon as you can. We'll be at the print shop in Charlestown."

"I'll come as soon as I can."

Fraser met Darcy at the precinct door. "What the hell was that? I've been watching you for the last half hour. Who was that man, and what was Olivia doing with him?"

She smiled at him. "Let's get some coffee. We'll talk."

"There's a Dunkin Donuts down the street."

"Send a rookie. We should probably stay here in the station. We need to talk privately."

As they walked into the squad room, he snapped out a coffee order to a uniformed boy who looked barely sixteen. "He old enough to be a rookie?"

"Police Explorer. It's like Boy Scouts, but all about being a cop. He gets coffee, photocopies, reviews cold cases. John's a good kid, and in a few years he'll have good cop instincts to take to the Academy."

Darcy nodded, a bit jealous. He was getting the training he needed for free, and she was getting nothing and had been paying Shaughnessey way too much for it.

They sat in a small conference room. "Better than the interrogation room," he explained.

Darcy looked around. "Much nicer. I hate those ugly gray rooms."

"That's the whole point. You're supposed to want to do anything to get out of them. Including confess to your crimes. Now, tell me what's up."

"Two things. First, Olivia found Camille Johnson.

"Where?"

"You won't believe it. She ran off to Vegas to get married. She's in Hawaii on her honeymoon."

"How did — ?"

"Just a hunch. She had a huge engagement ring so Liv started checking recent local marriage licenses. When those came up empty, she started checking Las Vegas. She found her hotel and talked to her."

"Nice work. What's the second thing?"

"Sniffers are in town."

"Really? I hadn't heard. But so what?"

"So what?" She was shocked. She thought everyone knew what the sniffers did. "They're trying to agitate the telepaths in town so they can make mass arrests. They want another New Year's roundup."

"We can't do anything. The Telepathic Corps is out of our jurisdiction," said Fraser.

"Once a sniffer captures a telepath, that person is never heard from again. Isn't that at least a civil rights violation?" She shook her head sadly. "I thought the lack of due process would bother you."

"We can't effectively monitor telepaths, so why

shouldn't they take care of themselves? Telepathic Corps is out of our jurisdiction."

"People disappear. It could be kidnapping, could be medical experimentation, could be murder. George and my other telepathic sources say they're bad news. Any telepath caught doing anything illegal is swept up off the street, all rights revoked in the name of national security."

"How does this relate to today?"

"My source was shocked at how strong they are becoming. It looks like they can push people to do things now."

"Aha! I knew they could do stuff like that."

"He says it's just the sniffers. The telepaths he knows aren't like that at all, and they don't want to be."

"Really?"

"Yes. He says most telepaths want to live and let live, just be regular people."

"Okay, so what was that with the gun? I was going to arrest him, but then he handed it to Olivia, and I thought I'd wait to see what happened."

"The sniffers had gotten into his mind and were amplifying his emotions."

Fraser just looked at her.

"It's something one telepath can do to another, apparently, not something a telepath can do to non-telepaths. It has to do with the two-way communication one telepath can establish with another. With a non-telepath, a telepath can only make a one-way connection, and they can't use it to force an action."

"That's exactly what was happening to that guy who kidnapped Olivia."

"I don't know how to explain that. Sue's

mental instability could affect her telepathy."

"He said the voice wouldn't let him rest until he did what she said, so it could be a one-way link."

John knocked and came in with their coffee, looking serious. "Thanks, kid," said Fraser. "Take the money from petty cash."

John retained his grim expression and nodded before he left the room.

"He always look like that?" she asked.

"It's his cop face. He's trying hard to be a man around here. I've seen him at home—he's a totally different kid, playing around and laughing."

"Anyway, Jose's feelings of loyalty to Wynton were being amplified to the point that he felt like all he could do was rush in here, shooting, trying to rescue him."

"That doesn't make any sense."

"No, it doesn't. Sniffers' priority is to get telepaths off the street, away from normals."

"But they are telepaths."

"Self-loathers, too. They feel the streets can't be safe with the likes of them running around."

"So what did Olivia do?"

"She calmed him down so he could push the sniffers out of his mind."

"Like the second time you saw Wynton and he had the headache?

"Yes."

"Is she ...?" He left the remainder of the question unasked.

Darcy didn't want to lie to Fraser, but saw no other option. "She's the kind of person who makes everyone else around her calm and relaxed."

"Like an empath?"

"No. It's just her kind personality. No one can

stay angry around her."

"So she talked him down. Then where did they go?"

"Jose took her to the other telepaths he knows, to explain what's going on. They need to keep the other telepaths calm."

"Think it'll work?"

"No idea. That's the reason I came back in here. You should be on the lookout for anyone else trying to 'rescue' Wynton. I recommend extra men on duty, stuff like that. Maybe send the kid home early."

"Not sure the chief will buy that."

"Try. Sell it for all you're worth. And if you can get George to get in touch with a few people to try to calm them down directly, that would help."

"He can't just use the phone whenever he wants to," said Fraser.

Darcy shook her head. "He doesn't need a phone."

Fraser's eyes widened. "Oh. I guess not. And what are you going to do?"

"I've still got a case to work on, so I'm going back out on the streets."

"I don't like the idea of you being out there alone. It's still my case, so we'll work it together."

Darcy sighed. Who is going to talk to me with a big cop standing behind me? I promise I'll check in with you every hour or two."

Chapter 23

A blinding headache woke Darcy early. She stumbled out of the bedroom, relying only on the pale glow from nightlight in the hall, afraid bright lights would hurt too much. She groped for a bottle in the bathroom medicine cabinet and took two aspirin.

It was clear the sniffers had finally made it to her neighborhood. *All I have to do is stay calm, and they will go away.* She sat on the couch and pulled the afghan her grandmother had crocheted over her shoulders. Closing her eyes, she began running though her exercises, hoping they would numb her headache along with her mind. Ten minutes later, headache receding, she looked up. It didn't matter whether the aspirin or the exercises had helped; she could see clearly again, and the dim rays of sunlight poking through the crack in the curtain did not hurt.

Gently, experimentally, she stretched. *No extra pain.* She stood without dizziness, another good sign. It was not even seven. *Maybe another hour in bed will help.* She walked toward the bedroom.

Olivia was moaning softly and thrashing in her bed.

"Liv?" Darcy shook her shoulder. "Wake up, it's only a dream."

Olivia moaned again, but she didn't wake. "Olivia. Wake up—now."

Olivia opened her eyes but closed them immediately. "Head."

"You have a headache?"

Olivia moaned again.

"I had one earlier. I took aspirin and started my exercises. Now it's almost gone. I'll get you some." When Darcy returned with aspirin and a glass of water, her sister was deep in concentration. She observed the enforced calm on Olivia's face. Fifteen minutes later, Olivia opened her eyes.

"Much better. But I'll take those aspirin, just in case."

Darcy handed her the pills and water. "What was that all about?"

Olivia's cell phone rang, the love song indicating it was Dan. "Yes, Dan?"

"Olivia, I just got off the phone with Wynton. He demanded I get a message to you. He said the sniffers are targeting his people, worse than yesterday, and that you have to protect them before they are all rounded up."

Olivia paled.

"Are you there?" asked Dan.

"What? Oh, yes. I'm here. Sniffers are targeting Wynton's people?"

Darcy jumped up and dressed immediately.

"That's what he said."

"They're still trying to provoke the local telepaths into some sort of rash action. We should go talk to them."

Darcy started throwing clothes to Olivia.

"They're a government agency, they don't go around picking fights. I don't have time for the ravings of a lunatic in prison. Just handle him, and make sure he doesn't call me unless it has to do with his case."

"I'll take care of it."

"Good. This foolishness has taken up too much of my time. I don't like the idea that you're involved with these telepaths."

"You're the one who gave us the case to start with. And does this mean you're hiring us back?"

"Believe me, Gray and Shalek won't make the mistake of taking another telepath as a client ever again. And yes, I'm hiring you back. I can't find anyone else will deal with them."

Olivia gazed off into the distance for a moment. She put her phone down, hand shaking. "We've got to get out of here. If we just get out of Boston—"

Darcy grabbed Olivia's hands. "That's the sniffers. They're trying to make us run."

"But—"

"Look at me and focus on my eyes. We'll be safe if we're together. George said we have to protect his people," she paused, "Our people."

Olivia took a deep breath and breathed it out as hard as she could. "I'm still afraid, but we can stay."

"Good." Darcy let her hands go and dialed Joyce.

"Joyce? It's Darcy Morrison."

"Can't talk now. I have to go save George."

"Joyce, listen to me. That's the sniffers. They're targeting the underground and once you make a move they'll take you."

Joyce gasped. "I warned him that too much publicity would make life harder for every telepath in the city. I've got to get everyone back together."

Darcy hung up. "She's taking care of the rest of them. We've got to get back to work."

"Let's just go, get out of town," Olivia pleaded.

"Stay with me, Liv. We can't run. If they're targeting us and we look suspicious, they'll haul us in. We've got to act normal. The sooner Wynton goes to trial and is set free, the sooner the sniffers will leave town and the better off we'll be."

Olivia looked frantic. "They're hunting us, Dar."

"No, they're not. Unless we draw their attention, they'll never know who we are."

She jumped up and started pacing. "I can't just sit here!"

"No. And we won't. We'll go see George, wait it out in the precinct, and stay safe. Once they're gone, we'll be fine." She took her sister's hand. "It had to happen sometime, Liv. We've been lucky it's taken this long for them to get here." She hugged her. "Be brave. Keep a tight rein on your ability; we'll get through this just fine."

Olivia wiped a tear from her eye. "I'm afraid. There's nothing we can do. If they find us ..." Her voice trailed off.

Now it's my turn to take care of her. "Courage. We are Morrisons, and no one does anything to us we don't want them to do."

Darcy knew Olivia would buck up once she heard the phrase that her father had used so many times when they were children. They both believed it, too, to the core of their being, even though sometimes they had to be reminded.

"You're right. So, on a normal day, we'd have breakfast and go to the office."

"I suggest we get breakfast and then go straight to see George. More people will be around us, and that's still part of our normal activities."

"Right." Olivia stood. "Let me get dressed, and

we'll go."

After a silent breakfast where both sisters ran through their mental exercises, Olivia felt substantially better, and she was optimistic by the time they reached the police station without sniffers descending on them. "How's your headache?"

"Not bad," said Darcy. "I think I'll keep taking the aspirin all day, just in case. I wonder how George is doing?"

They parked next to their uncle's beat-up Hyundai. Broadbent smiled and said good morning as he opened the driver's door, and the sisters walked with him into the precinct.

Fraser was just coming on shift and held the door open for the three of them. "Good morning."

"Morning, Fraser. We're here to see Mr. Wynton."

"Wynton?" said Uncle Joe. "Got a call earlier this morning. He had a tough night, yelling about sniffers blocking him from reaching his people. Almost had to sedate him, I hear."

"Interrogation Two," Fraser directed the twins.

By now, they had been given permanent visitors' badges, and they knew their way around. The walk to the interrogation room never failed to depress Olivia. Knowing that the hallway and room were purposely dismal didn't help alleviate her feelings of doom.

George shambled into the room, supported by Fraser, who gently led him to the chair. Wynton sat. He immediately put his head down on the table.

"Can he have some aspirin or something?" asked Darcy.

"He hasn't asked for any."

"Please?" she asked again. "You can see he's in

pain, and I don't think it would be out of line for you to give him aspirin. I've got some in my bag, can *I* give them to him?"

"Yeah, that will be okay."

She took the bottle from her bag and handed it to Wynton.

"Some water?" she asked.

He closed the door softly. Darcy smiled. *Fraser is a good man, as considerate as he is able to be, given his job.*

"George," Olivia whispered.

"Wha—?"

"What's wrong?"

"Sniffers. Targeting me. Never been this bad before."

"Can you block them? Take deep breaths and push them back?"

When he didn't respond, Olivia said, "Be strong. You can block them out. Fraser is bringing you something for the pain, and then you'll be able to fight them off."

Wynton still didn't respond. Olivia moved her chair next to his and motioned for Darcy to do the same. "We're here, protecting you. Nothing can harm you as long as we're here. Now, take a deep breath and push them back."

He took a deep breath and pushed it out forcefully. A moment later, he did it again. After three minutes of concentrated deep breaths, he sat up and opened his eyes.

Olivia was shocked at the pain still visible on his face.

Fraser came in with the water, put them on the table, and then moved to stand in a corner. Wynton continued to push the pain away.

"That's right. Are you ready for aspirin?"

George nodded, and Darcy handed them to him.

After four more minutes of silence, George began to speak.

"They're going."

Olivia smiled. "Good work, George. Don't let them back in."

Just as Darcy was about to ask Fraser to leave so they could talk to their client, a blinding pain ripped through Darcy's mind, and she slumped forward, moaning. Olivia gasped and dropped her head next.

Fraser was at the table at once. "Are you all right?"

Darcy was first to raise her head. "Just a headache." She smiled thinly.

And then the pain was gone. Olivia and Wynton looked up, surprise on their faces.

"What the hell was that?" asked Fraser.

"I don't know. You didn't feel it?" said Darcy.

"Feel what?"

"A headache. There must be something wrong with the air in this room."

Fraser looked at her suspiciously. "We'll go out to the squad room."

The group rose and slowly moved out of the grim room.

They sat at Fraser's desk, collecting their thoughts.

Olivia took a deep breath and said, "I'm fine now. If I were you, I'd check into the ventilation of that room."

Fraser's brow furrowed. "I'll do that." He turned to Wynton. "You all right now?"

"Yes. I'm fine now. Must be the aspirin you brought me. Thanks."

Fraser shook his head. "You want to talk here, or do you want to go back to interrogation?"

"Here should be fine. Just step back a few paces."

Fraser rose and stood against the squad room wall, his arms crossed.

George looked at Darcy and Olivia. "You felt that?"

Darcy had hoped he hadn't noticed. "Yes. But no one knows."

"I'll keep your secret, don't worry."

She didn't know whether to believe him or not. "Thanks."

"We called Joyce, and she's getting the word out. Is there anything else we should do?"

"Stay safe. If you haven't been put on a list somewhere, you'd do well to make sure you stay off the radar. You don't need to disappear like my parents did."

Darcy nodded. They had heard stories since the sniffers had first appeared. They were hard to believe, but the sniffers claimed national security and were given carte blanche to do as they wished. She had no idea that Wynton's parents had been disappeared.

"Right."

"Can we do anything else for you?"

"Just find who killed Kathleen."

Darcy and Olivia stood up. "Thanks, Fraser. I think he'll be all right in the regular lockup now."

"You two going to be okay? We can get a doc in to look at you."

Darcy smiled. "I think we're fine now."

He frowned. "I don't believe you. I have half a mind to hold you here, on suspicion of..." he trailed off.

"I promise, Fraser, we're fine."

Darcy's phone rang. It was Joyce.

"I need your help. They're not listening to me. If you don't come now, they're going to try another rescue mission."

"I'll be there in ten minutes." She turned to Fraser. "On second thought, maybe he would do better in the quiet of isolation today."

Fraser looked at her suspiciously. "What's going on?"

"I can't really say, but it's nothing illegal." *Not yet, anyway.* If she could help Joyce convince the others, there would be nothing for Fraser to worry about. She grabbed Olivia's hand. "We've got to go, right now."

Olivia pulled her hand back. "What's going on?"

"I'll tell you when we get there. Let's go."

#

Darcy drove to Wynton's printing plant as fast as she could without getting pulled over.

As they walked in, they saw Joyce and Jose arguing on the raised platform. Jose was urging the crowd to fight, and Joyce was calling for calm. From the cheers that filled the room after Jose called for action, not many telepaths seemed to be siding with Joyce.

The sisters made their way to the stage. Olivia put her hand on Jose's shoulder. "The sniffers are pushing you again," she whispered.

Darcy moved to his other side and said, "Let's get to a quiet place so we can push them away."

"No," he said. "I'm done being manipulated by you two. I know what we need to do, and we've got to go now." He turned back to the crowd. "Who is with me? We'll go now. It's time to hunt the sniffers." He stepped off the platform and was immediately swallowed by the crowd of telepaths. They chanted, "Sniffers ... sniffers ..." as they left the building.

Joyce sat on the stairs and put her head in her hands. After a moment, she said, "It's all over."

"What do you mean?" asked Olivia.

Joyce looked up. "Jose has control. There's nothing I can do to bring them back."

Olivia's eyes widened. She turned to Darcy. "Call Fraser."

Fraser picked up his phone on the first ring. "It's Darcy Morrison. I've got some information; just don't ask where I got it."

"Slow down," he told her. "Start from the beginning."

"Can't. A group of telepaths is on the streets to hunt the sniffers."

Fraser laughed. "That little group that was here before? Thanks for the heads up, but I think we can handle them."

"No! There are about a hundred of them, and they're furious. Jose has them whipped into a mob."

"Oh, damn."

"I've got to run. The Chief is going to want to know about this." He hung up before Darcy could say anything else.

"Well?" asked Olivia.

"He's going to tell the chief and they'll take care of it. Meanwhile, we've got to get back to the case. Reggie texted me with a lead." She pulled her phone from her backpack and read the name he sent her. "Jerry Sands."

"Who's Jerry Sands?"

Joyce interrupted the conversation. "Jerry Sands is Senator Hill's assistant."

"Let's go. We're going to have to talk to him," said Olivia.

Darcy shook her head. *No. Not that.* There was no way she was going into the lion's den. She had always had a fear of men like Hill: bigots who hated her without ever even meeting her first. She knew she could rub some people the wrong way—Dan, for instance—but hatred based on nothing but fear terrified her.

"You know we have to. Fraser is about to have his hands full, so we can get to Hill's office first." Olivia stood. "I'm going. You won't let me go alone, so get up and get a move on."

Olivia was right, and that's the part that pissed her off so much. "Fine. But if we're caught, I'm blaming you." She turned to Joyce. "Joyce?"

"No. I've got to find my daughter and get out of here. She won't be able to handle all this. She's too fragile."

"Good luck."

Joyce nodded. "You too."

Chapter 24

Making the drive to Hill's Senate office tore at Darcy. To go into the home turf of the enemy seemed needlessly dangerous.

"Liv?"

"Yeah?"

"Why would Sands want to kill us?"

"I don't know."

"What if Sands can tell? What if he calls the sniffers?"

"They're all busy with the underground. We'll be in and out before anyone can get to us."

Darcy took a deep breath and held it. She exhaled and tried to release her fear with the warm air. The dread diminished, leaving a nagging feeling of worry in the back of her mind. She parked the car and headed into the building as fast as she could, before she lost her nerve.

"Hey, Dar!" Olivia called. "Wait up!"

She hadn't realized how far ahead she'd sprinted until she looked back. Once Olivia caught up, she smiled. "Sorry."

Olivia squeezed Darcy's hand and returned her smile. "Let's go."

Hill's office was on the third floor of a brownstone in Brighton. At his office door, Olivia gave Darcy's hand another squeeze and said, "Once more into the breach." She opened the glass front door.

"May I help you?" asked the receptionist.

"Yes," said Olivia. "We're here to see Jerry Sands."

The receptionist smiled and flipped through a calendar. "Mr. Sands is not taking appointments this afternoon. Perhaps I can schedule you for next week?"

Olivia smiled at her. "No. We will see him now." She breezed past the woman's desk and down the central hall, barely slowing enough to read the nameplates on each door. Darcy speed-walked behind her. When they arrived at Sands's door, Olivia knocked and barged in.

"Mr. Sands?"

He looked up from the box he was packing, panic in his voice. "Get out."

"I beg your pardon?" Olivia asked.

"Get out. I'm packing and have to leave before Hill gets back."

Olivia walked to his desk and put her hand on his. "What's wrong?"

"He's insane and I've got to—" He took a closer look at Olivia and his face paled. "It's you ..."

"I'm sorry. Have we met?"

"No—ah, not personally. But I know you two. You can't be here."

"Why not?"

"He'll kill you. Don't you understand?" Sands abandoned his box and tried to rush for the door, but Darcy blocked him. "Please, let me go. He'll think it's all my fault."

Darcy stepped into the room and closed the door.

"Lock it," demanded Sands. Darcy complied.

Sands rummaged through his box and pulled

out an almost empty bottle of scotch. He unscrewed the lid with shaky hands and drank straight from the bottle. Olivia led him to the small couch and sat him down. "Why don't you tell us what's wrong?" she said.

"Hill is trying to have you killed. I didn't like it, but, hey, it's my job to do whatever he says. But when that mob flunky turned the job down and Hill said I had to do it, I knew I'd had enough. I told him I'd take care of you two, but I'm a politician. I can't work for someone who expects … that from me." He shuddered and took another drink.

"So you're not going to kill us?" asked Darcy.

His eyes widened as Darcy pulled a gun from her bag. "N-no. I never was. Put that thing away. You never know when it's going to go off."

Darcy laughed. "My finger isn't even on the trigger."

Olivia brought his attention back to her by putting her hand on his knee. He jumped in surprise. "Don't hurt me," he whined.

"No one is going to get hurt," she assured him. "Not if you cooperate."

"I can do that. But can we get out of here first?"

"Answer my question, and then we'll take you somewhere safe."

He nodded desperately.

"Why does Hill want us dead?"

A look of despair crossed Sands's face. "He didn't say," he whispered. "Oh, God! He never told me. You have to believe me. I just had to bring money and photos to the guy and make sure he took care of you two. Hill never told me why."

"And you didn't ask?" said Darcy.

"When you work for a man like Hill, you learn

not to ask. You don't want to know what he's thinking."

Darcy waved the gun at him. "Fine, let's go. I'm putting the gun away, but I can get to it long before a weasel like you can even think about getting away."

Sands nodded.

Olivia threaded her arm through his, and the three of them walked out of the office and down the fire stairs. Darcy breathed a sigh of relief as they left the building, but her relief came too early. Senator Hill was walking into the building. He looked at Sands, and then at Darcy and Olivia. "Grab them," he said.

His guards grabbed the three of them.

"Ladies, if you'll come with me?" He gestured to a waiting limo.

Darcy thought about reaching into her backpack for her gun, but despite what she'd told Sands, there was no way she'd get it out in time. She followed Olivia toward the limo. When she heard the sharp crack of a gun butt hitting Sands in the back of the skull, she turned around. She saw Sands crumple to the ground. The other two men lifted him and dumped him into the trunk.

"You're not going to kill us, too, are you?" asked Olivia.

Hill laughed. "Too? No. Sands isn't dead. But am I going to kill you? Yes." He grabbed her arm. A guard grabbed Darcy, and both women were forced into the back of the vehicle.

Hill turned to the guards. "You two go up and clean out Sands's office. I only need one of you to drive. I can handle these girls on my own." He slipped into the backseat next to Olivia and closed the door.

When Olivia had managed to sit up, she stared at Hill. "Why?"

He examined her and shook his head. "You've been infected. It's my job to cleanse the country of both telepaths and those who have been infected by them."

Darcy stared at him from across the car. *Can he tell we're telepaths?* "What do you mean, 'infected'?"

"You work for Wynton. You are trying to prove he's innocent when it's clear to everyone that he shot Harrison after he broke down her door. Your mind has been altered by him, and you cannot be trusted. It's my God-given right to cleanse the earth of people like you and Wynton. I have to make it safe for the rest of us."

Darcy laughed. "You think we're—? Oh, no!" she snorted. "You think we actually believe he's innocent?" She leaned forward and grabbed her bag as she continued to laugh.

Hill waved his gun. "Hey, hands up!"

Darcy smiled at him. "Oh, no, really. I just need a tissue." She sniffed loudly. "I'm laughing so hard I'm crying."

Olivia barged in. "Did you really think a firm like Gray and Shalek would hire us to prove his innocence?" She chuckled, "Gray and Shalek hate telepaths. You should see the anti-telepath clause in their employment contracts."

While Hill's attention was focused on Olivia, Darcy slipped her hand into her bag. She felt the rubber grip of her Glock's handle and grasped it, but she left it in the bag. *Knee or head? Kill or incapacitate? It doesn't matter,* she decided. Without removing the gun from the bag, her aim would not be accurate.

Hill began to look toward Darcy, and Olivia touched his hand. "You know, Senator Hill, our real mission is to make it look like we're helping Wynton. We're actually trying to find out how he did it so we can put him away for a very long time." She leaned as far away from Hill as she could and said, "I've always been a great admirer of yours."

Once Olivia leaned far back enough to be out of her way, Darcy flipped the safety off and prayed she would hit Hill.

She angled the gun upward and squeezed the trigger. The sound was deafening, and the limo swerved and jumped onto the sidewalk before it came to a stop. Blood stained Hill's right shoulder and he began to moan.

"What the hell? Sir, are you all right?" asked the driver through the intercom.

Olivia grabbed Hill's gun from his loosened grip and trained it on the closed dividing window. "He's fine. He's been shot in the shoulder. Drive to the nearest police station."

The window rolled down. "I'm calling an ambulance," the driver insisted.

Olivia cocked Hill's gun. "Don't."

"He could —"

"What? Die?" Olivia asked. "There's no way we'd be so lucky. Now drive."

Darcy pulled her phone out of her pocket and dialed Broadbent's cell phone. "Are you at work?"

"Just going in now. Fraser called, something about telepaths hunting sniffers. Chief wants everyone ready to protect the sniffers."

"Good. We're coming in, and we need your help."

"Help? What's wrong?"

"I shot Aaron Hill, and we need you to take us in, safely. I hit his shoulder, and it looks like he's passed out."

"You what?"

"Self-defense, I swear. Please, wait outside for us until the limo gets there."

He let out a string of expletives but agreed.

True to his word, he and Fraser were waiting outside the precinct, along with an EMT. Fraser opened the driver's door and trained his gun on him while Broadbent opened the passenger door. "What the hell happened?"

"He kidnapped us. His assistant is in the trunk."

"Kick those guns over here." They complied, and Fraser put each into an evidence bag. "Now get out, nice and slow, and walk directly to the interrogation room."

As they left, the EMT went to work on Hill, Fraser standing guard.

They sat at the table inside Interrogation Room Two. Broadbent silently paced the floor. Then he seemed to reach a conclusion. He slammed his fist down on the table and said, "What the hell were the two of you thinking? You can't take on a man like Hill on your own. You went straight into the office of the man who hired a hit man to kill you, and you think everything will be all right? I ought to arrest you for being terminally stupid."

"We didn't know Hill was behind this. We knew Sands was the middle man, but we didn't think it was Hill. He's an elected official. We just wanted to talk to Sands, and then it all spiraled out of control."

Joe laughed. "Out of control? Is that what you

call this? Darcy shot a state senator. You two will be lucky to get out of this without jail time. And never mind getting your licenses. You'll never work a case again, in any state!"

Fraser knocked and walked in.

"What?" barked Joe.

"Sands is backing them up. Says he heard Hill promise to take care of them for good before he was knocked out. And their lawyer is here."

"Wait here." Broadbent heaved himself up from his chair, shaking his head, and left the room.

Fraser was unsure if the command included him, so he waited. After a minute, he asked, "Is there anything I can get you two?"

Olivia smiled. "I think we should talk to Dan now."

"I called Stevens for you, but he wouldn't come down. Says you're on your own if you shot a senator. Broadbent always carries on about his crazy brother-in-law the lawyer, so I figured I'd call him for you. He's probably arguing with Broadbent right now about who should represent you."

Olivia smiled. "Uncle Joe and Uncle Dean arguing?" She settled back in her chair. "Might as well get comfortable. This could take a while."

Olivia was surprised when her uncles came back in a few minutes later.

"We're following the ambulance to the hospital. We want to be there when he wakes up. If you two are there it will shake him up and he might let something slip."

"Excellent," said Darcy. "I'd like to see your interrogation technique close-up."

"All you'll do is stand there. He'll know we've already got your side of the story and I want to see what he comes up with."

The ten minute drive to the hospital took them less than five. "I've got to get one of these sirens for my car," said Olivia.

"Just as soon as you join the force and become an honest detective," joked Broadbent. "Until then, you're stuck driving like everyone else." He led them through a maze of corridors to the ER admission desk. When the gray-haired nurse didn't look up, he cleared his throat.

"Detective Broadbent, how can I help you?"

"Need to talk to a suspect. Aaron Hill."

"He's a suspect? Looked a lot more like a victim to me. You find who shot him?"

Darcy felt a twinge of guilt, but didn't let it show.

"We're working on that," said Broadbent.

"See that you do. There's no reason to shoot our politicians. What is this world coming to."

Broadbent interrupted her reverie. "Emily? His room number?"

"The Senator is in room four. Don't take too long, he's had a rough day and needs to rest."

"Of course not," said Broadbent.

As they walked away, Olivia muttered, "Ha! He's had a rough day?"

Broadbent pulled the curtain closed on room four and barked, "Wake up, Hill."

Hill opened his eyes and flinched. It took him a moment for his eyes to focus. He raised his bed, wincing with pain. "Get those two out of here," he said.

Broadbent ignored his demand and said, "I'm Detective Broadbent, this is Fraser. We've got some questions for you."

"I need to speak to my lawyer," said Hill.

"I can do that for you," said Broadbent. "But if I do, I can't offer you any kind of a deal, and you're looking at some pretty serious jail time."

"What? I'm the victim here. That bitch shot me!"

Darcy set her jaw. "Self –"

"Not now," commanded Broadbent. He turned back to Hill. "So, as I was saying, some serious jail time. Jerry Sands has already told us everything about you. He says killing these two was all your idea and that he never wanted anything to do with it."

"It's a lie! He's only trying to save his own skin."

"Then tell us what really happened," said Fraser.

"Not without my lawyer."

No way, thought Olivia. There's no way he's going to weasel out of this. She stepped forward and peered into his mind.

"Tell them, Hill."

"She doesn't belong here. She's been working with a telepath and I don't want her anywhere near me."

"Tell them how you went to Kathleen Harrison's home and knocked the bowl off the table."

Everyone in the room turned to stare at her.

"Tell them how you punched her, how you threatened her." She took a step forward. How you chased her up the stairs and shot her." Her lip trembled as she continued to look into his memories. "That poor woman. She never had a chance."

"No one else was there, Adams was certain. How can you know ..." Hill trailed off as he realized

Olivia was a telepath. "Out, now. All of you." He pushed the nurse's call button and began screaming. "Telepaths! All of you. Get out of my head. Get out of my room!"

Emily and two orderlies came running into the room. "Damn it, Broadbent. This isn't what I meant when I said not to disturb him."

The orderlies pushed Hill back down into his bed as Emily hustled the group out of the room.

"It's all right, Mr. Hill. The doctor will be coming soon and he'll help you rest," said one of the orderlies.

Outside the room, Dean was waiting for them. "Quite a show in there. Let's get you two home."

Chapter 25

Dean said nothing on the drive to the apartment. Once they arrived and went inside, it was a different story.

"I don't even know where to begin with you two. You could have been killed. You could have killed Hill. You could have been convicted for murder." He shook his head. "And Olivia is a telepath? That's not a secret you should have shared with *anyone*, never mind your worst enemy. You two are fooling around where you don't belong. This job is too dangerous. You can't put your lives on the line like that."

"Uncle —"

"I'm not finished yet. I will arrange to have someone come in and monitor your business and make sure you have the training you need, starting with when to say no to a case and how to keep secrets."

"But —"

"No buts. You two will take the weekend to reflect on how you screwed up this week, and on Monday you will arrive at the office at seven o'clock sharp, ready to learn. I will find someone to represent you during the investigation into the Hill shooting. I suggest you tell your parents about it before they read it in the paper." He sat in one of the newly delivered chairs and continued. "Also, to keep the two of you from making such foolish choices, I am now your silent partner. I am giving you," he paused as he thought, "fifty thousand dollars to run your business properly."

"But—"

"Don't interrupt me, Darcy. You will buy the equipment you need and you will not take on cases your new mentor doesn't sign off on."

Darcy couldn't believe it. He was handing her everything she needed. "What's the catch?"

"No catch. Keep yourselves safe, listen to your mentor and never, ever take on a job because you're desperate for money."

Darcy began to pace around the small living room. "I don't know when we'll be able to pay you back."

"We won't worry about that right now. And if it turns out you need more money, you will call me first. You will not take any crazy jobs that almost get you killed. Agreed?"

Darcy and Olivia nodded. "Agreed."

"Good."

Olivia stood up. "Thank you, Uncle Dean. I don't know what we'd do without your help." She crossed the room to hug him and plant a kiss on his cheek. He rose and, shaking his head, walked to the door.

As he left, Olivia's cell phone rang. It was Dan, and she debated not answering, but she did.

"Olivia? Great news. Wynton has just been released from custody. The partners have jumped me ahead of all the other associates and I've been made a junior partner. Philips said he called for the vote the minute Wynton was released, and it was unanimous. I knew hiring you was the right thing to do, with you by my side I can do anything."

Olivia was stung that Dan didn't ask how she was. "That's great news, really. I'm proud of you."

"There's a dinner for me in a couple hours. I won't have time to pick you up, so you'll have to meet me there."

"Oh, Dan, I don't know. It's been a hell of a day for me. I'm not up for a night out."

"Don't be silly. Take a little nap and meet me at L'Espalier at eight."

"No, I really —"

"I know things have been rocky between us, but I'm willing to make it all right.

Olivia sighed. *How can I make this work?*

"What's up?" asked Darcy.

"Dan's been made a junior partner, based on his work on this case."

Darcy smirked. "Based on *his* work? We got Wynton released. We found the real killer."

"And there's a party in his honor tonight. I'm going to take a nap and then get ready."

"Why? I thought you were done with him."

"I am. But I want to make sure people know we did the work, not him."

#

Olivia walked out of the bedroom and pirouetted for Darcy. "How do I look?"

Darcy, stretched out on the couch, looked up from her *PI Gear* catalog. "You look great. I knew that dress would fit you just right." *She looks too good for Dan, that's for sure,* she thought. *He doesn't deserve a woman like Liv. He deserves some vapid idiot who will have his children and then leave him for someone else, taking all his money while she's at it. Oh, and maybe leave*

him with a venereal disease as a fabulous parting gift.
Darcy smiled at the thought.

"What's so funny?"

"Nothing. Have a great night."

"It's not too late. You could borrow my short black dress. It's too tight for me, but it would look great on you." Olivia moved to the couch, looking intently at Darcy. "Don't leave me alone with those people.

"You'll be fine. You fit right in with that crowd."

"Not anymore I don't. Please?"

"No chance. I'm staying home, researching new equipment. I have everything I need right here."

Olivia wrinkled her nose. "On second thought, the party sounds like a better idea."

#

The party was in full swing when Olivia arrived. She took a glass of champagne from a white-gloved waiter and started circulating through the crowd, looking for Dan. As she moved through the crowd, she caught bits of conversation.

"Who would have thought the telepath was innocent …"

"Aaron Hill. I voted for him. Hell, I made calls for him in the last election. Going to have to distance myself from him now."

"Calls, ha! No one will remember that. I contributed to his campaigns for the last five years. My name's on the books forever now. No way to get rid of it. I'm going to have to scrap my campaign for Congress next year, let this all blow over."

"You know who I blame? Damned telepaths

and their need for equality. They aren't equal, and we normal people just have to protect ourselves from them. We must. Between you and me, I think Hill was more right than wrong."

Tears sprung to Olivia's eyes. She was about to turn and leave when Dan, speaking to a group near the window, spotted her. "And here is the little woman who helped me out on this case." He walked to her, took Olivia's hand, and pulled her to his side. "Darling, have you met Philip Gray? I was just telling him about the case."

Philip Gray, managing partner, whose great grandfather started the firm with gin money during Prohibition, looked at her. She smiled her most genuine fake smile. "Mr. Gray, it's a pleasure to meet you. Dan has, of course, told me about you."

"Miss Morrison, my pleasure. Dan tells me you had a hand in bringing the real killer to justice."

It's no time for false modesty, she thought. "Yes. My sister and I followed the clues to Aaron Hill and found the proof needed to exonerate Mr. Wynton."

"Really? Dan hadn't told me about that. I'm not sure he should have put you in such a dangerous position."

"There was only a bit of danger, and we handled it well. Hill was overconfident with us and dropped his guard. It's a real asset to be a woman in the private investigation field."

Gray smiled. "I hadn't thought of it that way. We all trade on information, and if you can get it without people even knowing what you're up to, all the better. But don't you feel bad, letting a dangerous telepath back out onto the streets? I'm not sure he can be trusted, and perhaps he should have stayed in jail."

"I hardly think a life sentence for a murder you did not commit is a just punishment for having an affair with a very unhappy woman, do you?" She looked up at Dan, who was pinching her side.

Gray smiled. "Dan didn't tell me about your liberal streak."

"Not to worry. I'm sure she just doesn't understand all the legal ramifications. Art history major, you know." Dan winked at the senior partner.

Olivia was furious. She had never been so summarily dismissed in her life. Still, she smiled as she said, "If you gentlemen would excuse me, I need to powder my nose."

She walked out of the party and into the restaurant's bar. She was about to order a drink, but decided staying at Dan's party would be a mistake. She turned toward the exit, shaking with fury over his treatment of her. Suddenly he grabbed her arm.

"You can't leave yet," Dan said.

"After that ... performance in there, you expect me to stay? No."

"Just until after the toasts, then you can claim a headache and go home. I have a surprise for you, and I think you'll like it."

"Do you even understand why I am leaving?" *I bet he doesn't.* When the blank look on his face didn't resolve into understanding, she continued. "You pinched me to make me stop talking. Then you dismissed my intelligence and my well-considered opinion while demeaning my education. In that one exchange, you showed me exactly what you think of me. And then you winked at that man! You showed not a shred of respect for me, for the danger I put myself in, or for the hard work Darcy and I did on your behalf."

He stood still but said nothing.

"And you have nothing to say for yourself?"

"I was waiting for your little tantrum to be over. It's time for the toast. Come with me, and smile." He pulled her by the arm back into the restaurant, toward the wall of windows looking over Boston's twinkling lights. "Smile," he hissed at her, "you're making me look bad."

Olivia tried to smile, but his grip on her arm hurt too much. The crowd quieted down when Dan reached the front of the room and raised his glass in a toast.

"I'd like to thank you all for coming out tonight. It's a great night for me, and a great night for Gray and Shalek. I can't take all the credit for winning this case, though I'd like to—maybe I'd have gotten a bigger raise." He paused for a smattering of laughter. "Anyway, I'd like to thank Philip Gray for his guidance; the metropolitan police for their quick thinking and apprehension of Aaron Hill; and my assistant Emily for her hard work and tireless dedication. Finally, I'd like to thank the most important woman in my life, Olivia Morrison. Without her support and love, I would not be the man I am today. Liv has spent countless hours listening to me as I worked things through, not to mention making sure I eat and sleep regularly. And tonight I'd like to make the arrangement formal." He reached into his pocket, extracted a box, and opened it for the crowd to see. Everyone smiled at the three-stone emerald-cut engagement ring. He turned to Olivia and showed her the ring. "Olivia, would you marry me?"

She looked at him in shock. *Is it possible that he is this incredibly clueless, or is this just a charade for the partners?* She reached up and rubbed the faint bruises Dan had left on her arm when dragging her back into the party. Clearly and without hesitation, she answered, "No." She lifted her head high and walked through the stunned silence out of the party, into her new life.

About the Author

I am 9 days older than Star Trek. I thank any and all deities that I have never had to live in a world without Mr. Spock.

I probably spend way too much time watching television. I blame the internet. Seriously, my lack of will power has nothing to do with it. Now that I can wait and watch an entire season of a show at once I get sucked in and don't come up for air until about 2 in the morning. I think this goes along with my love for long songs, multi-book series, and four hour movies.

My life seems to be a series of crazy ideas, from 'go to college across the country where you don't know anyone' to 'four kids sounds like a great idea' to 'writing novels for a living sounds like a great plan'. My latest crazy idea is to hike the Appalachian Trail all at once with my long-suffering husband. He's taking it rather well.

I live in southern New Hampshire with my husband and our four children. I am the author of the Morrison Investigations series. Please visit me at www.LisaBouchard.com.

www.ingramcontent.com/pod-product-compliance
Lightning Source LLC
Chambersburg PA
CBHW071252170626
46809CB00001B/189